# Booted

## PAM GODWIN

# Disclaimer

Each book in the TRAILS OF SIN series
is a different couple,
but they should be read in order.

KNOTTED (#1)
BUCKLED (#2)
BOOTED (#3)

# Raina

The silence in the master suite makes my blood run colder than the air blasting from the floor vent. It's an accusing silence, articulation without voice, howling with my failures.

Tensing against the tremors is useless, but I do it impulsively, trying to deaden the bleed of anguish.

The bruises and cuts John Holsten left on my body mean nothing. It's the other damage, the deep hole he cleaved through my heart that wracks me with inconsolable pain. I can't undo what he did. I have no choice but to survive it.

I drink in the silence and hear what it's telling me.

It says to end the pity party, pull my ass from this bed, and go.

How long have I been at Julep Ranch? Two nights? Three? I haven't eaten. Haven't bathed. Haven't left this room. I'm bereft of strength, my limbs hanging boneless and brittle, as if karma is conspiring to keep me here. *In*

*John Holsten's family home.*

I owe Maybe Quinn for risking her life to save me, but the unexpected freedom doesn't dare whisper the reassurances I need. I have nothing. Not here or anywhere.

She should've left me chained in that room in Texas. I would've killed the son of a bitch eventually.

Lying on my side with my back to the door, I've only been awake for a few minutes. Daylight fades beyond the window, sharpening the jagged edges of my existence.

A fuzzy sheen glazes my good eye. The swelling in the other has gone down since the night John rammed his fist into it. But it waters and stings unbearably. If the cornea is scratched, there's no fix for that except time.

Time will heal the small stuff. The worst of my wounds, however, may never stitch back together.

Behind me, the quiet intrudes like a thief, bristling with menace and plundering the cavernous suite. Is someone here?

I hold my breath, listening. Then I feel it. A knot of air. An undeniable presence. I'm not alone.

Maybe checks on me every few hours to treat my wounds, nag me to eat, and ask questions I don't have the energy to answer. She stomps around and makes too much noise for the presence behind me to be her.

Curiosity shifts me to my back, but I misjudged the weakness in my body. My muscles struggle to take orders, my breaths rasping in my exertion to re-position. I turn my neck and wait for my vision to clear, hoping for a feminine face or friendly expression. I get neither.

Cold green eyes hijack my pulse. Long, lean, and packed with power, the formidable cowboy sprawls on a folding chair a few feet away and glares out the window from beneath a black wide-brimmed hat.

Immersed in the beauty of his dangerous

superiority, his gaze slides to me and narrows into judgmental slits. It's a look without morals or manners, one that says killing me would cause him less grief than putting down a horse.

A gasp hitches my chest, but I keep my eyes steady on his. Two years ago, I met John Holsten's sons, Jarret and Jake. Yesterday, I met Conor, the only daughter at Julep Ranch. This man must be Conor's brother, the elusive fourth in their tight-knit quartet.

Lorne Cassidy.

When I stayed here before, a photo of him graced the fireplace mantle. The smiling boy in that picture has no resemblance to the felon scowling at me now.

If an ex-con has a look, Lorne personifies it. The icy allure reflected on his face makes me shudder as his thumb mindlessly strokes the scar on his palm. Chillingly intense and devoid of sympathy, the man is chiseled in hostility.

Where his eyes are the vivid green of fresh dew on a pasture, his lips are pale and pressed into a severe line. Short black hair peeks from under the hat. A slender nose and prominent, clean-shaved jaw accentuate his bold angles.

Beautiful doesn't begin to describe him. He's arresting in the way a viper is deadly. Entrancing. Calculating. Patient. If he strikes, I won't survive the bite.

His strength flows through the twining cords of muscle that shape his physique—thick biceps, powerful thighs and calves, rock-hard chest and abdomen. The jeans and t-shirt fit too tightly, his broad frame stretching the fabric and testing the seams.

Incarcerated at age eighteen, he must've grown over the past eight years. But little inconveniences, such as needing new clothes, are probably not high on his *give a fuck* list.

He sweeps a cursory glance over my bandages. The marbled coloring on my arms and chest blends together in layers of yellows, blacks, and blues. Every inch of my body narrates the story of my life as John Holsten's whore.

"Tell me what happened." His voice scratches, low and rusty, as if out of practice.

"Isn't it obvious?"

Leaning forward, he rests his elbows on spread knees. Rather than drilling me on how I became a punching bag, he pins me with threatening silence. The kind of silence that wraps my lungs in razor wire.

He stares, and I stare right back, as much as I can with a busted eye. His demeanor is unnerving. Downright scary. It probably earned him an empire of respect in prison.

There's no denying he's the alpha among men. The biggest wolf of them all. And he just graduated from a maximum-security school for gangsters, predators, and murderers.

I brace for another growly order, but he doesn't need his voice to intimidate. He commands with a rigid posture and unwavering eye contact. His terrifying calmness demands I explain myself and promises pain if I don't.

Goosebumps skitter along my arms. Pain isn't something I'm ready to experience again so soon. But I'm even less inclined to lie here and tolerate his silent attempt to terrorize me.

Fear doesn't control me. He doesn't know that, but he's about to find out.

I swing my legs off the bed. "I'm leaving."

He glares at my bare thighs. "Cover yourself."

Wearing the sundress Maybe gave me, I tug the fabric to my knees and cringe at the dried red stains amid the flowery pattern.

# Booted

My wounds are no longer bleeding, my memory a fog of constant agony. Pointy-toed boots, leather belts, angry knuckles, whips, blades, the floor, the wall—anything and everything was used as a weapon to punish me.

I'm physically beat down, but beneath the bruises, I seethe with determination. If Lorne, John's sons, or anyone else tries to hurt me, I'll stand up to them with everything I am.

If they want to help me, I'll return the kindness with kindness. They lived with John, too, after all. Since we share that misery, maybe we can help one another.

"I need to get moving." I peek at the devil with green eyes. "If you'll help me—"

"No."

"I just need something clean to wear and—"

"You're not going anywhere."

That answers that.

My toes curl against the hardwood flooring. I need shoes. Guess I'll figure that out after I find the strength to stand.

I push off the bed and lock my knees against a vicious wave of shaking. Dizziness plummets through me, and I sway to remain upright. I should've eaten something. But even now, the thought of food makes my stomach shrivel in on itself.

I take a step and lose my balance, faltering.

Detached and expressionless, Lorne watches me wrestle with gravity without offering a hand or a word of encouragement.

Fuck him.

I attempt another step and careen toward the bed, missing it. My knees hit the floor with a bone-rattling smack.

A hot river of tears streams from the burn in my bad

eye. I cry out in frustration and pound a fist against my thigh, hurting to the point of nausea.

Pain medication would be a blessing right now, but I said no doctors and no cops. For good reason.

Lorne observes my debility with indifference. I swear if he had a gun, he would raise it to my head and gently apply pressure to the trigger, just to play with the action between firing and not firing.

After a loaded span of breaths, he rises and exits the room, leaving me to fend for myself on the floor.

I slap at the tears streaking from my injured eye, which only aggravates the broken skin on my cheek. I'm not crying. It's just... Dammit, everything hurts.

Indiscernible whispers sound from the hallway as I brace my hands on the mattress and attempt to hoist ineffective muscles.

Sweat beads on my temples, and my arms tremble uncontrollably. I make it to my feet as the tread of boots scuff behind me.

Lorne prowls into the room and returns to the chair without glancing in my direction.

"When did you get out?" I slump onto the edge of the bed, out of breath.

"Four hours ago." He rests a loose fist beneath his mouth and stares at the window.

It's a two-hour drive from the prison, and he was here when I woke.

"You spent your shiny new freedom watching me sleep?" I flex my hands on my lap.

"This is my room."

"I'm on my way out."

As soon as I muster the energy to walk. And eat. And steal a pair of shoes.

I press my bare feet together and blink at the floor. "If you could call me a cab and loan me a few dollars—"

# Booted

The door opens, and Maybe breezes into the room, carrying a small tin box.

"You're up." She bathes me in the brightness of her smile.

"I'm working on it."

She gives me a once-over and settles on my face. "Your eye is still watering."

"It's fine." I wipe away the cascade of tears. "How long have I been here?"

"Two days." She pats my shoulder and offers the box to Lorne. "Is this what you wanted?"

"Yes." He takes it from her, lifts the lid, and removes a marijuana cigarette.

She purses her lips. "I really don't think she should—"

"I didn't ask for your opinion." He hands her the joint and a lighter from the box. "Light it."

Why doesn't he light it himself?

On the way here, I overheard Jarret and Maybe discussing Lorne's prison sentence. He earned an early release. No parole. No checking in. No routine drug tests. He's a free man.

Perhaps he has an aversion to drugs? God knows I do.

I meet his frosty green eyes and shiver. "I don't do drugs."

"But you'll do a man three times your age?" His jaw sets. "Didn't realize you had standards."

My hackles bristle. This is one of the reasons I need to leave. They will never understand why I did the things I did, and I don't care enough to enlighten them.

Maybe coughs through an inhale and passes the joint back to Lorne. "Are you always such a dick?"

"Every day. Every breath." He snatches it from her and motions toward the door. "Leave us."

She slams her fists on her hips. "If you're trying to scare me away, it won't work. I love Jarret, and he loves me." She holds up her hand, wriggling the engagement ring with a surly smirk. "This means I'm not going anywhere. Deal with it."

I smile inwardly, in awe of her fire. I liked her the moment I met her, when she showed up at John's door two years ago demanding answers about her husband, Rogan Cassidy.

She was married to Lorne's half-brother. Now she's engaged to Lorne's... What is Jarret to him? They grew up together on the ranch. They might as well be brothers.

Jarret and Jake killed her husband before they knew about his relationship to the family. Not that it would've stopped them. The Holsten men are murderers, through and through.

"You just keep on scowling at me, Lorne. It only makes me want to *boop* your nose." Maybe reaches toward him, as if to tap his nose with a finger.

His lips curl, exposing straight white teeth that look dangerously close to biting off her finger.

She yanks her hand back. "Okay, you're clearly not ready for that. But we'll get there." She turns her blue eyes to me. "You need anything?"

"Shoes?" I sit taller.

"She doesn't need shoes." Lorne flicks a finger at the door. "Get out."

"I'll see what I can do." She winks at me and strides from the room in a whirl of wild blond curls and cowboy boots.

I glance at Lorne, trying to get a read on his reaction to her. "She's...different."

"She's a vegetarian," he says, as if that explains everything. He holds out the joint between two long fingers, his voice void of emotion. "This'll help with the pain."

Is he actually showing a glimpse of concern?

I don't know why that makes me soften. Maybe because I really want these aches to go away, and he seems to understand that.

Accepting the herb, I lift it to my lips. The first draw sets my throat on fire, and I hack out a lung. I used to steal my mom's cannabis when I was a kid, but that was forever ago.

After a few more attempts, I get the hang of it, pulling in the pungent smoke, holding it in my chest, and slowly releasing it.

He cracks the window and reclines in the chair, glaring at me like it's a completely normal thing to do. As I smoke down half of the joint, I glance between him, the window, the floor, back at him. He really knows how to make a person feel awkward.

"Why did you call Maybe for help?" He holds himself unnaturally still, moving only his lips.

"She offered." I shrug and flinch at the pain that small movement produces. "Two years ago, she visited John and gave me her phone number. Or rather, she gave it to him but—"

"I know how she did it. Why not call the cops? Or family? Someone you know?"

My heart collapses beneath a deluge of irreparable mistakes. "I have no one."

"No family?" His gaze dips to my throat.

"No." I touch the leather choker that holds his attention, and my shoulders loosen.

My Cherokee grandmother made me the necklace before she died. The leather connects to a silver ring at the base of my throat, and a web of woven wire with a turquoise bead at the center fills the hoop.

My ancestors believed these dream catchers warded

off the badness in the air. There used to be three silver feathers dangling from mine. I must've lost them during one of John's rampages.

Heaviness seeps into my muscles and desensitizes my brain. The devil's cabbage—as my grandmother used to call it—is doing its job, the medicated high magnified by the sadness creeping around my armored walls.

Stoned and despondent. A terrible combination in the company of this man.

"I'm gonna go." I hand him the roach.

He crushes it out on the bottom of his boot and returns it to the tin box. "Tell me why you're avoiding the cops."

A rush of lightheadedness bears down on me. My face loses feeling. The room spins, and my insides threaten to heave.

I'm a lightweight, but the weed shouldn't affect me like this. Except I haven't eaten in days. I haven't smoked in years, and my emotions are leaking all over the place.

"I need to..." My vision blurs. "Lie down."

I topple over, straight off the side of the bed.

As I brace to hit the floor, strong arms catch me instead.

Cradling my back, he settles me on the mattress. The intoxicating scent of clean, musky spice hits my nose and works its way through my muddled mind like an aphrodisiac. He smells divine. Like warm skin, soft linens, and insatiable sex.

He's unbelievably tense. His fingers, arms, chest— every part of him that comes in contact with me is coiled tightly, his teeth grinding to the point of fracturing. He might hate me, but if I shoved a hand down his pants, I bet he'd fill my grip like a loaded shotgun.

"Why no cops?" The wavy mirage of his perfectly symmetrical, gorgeously masculine face hovers over me as he braces his hands on either side of my head.

I moan, swaddled in doped exhaustion. "You don't want cops involved."

"No, I don't. But why don't *you*?"

"They'll stop me." My tongue feels too big in my mouth, lolling in slow motion and slurring my words.

"Stop you from doing what?"

"Gonna take a nap." My hundred-pound eyelids shut out the world, and I bask in the solace of darkness.

Until painful pressure ignites through my jaw.

I snap back into consciousness to find his fingers squeezing the hell out of my face.

"What are you planning?" His green eyes blaze down on me.

I gently clutch his muscular forearm and caress my thumb across his wrist. The soft touch does exactly what I intended. He lets go.

Working my jaw, I blink slowly, heavily. "I'm going to kill John Holsten."

He straightens and rests his hands on his trim hips, his expression unreadable. "You think I won't stop you?"

"You won't."

"There's a reason he's still alive." He glances at the door, no doubt considering John's sons.

I was here the day Jarret and Jake evicted their father from the ranch. They could've killed him then. I wish they would have. They knew enough about his crimes to justify it.

But they don't know everything.

"I'll tell you why he needs to die." My voice fades to a whisper as sleep threatens to pull me under.

"I don't care how you got involved with him or what he did to you."

"This isn't about me." I mean, it partly is. I have my own reasons for gutting that monster, but like Lorne said, he doesn't care. "He's a murderer."

"I know that."

"You don't know." A swallow sticks in my cotton throat as I meet his distrustful glare. "John Holsten killed your mother."

## 2
### Raina

Lorne goes eerily still, his expression closed off and voice monotone. "My mother died in a car accident when I was four."

Ava O'Conor did die in a car. That part is true. She was driving, and John's wife, Julep, was with her.

Julep and Ava were best friends. When Ava inherited the land from her parents, Julep helped her turn it into a successful cattle ranch, which Ava named after her. *Julep Ranch.*

All of this is common knowledge. The truth surrounding their deaths, however, was buried twenty-two years ago.

"The accident wasn't accidental." I float on a groggy high that's too lofty for this conversation. The rounded edges of my thoughts blur together, garbling my voice. "Julep wasn't supposed to be in that car."

"John told you this?" He stares at me, incredulous.

"All the time. Usually while drunk." A yawn

stretches my jaw as I muse, "He loved his wife."

Air hisses past his teeth. "The man isn't capable of love. You know what he did to my sister."

Eight years ago, John put a hit on Conor and Lorne. That night left a tragic mark on this family. It's the reason Lorne went to prison. He has every right to kill John himself.

"I know what he did." I gentle my expression. "I also know he loves Jarret and Jake."

"You're defending him? A man who beat you and raped you?"

"Not at all, and he didn't rape—"

"There was blood between your legs when Maybe found you chained in that room."

My skin heats. Did she tell the whole family about that? These people have no sense of privacy.

John did a lot of disgusting things to me, but I put myself in that position and accepted the consequences.

Until I couldn't.

The night I fought back, my world turned inside out.

Lorne's mouth twists into a cruel snarl. "Did you or did you not willingly fuck that son of a bitch?"

My brain sloshes through a sedated state of confusion. The answer isn't black and white. I let him fuck me, but did I have a choice? Maybe if I was stronger, smarter, I could've steered the past two years in a different direction. "I was willing, but—"

"You fucked him, knowing he killed my mother?"

"I didn't know at first."

He steps to the window and rests his hands on the sill, staring out into the fall of darkness. "I have a hard time believing anything you say."

"I don't care what you believe as long as you don't stop me from killing him."

He looks at me like I'm incapable of hurting a fly.

"How did he kill her?"

"I don't know. He bemoaned the fact that his wife was in the car, that he only meant to kill Ava O'Conor."

"Because he wanted our land?"

"I don't know."

I don't remember his words, but I remember his fists. He swung them hard whenever I asked questions.

Lorne turns back to the window, absorbed in brooding silence.

"I want you to know..." I sink into the bed, extraordinarily drowsy and fading fast. "I meant what I said about no cops. Jarret and Jake did the right thing by killing those men, and I would never turn them in for that. Your secrets are safe with me."

He gives a tight nod, his gaze on the darkness outside.

The sting on my cornea dulls, but every blink is an irritating scratch. So I hold my eyes closed, for just a moment of relief.

The rigid stillness in the room stretches around me as I fight sleep. I intend to leave tonight. I don't know how, but I need to stay awake. I try for long minutes, straining to open my eyes.

It's a battle I eventually lose.

When I wake, the suite is empty, the stark space illuminated by a dim lamp. The clock on the nightstand reads two in the morning.

Blank walls, no personal touches or color, boxes piled in the corner—there's no warmth or life here. This space has been waiting a long time for Lorne to come home, and I hate that I've stolen it from him.

I need to go.

A plate of fruit, vegetables, and cheese sits beside the clock. I'm sure I have Maybe to thank for that.

Gripped with a voracious case of the munchies, I fall

upon the food, inhaling every bite and gulping down both bottles of water.

The walk to the en-suite bathroom is murky. My head feels too heavy for my shoulders, and it's all I can do to put one foot in front of the other. But I manage to stay vertical, empty my bladder, and return to the bed without colliding with the floor.

I'm just going to lie down for a few minutes until this throbbing hangover passes.

I shut my eyes, and when I open them again, sunlight stabs into my retinas.

"Fuck!" I lurch upward and glance at the clock.

Fucking fuck, fuck! I slept for twelve hours?

A sinking feeling hits my stomach. Last night was Lorne's first night out of prison, and I took his bed. Where did he sleep? On the couch?

Fuck me, I'm such an asshole.

The fresh plate of fruit and bread on the nightstand makes me feel worse. This family didn't give me the warmest reception, but they took care of me. They don't deserve what I'm about to do next, but I don't have any other options.

I eat quickly and crawl out of bed, surprised by my energy. It seems food and sleep were exactly what I needed.

In the bathroom, I peel off the dress. The bandages follow. The recent knife wounds are the ugliest of my injuries, but they aren't deep enough to require stitches.

John was more of a slasher than a stabber, every cut meant to make me less attractive so no one else would want me. His words.

After a quick shower, I clean my teeth with toothpaste on my finger and glance at the mirror.

Holy fuck, my face looks like ten miles of bad road. At least the bruises and cuts aren't swollen today, and my bloodshot eye appears a little less red.

I wrap a towel around me and creep through the estate.

A peek at the kitchen, living room, and front and back porches confirms I'm alone. Having lived here before, I know the guys work long hours in the field.

I'll be gone before they return to the house.

I grab some protein bars, canned goods, and bottled water from the pantry and head back to the wing that once belonged to John. It's been remodeled since I was here. Not a hint of his toxicity left in this space.

Bypassing Lorne's suite, I slip into the bedroom Jarret shares with Maybe.

In the closet, I find a small backpack and stuff it with the food and a few of her comfortably loose sundresses. If I weren't so malnourished, her jeans might've fit.

Guilt pinches my stomach as I rummage through her shoes and take a pair of scalloped cowgirl boots. I slide on a casual dress that covers the bruises on my chest and thighs. And panties... I'll have to get some later.

I hurry back to Lorne's room. His wallet and key ring sit on the boxes in the corner. I overheard Jarret and Jake discussing how they kept Lorne's old pickup truck in working condition while he was in prison. I loathe the idea of stealing from him, but I must find a way back to John Holsten *before* he finds me.

Assuming the boxes belong to Lorne, I dig through them until I find what I'm looking for. Amid books, clothes, and old boots, I remove a mid-sized hunting knife in a leather sheath.

Wrapping my fingers around the wooden handle, I imagine driving the steel blade into John's chest. Adrenaline fires through my system, and my spine forges with determination.

I slip the knife into the backpack.

There's a hundred dollars in Lorne's wallet. I take forty bucks, swipe the keys, and give the room a final glance.

I'll leave his truck in town and hitch a ride to Texas. I can't, however, repay the things I've taken. I have no one and own nothing. Except...

My hand lifts to the choker at my throat, and my eyes burn. The necklace is only worth its sentimental value, but Lorne will know that. He might not understand what it means to me, but he'll know it's the only possession I have to give.

With trembling fingers, I release the clasp and position the dream catcher on his wallet. "I'm so sorry I stole from you."

After I kill the man who took his mother's life, maybe he'll forgive me?

My fingers linger on the handmade choker, my breath trapped in my chest.

*No more delaying.*

I have a monster to hunt.

Releasing my lungs, I square my shoulders and make my way to the truck.

# Lorne

Garish neon lights blink on and off, illuminating a sign in the crude shape of a naked woman. There are no words or anything to advertise the grungy, one-story strip club. Just the pink neon lady, flickering erratically.

I try to time the rhythm of the buzzing light, but it's too sporadic. Irritatingly so. There must be an electrical short.

Parked in a dark corner of the weedy lot, I've been sitting in my truck for an hour, working up the nerve to go inside.

I found my truck abandoned in Sandbank yesterday. Raina's lucky I haven't found *her*.

The bitch disappeared twenty-four hours ago. She stole my knife and my money and dumped my pickup on the side of the road. Where she went after that is anyone's guess.

The moment I discovered her missing, Jarret and I drove to Texas, expecting to find her chained in John

Holsten's house.

Except no one was there. John must've left right after Raina escaped with Maybe, given the platter of rotting chicken and half-finished tumbler of whiskey beside the recliner.

We found the wall safe open and empty, four days of mail in the mailbox, and the clothes in his bedroom closet all gone.

Did he run because he thought I'd come for him? He sent hit men after my sister and stole eight years of my life. Killing him would be a mercy. I'd rather torture him for the next twenty years.

My hands flex on the steering wheel as I glare at the aggravating neon sign. How long has it been shorting out like that?

Why am I even here?

When we left John's house, Jarret dropped me off at my truck. From there, I drove up and down the streets in every town between Sandbank and the Texas border.

That's how I ended up at a strip club an hour away from home. The obnoxious sign caught my eye, and some irrational part of me decided I needed sex more than food or sleep.

It's after midnight. I haven't slept in two days, and I want nothing more than to walk into that club and shove my cock into the first available hole.

Since I've been behind bars my entire adult life, I've never been to a place like this. But I heard these girls will do anything for extra cash. I could grab one on her break, bust a nut, and be home by morning.

The idea doesn't arouse me. The thought of sticking my dick in a drugged-out stripper makes my balls shrivel. But after fucking my fist for eight years, I need to know I can still get it done, that I can engage with a woman like a normal man.

# Booted

I'm ready to be normal again.

That means spending time with my family. They were the ones fighting for me when I was inside the barracks.

It means taking over the ranch I was always meant to run.

It means giving up my ridiculous search for Raina.

Problem is, I feel responsible for her. Only because I should've told her John Holsten called the day I was released from prison. I should've told her he intends to get her back, by force or any means necessary.

He might be old and destitute, but that didn't stop him before. The motherfucker is resourceful. If he wants her badly enough, he'll find people and ways to make it happen.

What if he already found her? He could have her shackled somewhere right now.

I grew up under his thumb, and I know how he operates. He's selfish, greedy, and indulges in whatever he wants, whenever he wants. I bet he wants Raina for no other reason than because she's the sexiest woman to ever step foot in Sandbank.

Hell, even with her face swollen and bruises discoloring her body, she's so goddamn gorgeous I can't breathe when I look at her.

But I haven't forgotten she stole from me. Christ, I'm angry. Fucking enraged. I can't blame her, though. She has nothing to her name, not even a shirt on her back. She wants revenge, and she did what she had to do to go after him.

It's a strange contrast, these feelings she stirs in me. I want to punish her for stealing and reward her for being so tenacious. A spanking would accomplish both. Ruthless strikes to teach a lesson. Erotic swats to arouse hunger. Fucking hell, to see her naked, bound, and trembling...

I adjust myself, hard and annoyed by the direction of my thoughts.

She shouldn't have gone after John alone. But if she waited, would I have helped her? At the risk of losing my freedom?

I was arrested, convicted and incarcerated in a maximum-security state penitentiary a month after my eighteenth birthday for second-degree murder.

I pleaded guilty because John and my father promised me that Conor would be safe as long as I was locked up. Any other eighteen-year-old kid would've pleaded self-defense and gotten off.

To say I'm carrying a massive fucking grudge is an understatement.

I served eight years of a ten-year sentence, because I kept my head down and my ass squeaky clean. It was the hardest thing I've ever done. I lived with seven-hundred violent men who were ready to kill me at the drop of a hat, and I know that mentality rubbed off on me.

But would I kill again at the risk of returning to that hell? Even if I had proof that John murdered my mother?

My stomach hardens at the thought.

I know prison changed me, but it's difficult to remember who I was prior to incarceration.

I lost my adolescent innocence the night I watched two men violently take my little sister's virginity. Vaginally. Anally. I can still hear her muffled screams.

I've slept with those demons for eight years.

That said, it's possible I came out with more emotional trauma than I went in with. PTSD is unavoidable. No one leaves prison without it.

I received an education in human depravity and criminal behavior that can't be learned in a school psychology course. I survived by mastering indifference, by forcing myself to become numb to things that would bring the average person to tears.

Now that I'm out, I don't know how to be un-numb.

What I do feel, however, is a strong attachment to common things. A cup of coffee, a starlit sky, a sexy song, a woman's smile—the tiniest things are luxuries behind bars.

I twist the leather rope around my wrist, where it wraps twice to make a bracelet. As far as I know, this necklace is the only thing Raina owned. Her sole possession. And she left it behind.

For me.

A strange warmth shifts in my chest as I run my thumb over the wire in the dream catcher pendant. It looks handmade and lovingly worn, and Christ, it smells like her. I lift the leather strap to my nose for the hundredth time and breathe deeply. *Sweet, botanical, feminine.*

It's the damnedest thing, but when I wrapped the necklace around my wrist, I knew I would never take it off.

The door to the strip club opens, and a middle-aged man stumbles out. He ambles across the parking lot and stops beside a red sports car. His hands lower to his zipper, and he proceeds to urinate on the concrete.

Every muscle in my body turns to stone. It's an instinctual response, one I acquired in the Gladiator-like environment in prison. There's a level of respect inside that doesn't exist out here. Pissing on the ground or hacking loogies at the dinner table would get a man killed in there.

This jackass doesn't think twice about it, because the world he lives in is a disrespectful free-for-all. As he climbs into the car, I'm tempted to chase him down and teach him a lesson with my fists.

But I didn't come here to pick a fight.

I need to get laid. Because I'm a man, and I've gone

eight years without. That's the only thing I should be thinking about.

Given the half-empty parking lot and dearth of traffic coming in and out of the building, it shouldn't be crowded inside.

From the glove box, I remove a condom and stuff it into my pocket. Then I step out of the truck.

My heart pounds a mile a minute, quaking my limbs. My gait is slow, my shoulders back, my jaw rigid beneath the shadow of my hat.

Weakness isn't allowed in prison. Running and hiding from problems is like waving a flag to become someone's bitch. That was the first lesson that stuck with me.

I remind myself of this as the door opens and a throng of patrons pours into the parking lot.

My hands clench and release at my sides, and sweat saturates my shirt. Prickles assault my skin, my nerves raw and senses on high alert.

I have an extremely short tolerance for people now. I lost the ability to socialize and connect with others. I'm even fumbling through my relationships with my family. Jarret, Jake, and Conor don't know how to relate to me. They're trying, but my carefully constructed shields don't make it easy.

It doesn't take long for the crowd to disperse. Car doors open and shut. Engines rumble. The crunch of gravel beneath tires follows them out of the lot.

With a steadying breath, I make my way toward the door.

Until it opens again.

A man and woman emerge, his arm hooked around her shoulders as he leads her toward me.

No, not toward *me*. I'm standing beside the only car at this end of the lot.

# Booted

With a racing pulse, I step out of their way.

The raven-haired woman lifts her head. Her dark eyes collide with mine, and the smile on her bruised face drops.

I slam to a stop a few feet from her. What the almighty fuck?

"Lorne?" Raina jerks away from the balding man and clasps her throat. "What are you doing here?"

Red. It's all I see, smell, feel. Fire seethes from my pores, coloring the world with my rage. A fire so potent and deadly it claws through my chest and grips my windpipe with flaming fingers.

John Holsten's looking for her, and here she is, hanging out with some asshole at a strip club.

I probe the dark fields around the building, every nerve in my body on edge.

"I'm so sorry." She digs into her stolen boot and pulls out a wad of cash. "Here." She separates two twenty-dollar bills and holds them out with a trembling hand. "I have the knife, too."

She lowers a backpack from her shoulder and rummages through it.

Blood rushes to my extremities and pounds in my ears. Where did she get the rest of that cash?

I turn my gaze to the man. His department store trousers, collared button-up, and squishy dad bod announces his status as a bored office clerk in middle-income America.

He's with her to squeeze out an hour of pleasure away from his nagging wife.

Then it dawns on me.

Raina's with him because she needs money.

"Did you already pay her?" I ask the man.

"Um... Yes?" His eyes tick between me and the woman he will *not* be fucking. "Are you her pimp or something?"

"Return his money." My voice sounds like breaking teeth and punctured lungs.

She stares at the cash in her hand, her expression stark.

"What's going on?" The man stands taller despite the quiver in his jowls. "Is this the guy who banged up your face?"

Adrenaline surges through my body. I plant my feet wide apart, burning to crack bones and spill blood.

"No." Her eyes lift to mine, watching me from beneath her lashes. Whatever she sees in my expression tightens her shoulders and stutters her breath.

I need to reel myself in.

I'm not a religious man, but in some ways, I have the wisdom of Solomon. I've been to the very bottom, a place where there's nowhere to look but up. The belly of hell. Nothing compares to that darkest hour of my life. Not the threat of John Holsten. Not this sickening situation with Raina.

"I made a mistake." She grabs the man's wrist and presses the money against his palm. "You should go."

He glances at me and back to her, working his jaw. "But we—"

"Go home to your wife and kids." I step toward him, forcing him to back up.

My I.Q. was higher than every prisoner and prison employee I encountered. Yet I learned to accept other men's shortcomings. Beneath every hard, scarred, tattooed surface is a story of tragedy and strife.

Even this guy. He raises his chin and meets my gaze head-on, as if he's more concerned about Raina's safety than getting his face smashed in. As much as I want to do exactly that, I remind myself that everyone is suffering.

"I won't harm her." I nudge up my hat so he can see

26

the truth in my eyes.

"Okay." With a parting glance at Raina, he hurries to his car.

I pull out my keys and press the remote to unlock the doors. "Get in the truck."

"Lorne, I..." She watches the man speed out of the lot, his taillights glowing red in the darkness. "I can't."

"You haven't been to John's house."

"No." She glares at the empty road. "I'm working on that."

"He's not there."

"What? Are you sure?"

"I went there yesterday." A crawling sensation itches between my shoulder blades, and I scan the surrounding fields. "Wherever he is, he's looking for you."

"I'm sure he is." She crosses her arms, her beautiful face a picture of stubbornness. "Julep Ranch is the first place he'll look."

"He wouldn't dare step onto my land, but I'd love to see him try." I point at the truck, a silent order to obey me.

Her eyes hone in on my raised arm, on the necklace that ropes around my wrist. "I'm so sorry I stole..."

Tuning her out, I stride toward the pickup and climb in.

I itch for a drink. A numb haze would make all this go away. My hands clutch the steering wheel and squeeze.

She stares at me through the windshield, her jaw wriggling back and forth. After an eternal minute, her shoulders lift with a sigh. Then she grabs the backpack and joins me.

Lorne

4

As I pull out of the parking lot and steer the truck onto the dark street, Raina's proximity presses against my senses.

Warm femininity teases my nose. The skin on her toned arms lures my gaze. The rasp of her gentle breaths dries my mouth. She's too damn soft and delicate and all around me, caressing my need for female company and making me uneasy.

I scowl at the road and try to relax the tension in my muscles. "That wasn't the first time you solicited a man for sex."

"No."

"Was John Holsten the first?"

At the edge of my vision, she shakes her head and stares straight ahead, her eyes watering in the glow of passing headlights.

Very few things surprise me anymore, but fuck... Not once did I suspect she's a prostitute.

I fail to keep the judgment out of my tone. "How

many johns have you had in the last twenty-four hours?"

"None. I can't exactly advertise on the streets around here. So I found a strip club."

"You dance, too?"

"No, but men go there with one thing on their minds." She glances at me. "I mean, that's why *you* were there."

My neck tightens. "I don't have to pay for sex."

"But it's easier, right? No attachments. No small talk or expectations beyond a thrust and release."

If I had a woman wrapped around my cock, I'd give her a lot more than a thrust.

Her seductive brown eyes stroke the side of my face. "I can repay the money I owe you." She drifts a hand toward my thigh, her voice melting through several octaves. "I can give you relief—"

I capture her wrist in a ruthless grip and shove her away.

She rubs her arm and shoots me an offended look. "You don't have to be cruel."

"Don't try to sell yourself to me again. Just because I've been in prison doesn't mean I'm a walking goddamn hard-on. I know how to take care of myself."

Jerking off was one of the few ways to pass time in a place where every minute felt like an eternity.

She looks out the window, her chest hitching and falling into the stiff silence.

My attention flicks between the street and the rearview mirror. I don't know if John has the balls to run me off the road. To get this woman back, I suspect he'll do anything.

"I get that you're not interested in me," she murmurs. "But even the hardest man craves a soft touch."

Her hands rest on her lap, her fingers slender, with short, unpolished nails. I imagine them gliding up my chest and over my shoulders like feathers, teasing, stroking.

A shiver sweeps through me, and I lock my grip on the steering wheel. "Start talking."

I want to know about her relationship with John, why she stayed with him for two years, and what she's been doing for the past twenty-four hours.

I find her eyes, huge, liquid brown, and mesmerizing in the moonlight. Her brows knit together, and I harden my expression.

A swallow jogs in her throat, and she turns her attention to the backpack at her feet. Opening it, she removes my hunting knife and sets it on the seat between us. A water bottle comes next, which she offers to me.

I shake my head and veer onto the highway, scrutinizing every vehicle in my path.

She unscrews the cap and takes a long drink. "After I left your truck in Sandbank, I hitched a ride west. The driver could only take me halfway to John's house, but I needed to prepare anyway." She puts the water bottle away and glances at the sheathed weapon beside my hip. "I took the blade in case I ran into trouble hitchhiking. I knew I couldn't use it against John, because you know what they say. Never take a knife to a gunfight, and John has a lot of guns."

All of which he took with him when he abandoned his house.

"Your forty dollars paid for my motel room last night." She straightens the skirt of her dress. "I needed money to buy a gun. That's what I was doing tonight. Earning some quick cash."

At her pause, I give her a firm glare, ordering her to keep talking.

"You want to know how I started..." She smooths her long black hair behind her ear. "How I started in this profession?"

I want to know everything, and she won't leave this truck until she tells me.

She reads my silence and licks her lips. "I grew up in McAlester, right down the road from the Big Mac."

My head jerks back. Big Mac is the nickname for Oklahoma State Penitentiary, where I was incarcerated.

"When I was young," she says, "I hung around the prison and met a lot of inmates as they were released."

"Not the best place for a kid. Where were your parents?"

"Never knew my dad, and my mom spent more time with her drug dealers than she did with me. She couldn't keep a job. Couldn't pay the bills. Meanwhile, I matured early. Boobs, ass, all the things that attract older guys." She lifts a shoulder. "Didn't take me long to learn how to use my body in the world's oldest profession."

My blood chills. "How young?"

"I was fourteen the first time. He was just released from prison for—"

"Pedophilia."

"Assault with a deadly weapon, actually.

A growl vibrates in my chest.

"Okay, maybe he had a thing for young girls." She presses her knees together. "He was gentle with me. I've heard horror stories about girls losing their virginities. Mine wasn't so bad. For a guy in his twenties, he seemed to know what he was doing. Afterward, he took me to a diner and fed me the best meal I had in years. He also told me which convicts to steer away from, what to look out for, and how to protect myself from diseases."

If I hear much more of this, my molars might crack from the pressure.

"I never saw him again." She falls quiet for several minutes, seemingly lost in thought. "I didn't do it all the time. Not until after high school. By then, I was desperate. I figured out when inmates were released, how to catch their interest, and which ones had the money to buy an hour with me."

A bitter taste floods my mouth. "You could've flipped hamburgers."

"I didn't have that luxury." Her voice cracks. "Minimum wage doesn't pay hospital bills."

"Hospital bills?"

"Three years ago, my sister was diagnosed with Chronic Renal Insufficiency." She draws her arms tight against her ribs and stares down at her empty hands. "By the time I met John Holsten, she was in severe kidney failure."

Two nights ago, she said she had no family. Did she lie?

"Tiana was just a baby at the time, barely a year old." She hugs her waist. "I was willing to sell my soul to save her life. The doctors kept delaying organ transplantation, and the bills were stacking up. Her illness inspired my mom to get clean for a while, but she still wasn't working. If we had insurance and money, Tiana would've had options. Longer hospital stays. Better medical care." Sniffling sounds break up her words, and she wipes her nose. "I was just one person, juggling the bills and Tiana's around-the-clock care on my own. And failing."

My chest constricts, and my fingers twitch to touch her. The impulse is so unfamiliar I instinctively shut it out and return to numbness.

"I was in the parking lot of the prison when John rolled up beside me in his fancy truck." Her hands ball into fists. "I assume he was there to visit you?"

"He liked to check up on me, but I refused to see him."

33

A glance at the rearview mirror reveals miles of darkness. A sick part of me wishes John would show up. I'd love to drag his ass into the street and drive over him a few hundred times.

"Before John, I'd only been with convicts," she says. "But he had that huge expensive truck, designer suit, and an aristocratic air about him that screamed money, like a big businessman or oil tycoon. The way he looked at me, I knew he saw an easy lay in a cheap motel. When I looked at him, I saw an opportunity."

"It was all a front. He didn't have a pot to piss in or a window to throw it out of."

"I didn't know that at the time, but I should have. My gut whispered to run, and I ignored it."

According to Jake, Raina is twenty-four, the same age as Conor. At least she wasn't under-aged when she met John.

That doesn't stop my blood from boiling.

She releases a sigh. "He offered twice my usual rate and took me to a nearby motel, where I made it my life's mission to give him the best damn hour he ever had. I wanted to ensure he came back. I thought if I could turn it into a regular thing, maybe add some overnights and long weekends, I could earn enough money to make a difference in Tiana's treatment."

"Did you tell him about her?"

"No. But when he showed up at our apartment two days later, he knew. I hadn't given him my address, hadn't told him anything about me, but he knew every aspect of my life and exactly how to manipulate me." Her voice shivers into a silent whimper that makes the hairs stand up on my neck.

Once her tears start falling, she seems unable to stop them. It's a reluctant cry, buried in her small hands, eking out in soft, muffled sobs.

# Booted

Her vulnerability tightens my skin and fucks with my heartbeat. I haven't seen tears since the night Conor was raped, and I didn't stick around to watch it. I hungered for blood and death so ferociously I couldn't think past revenge.

If only I reacted differently, I wouldn't have ended up in prison.

It's on the tip of my tongue to tell Raina to pull her shit together, but I won't do that. She doesn't strike me as a woman who cries often. Maybe she needs this.

She curls toward the door, hunching her shoulders and hiding her face. She needs privacy, but I can't give her that. She's trapped in this truck with me until I reach the ranch. The best I can do is give her some background noise.

I turn on the radio and adjust the volume to balance the sounds of her misery. *Better Man* by Little Big Town drifts through the speakers, and her posture loosens, slipping deeper into the seat.

I'm anxious to hear the rest of her story, but I force myself to wait and focus on the landscape, the light traffic, anything that might indicate we're being followed.

Forty-five minutes later, I navigate the truck into Sandbank and turn onto the dirt road that leads toward home.

Her head lifts from the window to watch the dark fields blur by. "I can't stay with you."

"Finish your story. Then we'll discuss what happens next."

"You can guess the rest of it."

"Tell me anyway."

She releases a shaky breath and rubs her palms on her thighs. "When he showed up at our apartment, he offered me a deal. If I went to Sandbank with him, he'd make sure Tiana received the best care possible. It was

35

more than I ever hoped for. My mom decided the sun rose and set in his wallet and agreed to look after Tiana in my absence. So I went with him, and when I arrived at Julep Ranch, I thought he was the richest man in Oklahoma. He lived in a sprawling estate and was drilling oil in his own backyard. It was easy to believe he had the power and money to help my sister. The promise of that made up for the..." She averts her gaze and swallows. "For the job I was there to do."

My stomach twists at the thought of her spreading her legs for John Holsten. "When did you find out he was broke?"

"A couple of weeks after I moved in. Tiana still didn't have the promise of a new kidney, and my mom hadn't seen a dime of financial aid for the ongoing dialysis. When I confronted him, that's when the threats began.

"He confiscated my phone and told me if I left the ranch or communicated with anyone, including his sons, he wouldn't just kill my mother and put Tiana in foster care. He would make sure my sister got lost in the system without the treatment she needed. He swore he had the power to place her with a family who had a history of preying on little girls and he would see to it that she suffered unspeakable nightmares before she died of her illness." She pulls in a ragged breath. "I believed him."

He doesn't have money, but he's proven to have powerful connections with unsavory people. I wouldn't put it past him to do exactly what he threatened.

"He didn't put me in chains until later, but I was in a prison, nonetheless." Anger leaks into her voice. "As long as I didn't disobey him, he gave me updates on Tiana. Every communication device within my reach was locked, but I managed to steal Jarret's phone a couple of times to contact the hospital and validate her health. Those calls brought me some semblance of peace. Until we moved to the middle-of-nowhere Texas."

"Jarret said he tried to talk to you the day they forced John to leave." I slow the truck on the dirt road, delaying our arrival at the ranch. "Why didn't you tell him?"

"I was scared. I didn't know if I could trust him or if he could even do anything to help me." She finds my eyes in the darkness. "Could he have stopped John from killing my mother and putting Tiana in foster care?"

"He could've threatened John the same way he threatened him to leave."

Her face crumples. "Oh, no." She buckles at the waist, hugging her chest. "I should've..." Tears saturate her whisper. "I should've told him. If I had, maybe Tiana would've—"

"Raina."

She clamps a hand over her mouth, trapping a sob.

"Raina, look at me."

Her damp eyes lift to mine.

I roll the truck to the side of the road and stop. "Do you think John would've let you go as easily as he let go of the cattle business?"

Her hand lowers to her lap, and she shakes her head, her voice hoarse. "I don't know."

Tears slip over high elegant cheekbones, and slender shoulders hunch around the prettiest face I've ever seen. Her hair hangs like a velvet black curtain around her arms, her curvaceous body flawlessly shaped in the form of every man's erotic dream.

I only need to look at her to know John Holsten covets her above all else.

"He wouldn't have surrendered you." I turn back to the road and slowly hit the gas. "Not under any threat."

"Maybe you're right." She straightens in the seat and clears her voice. "He openly discussed his dealings in front of me—the manipulations with the land, his efforts to keep you and Conor away, his shady partnerships with creditors and local law enforcement. I heard it all, because he had no intention of ever letting me go."

"What happened when you moved to Texas?"

"My mom started using drugs again and stopped taking Tiana to her dialysis appointments. No one was there to hold her accountable. *I* wasn't there." She yanks a hand through her hair. "I fucking left Tiana with that worthless fucking whore and... My baby sister died." Her voice deadens to a hollow whisper. "She died eight months ago, and I didn't find out until two months after she was cremated."

I approach the ranch and slow the truck to a crawl, my limbs stiff, my insides sick with shock.

"I kept asking him about her." She stares out the side window, trembling. "When he wouldn't tell me, I threatened to leave, to find a phone, to do whatever I needed to check on her. She was the only reason I was with him. The only reason I let him...in my body." She makes a pained noise. "He finally told me she passed. That's the night he chained me in the spare room."

He lost his leverage and locked her up to keep her from fleeing. That was six months ago? She was chained up for that long?

My fingers clench, creaking the leather steering wheel.

I spent eight years in prison, mourning my sister's assault. But this is worse. She was shackled in a room like an animal, alone, beaten, and raped while mourning her sister's *death*.

"Christ." I rub a hand down my face. "No wonder you want to kill him. How did you manage to call Maybe?"

"He locked me in the bathroom every night so I could shower. That night, he'd been drinking, and I was able to swipe his phone from his pocket." She leans her head back and closes her eyes. "The moment I was alone in the bathroom, I called the only number I'd memorized. When Maybe answered, I checked the door and realized he forgot to lock it. Through the crack, I saw his pistol sitting on the coffee table in the living room, and he was nowhere in sight."

"So you changed your mind and told her not to come." My head pounds as everything clicks in place. "That's why you told her not to call the cops. You hung up on her and went after the gun, intending to shoot him."

"Yeah. I cleared the call history and dropped the phone on his recliner. Just in case. I didn't want him going after Maybe. Then I grabbed the gun and figured out how to turn off the safety. When he walked around the corner, I aimed and squeezed the trigger."

Maybe Quinn saw him the next day and never mentioned a gunshot wound. Raina either missed or...

"The pistol wasn't loaded." Her breath slips out with a shudder. "I can still feel that hollow click. I was stunned, frozen, and knew my time was up." She touches the bruise around her eye. "When he punched me, it was like a hammer. Knocked me out cold. I woke in that room, chained to the wall, with him rutting on top of me and beating my face into... Well, you're looking at it. I don't remember much after that. Until Maybe showed up."

John was smart enough to remove his bullets before he started drinking. He's a dirty dealing bastard, but when it comes to gun safety, he's a fucking saint. He drilled that shit into my head growing up.

Thank Christ Raina had the foresight to clear his phone logs. Otherwise, he would've known she made a call and dealt with Maybe when she showed up. I wonder if Raina knows she saved Maybe's life.

The moon's rays kiss Raina's marred cheeks and

illuminate the torment in her eyes.

My hands burn to cradle the fine bones of her face and feel her silky hair fall against my touch. At the same time, every muscle in my body flexes to destroy the man who hurt her. The existence of such strong and contradictory feelings leaves me breathless and off balance.

I wish she would've succeeded in killing him. Not just to save my family the trouble. She deserves restitution as much as we do.

The fucker's out there somewhere, gathering resources and waiting for the moment to snatch her back. He must be dealt with.

I pull the truck under the archway for Julep Ranch and park beside Jake's pickup in the lot.

She glances at the estate, then the door handle beside her hand, but doesn't move to step out. "Why am I here?"

We weren't followed, and I haven't seen another car since I hit the dirt road. John won't come here, but he could hire or blackmail someone else to come. Nowhere is safe for her.

I turn off the engine and tilt my head, watching her from beneath the brim of my hat. "Have you ever fired a loaded gun?"

"No."

"Ever killed anyone?"

Her head gives a slight shake. "No."

"Do you know how to defend yourself against a man twice your size?"

She looks down at the bruises on her arm and blows out a sharp breath. Then she finds my eyes. "Where are you going with this?"

"I'm going to help you."

# 5

## Raina

"You want to help me?" My heart gallops into a thundering sprint. "How?"

"I'll keep you safe here." Lorne nods at the estate, his face hidden in the shadow of his hat. "And I'll teach you how to shoot a gun and fight with your hands."

A spark of life ripples beneath my skin. He could give me a wealth of knowledge. Hunting was part of his upbringing on the ranch, and he probably learned how to scrap in prison. Although, as intimidating as he is, I imagine he only needs to stand tall, look a man in the eye, and growl.

I'm dying to accept his offer, except... "You're a felon. Pretty sure that means you can't be around firearms."

"I cannot *possess* a firearm. If it's attached to you and you're in control of it, I won't be breaking the law."

"But you were advised to not be in the vicinity of a gun, right?"

"I don't give a fuck. I live on ten-thousand acres. No one's around to witness what I'm doing."

It's a risk, but a small one in the scheme of things.

"Shit." He pushes his hat down his forehead and slumps in the seat.

I follow his gaze to the front door, where Conor explodes out of the house and charges toward us, her eyes blazing in the moonlight and red hair whipping behind her.

My stomach sinks. She has every right to be pissed at me for stealing from her family.

"This should be fun." He rolls down the window and rests an elbow on the frame. "She's fixing to chew me up and spit me out."

Him? What did he do?

"Evening, darlin'," he drawls as she reaches the truck.

"Speak of the devil and he shall appear." She sets her fists on her hips and scowls at him. "You better give your heart to Jesus, because your ass is mine."

"Conor—"

"You think you could've bought a cell phone and called your sister while you were missing for *twenty-four hours*?" She stomps a boot. "I oughta jerk you bald for making me worry."

He's been gone since yesterday? Looking for me? He sure as hell didn't spend twenty-four hours at the strip club. He didn't even go inside.

"I'll get a phone tomorrow." A muscle flexes in his cheek.

Her frown deepens, and she crosses her arms.

Seeing them side by side, I realize beauty isn't in the eye of the beholder. It's in perfectly designed genetics. The Cassidy genes should be bottled and cloned.

They share the same vibrant green eyes, except his

42

are darker, harder. She has the feminine version of his nose. Same oval-shaped face, pouty lips, and alabaster complexion. Her hair is every shade of fire, and his is as black as mine. She's soft and petite where he's solid and angular. They're proportionate, symmetrical, unlawfully easy on the eyes.

Sleeves of ink paint beautiful murals of color from her wrists to her shoulders, and I wonder if he has tattoos. A lot of inmates get them in prison, but it's rare to see ink in Sandbank.

"I'm sorry." His lips flatten. "I should've called."

Her expression softens. "Don't do that to me again."

"Yes, ma'am."

My eyebrows lift. His heart might be a thumping gizzard, but it sure loosens up for his sister.

"And while you're shopping for a phone, get yourself some clothes. Or I'll do it for you." She hooks a thumb under the strap of her yellow tank top. "Pastels are in. You'd look as cute as a bug's ear in pink."

"I'll take care of it." He shifts in the seat, adjusting the denim on his thighs.

His shirt and jeans fit him better than the ones he wore two nights ago. He probably borrowed clothes from Jake or Jarret.

She turns her attention to me. "I'm surprised to see you again, Raina."

"About that..." I grimace. "I might be the reason he disappeared. I'm sorry."

"Did you hold a gun to his head and prevent him from calling me?"

"No."

"Then don't apologize for him." She cocks her head, studying me. "You sticking around this time?"

"No, I'm—"

"Conor." He flicks a dismissive finger at her. "Give

us a minute."

"You're not going to abandon me again." Her jaw sets.

*Abandon?* I don't think she's referring to last night. When Lorne went to prison, he refused contact with her for six years. John made comments about how well that worked at keeping her away from Sandbank. But Lorne didn't have a choice. Shutting her out of the family was the only way he could protect her while locked up.

"Never again." He reaches through the window and cups her cheek. "I promise."

"Okay." She holds his palm against her face, her eyes glistening as she lowers their hands. "We're out back on the porch."

She pivots away and strides toward the house, peeking over her shoulder a few times, as if she doesn't quite believe he's not going anywhere.

He releases a long breath. "I really fucked things up with her."

"You did what you had to do."

His mysterious eyes shift to mine. "Where's your mom?"

The change of subject gives me whiplash, and I take a moment to gather my thoughts.

"She died from a Fentanyl overdose the day after Tiana passed." I never felt sadness about that. Hard to feel anything but anger for a woman who chose drugs over her three-year-old daughter.

"Do you have proof of death? Or is this just what John told you?"

"John was all too happy to provide police reports and death certificates."

Hospital workers contacted the sheriff's offices when they were unable to find anyone to take custody of the remains. No one located me as the next-of-kin. I was technically missing, but my mom never reported it. So she and Tiana were cremated without a funeral service.

There's no grave. No ashes. I have nothing to visit or hold onto.

I have nothing.

Lorne watches me, his expression frosty. But there's something gentle behind the shadows in his eyes. A flicker of understanding? I peer deeper, and he looks away.

"Why would you help me?" I ask.

"I want him dead, but if I do it myself, I risk returning to prison."

"Better to let me kill him and take the fall?"

"You're going after him, with or without my help."

He has a point.

I can go to the cops, kill John Holsten, or wait for him to snatch me. Involving the police would launch this family into a hairy investigation, one that could uncover a trail of murders. Jake and Jarret murdered every hitman and creditor who threatened Conor's life. I won't be responsible for sending them to prison.

Going after John is my only option.

"I'm your only chance at succeeding." Lorne opens the door and unfolds his muscled frame from the truck.

Without waiting, he ambles to the front porch, his boots falling heavily on the gravel path.

The chiseled definition in his back and shoulders flexes beneath the shirt. Broad on top and narrow around the hips, his dark silhouette cuts a powerful outline against the backdrop of the porch light. Every movement radiates virility, his bearing confident and deadly.

He's the kind of handsome that leaves a profound, unprecedented impact. Doesn't matter how mean and unfeeling he is. Most people would revere him anyway, just because he's so damn pleasing to look at.

If he'd accepted my offer for sex, I might've liked

the job for the first time in my life. There would've been no love in it. There never is. But I wouldn't have minded running my hands all over that sculpted physique and pretending, just for a little while, that he wasn't a job, that we were together because it felt right. What would that level of intimacy be like?

My heartbeat flutters as I imagine his arms around me, our tongues tangled, eyes connected, skin on skin, hips rocking in a maddening rhythm. Ten minutes with him and I'd blow his fucking mind.

It's better this way. Lorne Cassidy might be insanely attractive, but his insides are razor blades and dry ice. I'm under no illusion that he's the one who could change my attitude about sex.

Besides, fucking him would complicate an already complicated situation.

I grab the backpack, slide out of the truck, and jog to catch up with him. "I don't think John's sons will be happy to see me again."

"No." He steps into the house and holds the door open for me. "They won't."

My insides pinch. Would it hurt him to sugarcoat the truth a little?

I pause on the porch and stare down at my stolen boots. "Maybe I should just—"

He releases the screen door and turns away, letting the heavy frame whack my bruised shoulder.

I bounce out of the way and rub the hurt, glaring at his back.

The door clicks shut, leaving me outside as his hulking frame moves deeper into the house and vanishes around the corner.

My throat closes. It's not like I expected him to hold my hand or anything. He doesn't like me or want me here. But damn, if he's going to help me, he could make an effort to remove his head from his clenched ass.

Now I have to go in there by myself. Where I'm not welcome. Dread knots in my stomach, and my ears burn.

The family's probably talking about me.

*Let them.*

I refuse to walk around with my head hanging.

The only thing I own is my body, and I sold it to survive. I promised myself that the *better* would come after the *worse*, and through the years, that hope burned stronger inside me than the hell around me.

I don't think anything burns in me now. Hope died with Tiana. The worse happened. I'm due for a little dose of better, but the odds aren't in my favor. Not with John aiming to put me back in chains.

Nightfall squeezes around the house, the dark depths stirring with shadows and skittering noises. Lorne doesn't think John will return to the ranch, but I'm not so sure. John could be watching me right now.

Being his whore again is less enticing than being dead.

If I stay here, I'll be surrounded by three lethal cowboys who would put John in the grave before allowing him on their land. I'm safer on the ranch than out there on my own. And if I learn how to shoot a gun, my chance of survival greatly improves.

With a resigned breath, I head inside and lock the door behind me. Creeping through the house, I follow the muffled sounds of voices on the porch.

At the back door, I set down the backpack and peer through glass.

Outside, Lorne leans his butt against the railing, fingertips in his front pockets, and boots crossed at the ankles, epitomizing the casual cowboy pose. But there's nothing casual about his expression.

His gaze locks onto mine, jaw squared with sharp

angles and mouth pressed in a tight line. He lifts a hand and crooks a finger at me through the glass.

Jake paces beside him, all tense and scowly. Conor perches on the small outdoor sofa, and across from her, Jarret sprawls in a cushioned chair with Maybe on his lap.

Expressions are strained, postures stiff and voices heated.

I open the door and step out. When all eyes turn in my direction, I focus on Maybe's.

"I'm sorry for stealing your clothes." I brush a hand down the sundress. "And boots. I'll clean them and return them tomorrow."

"That's okay. Just ask me next time." She nods at my feet. "Keep the boots. I don't know why I bought them. Jarret's are the only ones I wear."

"I can't—"

"I insist."

"Thank you." My shoulders relax a fraction, and I glance at the others. "I rifled through your pantry and took some of your food. I'm sorry—"

"I don't care about the food." Jake folds his arms across his chest, staring down at me from a few feet away. "Lorne says you intend to kill John Holsten."

"That's right." I raise my chin.

"Did you consider how that might affect my family?"

My ribs squeeze. "I thought you'd approve."

"You also thought it would be a good idea to fuck my worthless cunt of a father." His nostrils flare. "Keep thinking, Raina. Someday, you might come up with something intelligent."

"Jake," Lorne says in warning tone.

"It's fine." I stand taller despite the hurt in my chest. "Jake can be an asshole all he wants in his own house."

"I 'preciate your permission," Jake says in the

coldest drawl I've ever heard.

"I agree with Jake on this." Jarret sets Maybe on the chair and rises to stand beside his brother, his gaze on Lorne. "You brought her here—"

"Actually, you and I brought her here," Maybe says.

"But Lorne brought her back, knowing she's a target." Jarret turns to Lorne. "You might as well invite dear ol' Dad to move back in. We can be one big happy fucking family again."

"That's enough, Jarret." Conor shifts to the edge of the couch.

"He's right," I whisper.

My presence here will pull John back into this family, and they've suffered enough under his tyranny.

"I'll leave." I move toward the door.

"Stop." Lorne's harsh tone freezes my steps. He waits until I turn around before addressing the others. "I'm going to teach her how to use a gun and protect herself. What she does after that is up to her."

"*That's* your plan?" Jake widens his eyes, the whites around his brown irises glowing in the light.

Silent objection pulses from Jarret. The tension in the air steeps in testosterone. The porch isn't big enough for three alpha men locked in disagreement.

The strange part is, I'm not exactly sure what they're opposing. Every person here wants John Holsten dead.

"This isn't *her* decision." Jake paces in a tight circle, hands clenching at his sides. "If she's arrested for murder, she'll rat us out to enter a plea bargain."

"I wouldn't—"

"You don't know what you'll do when facing life in prison." He turns to Lorne. "This impacts all of us, and we'll deal with it together, just like we always have. The four of us."

"There's five now." Jarret nods at Maybe.

"Six." Lorne's eyes cut to me and return to Jake. "She's part of this, whether we like it or not, and she has a better reason than any of us to spill his blood."

"Bullshit." Jake gestures angrily at Conor. "Have you forgotten he tried to kill your sister?"

"You know he hasn't." Conor rises from the couch and rubs her hands along Jake's contracting biceps. "You need to calm down."

"Not until he explains this." He jabs a finger in my direction. "She fucked the old man and paid the price. That doesn't give her a vote in what happens to our family."

I flinch at his scathing tone, my eyes and cheeks hot with humiliation. I feel naked, on display, and would do anything to make this end.

"There's more to it." Lorne glances at me, his gaze a storm of dark splendor.

"Like what?" Jake asks.

I close my eyes. If they hate me now, they'll really hate me when he reveals what I do for money.

"That's her story to tell." Lorne lets that settle over the group, surprising me into breathlessness.

I open my mouth to come clean, but he's not finished.

"She can either kill him or go to the cops." A twitch feathers across his jaw. "She's doing us a favor by dealing with John on her own. The least I can do is give her some training."

The mood in the air shifts, their expressions pinched with puzzlement and curiosity. I don't know what they assume about my story, but one thing's for certain. They're furiously protective of their bond with one another.

"I can't let you risk going back to prison." Jake steps

toward him.

Lorne straightens away from the railing, his hands falling at his sides. "That won't happen."

"Think carefully about this." Jarret approaches Lorne's other side, closing him in. "All it takes is one ranch hand to see you with a firearm. If this turns into an investigation, our employees will be questioned, and you'll be arrested."

Jarret moves into his space, and Lorne's face pales beneath the brim of his hat. He steps backward, but Jake and Jarret stay with him, their body language assertive and tense.

The cords in Lorne's neck go taut, and his breathing accelerates. I don't think the conversation's setting him on edge so much as the proximity of two men corralling him.

I inch closer, debating whether to intervene.

"It's not worth the risk." Jake puts his face in Lorne's, his voice rising. "We just got you back, dammit. If you returned to prison, think about what that would do to Conor. To all of us!"

"I made my decision." Lorne turns toward the porch stairs to leave.

"We're not done here." Jarret reaches out and clasps Lorne's shoulder.

I see the next few seconds play out before it happens.

Whirling around, Lorne reacts like a man who's been repeatedly attacked from behind. He seethes past clenched teeth, his arms swinging to block, punch, and defend against a gang of brutal inmates.

Jarret grabs for him again, but Lorne doesn't see his family or their attempts to calm him. He sees memories. Aggression. Pain.

Maybe I'm wrong, but I've received a few black eyes during sleepovers with ex-cons who woke in the throes of flashbacks.

"Don't touch him." I launch into the gridlock of muscled arms and labored breaths.

Jake knocks me out of the way as he wrestles to get a handle on flaring tempers. But his impulse to restrain and control only adds to Lorne's distress.

"The fuck?" Jake dodges a punch. "Calm down."

They continue to grab at Lorne in an attempt to subdue him, arms flying, boots scuffing, and hats tumbling off. Can't they see that Lorne just wants to get away?

"Stop it!" Conor grips Jake's shirt. "All of you."

"Let him go." I throw myself between the men, ramming a shoulder into Jake's chest and screaming over the ruckus. "Step back!"

Jake and Jarret freeze, and their hands drop. Lorne staggers backward, eyes haunted. He grabs his hat from the floor and bolts off the porch.

Jarret moves to chase him, and I step into his path.

"Let him cool off." I tilt my head back and wince at the flames in Jarret's golden eyes.

"Move." Muscle and veins strain against his skin as he glowers at me, panting.

I stand my ground, fully aware he can shove me out of the way. "He needs a minute."

"What the hell do you know about what he needs?" Jake growls behind me.

"I don't, but—"

"Something triggered him." Conor approaches, her face pallid as she stares into the darkness that swallowed her brother. "He never loses his shit like that. It exploded out of nowhere. You guys were just talking. There had to be a trigger, but I don't know what—"

"Jarret grabbed him." Maybe moves to stand beside her fiancé, lacing her fingers through his. "Does he not like to be touched?"

"No, that's…" Jarret rubs a hand down his face, his mouth slack. "He doesn't have issues with personal space. I hugged him the day he was released."

"But tonight he was on edge, and you crowded him in." I rest my hands on my hips, replaying the confrontation in my head. "He turned to leave, to escape the discomfort, and a hand landed on his back." I scan the distraught expressions around me. "He's trained himself to be in survival mode at all times. He had to. That's not something he can unlearn overnight."

"What makes you an expert on the prison psychology?" Jake crosses his arms.

"I'm not an expert. But I spent a lot time around men dealing with post-prison adjustment."

"Why is that?" Jake scowls at me.

I stare at the black field with longing, wishing I could escape like Lorne did rather than rehash my life for the second time tonight.

Stepping toward the railing, I lean a hip against it and turn back to Jake and Jarret.

"Before I met your dad, I had sex with ex-cons." I straighten my spine. "For money."

Raina

Four pairs of eyes widen at my announcement. Lips part. Heads tip to the side. Their stunned silence sweeps a tingle up my nape. I turn away and grip the porch railing.

Stillness creeps in until all I hear is the occasional chirp from the shadows in the field. John's family might be wordlessly judging me, but I won't give them excuses. Living in poverty, sharing DNA with a drug addict, selling my body—none of those things define the worth of my soul. They're circumstances, trials, the ugly parts of my journey.

The last two years, however, shaped the person I am today. John Holsten, my sister's death, and my thirst for revenge are the reasons I'm here.

"I don't need to defend myself. So I won't." I twist back to face John's sons. "But I'll answer questions."

Jake picks up his hat and sets it on his head, his expression blank. "I want to hear your story."

He lowers onto the couch and pulls Conor down

beside him.

Maybe joins Jarret on the seat across from them, curling up on his lap.

I sit in the remaining chair, draw a deep breath, and tell them everything. As I talk, their features morph through every emotion, from shock and outrage to sympathy and pity.

After crying in Lorne's truck, I thought I might break down again. But the narration's easier this time, my voice steady and remote. Perhaps it's because my mind is elsewhere, on the man who's fighting his own demons out there in the dark.

I finish with the explanation about my phone call to Maybe, why I hung up on her, and my pathetic attempt to shoot John.

"You know the rest." I meet Maybe's damp blue gaze. "Thank you for coming for me."

"I'm so sorry about your sister." She squeezes her fingers around Jarret's hand.

I nod, grateful for her kindness.

Conor stares at her lap, eyes watering. "When Lorne told us John killed our mothers, I didn't believe him. But after everything he did to you and Tiana..."

My chest tightens. "And what he did to *you*..."

"I'm still trying to process that." She rests her head on Jake's shoulder. "He wasn't like that when we were kids. He was hard, but not so...*vicious*."

"You're remembering him through the innocent eyes of a child." Jake touches his lips to her hair. "He's always been cruel."

They talk among themselves, recounting events from their childhood and examining their perceptions of the man who raised them.

Jarret doesn't say much, but the transparency in his mannerisms and expressions speaks for him. Jake, on the other hand, has no problem voicing his thoughts. Meanwhile, his eyes give off a brooding kind of elusiveness that makes me shiver.

As they continue to share memories, my mind wanders to Lorne. I should check on him. But what can I do to help him? Sex is the only way I know how to distract a man from his troubles, and he doesn't want that from me.

Jake props a boot on the coffee table and rests his dark brown gaze on me. "So you're a hooker."

"I've been called worse."

Conor elbows him in the ribs. "Mind your manners."

"Don't need them." He absently rubs the wide leather cuff on his wrist.

"You do if you want to get laid again."

He fists a handful of her fire-red hair and drags her to his mouth. "We both know the opposite is true."

A slow smile builds on her face, at odds with her sharp whisper. "Let go."

His lips bounce, and he releases her, draping an arm around her shoulders and tucking her against his side. His flinty gaze drifts to me, to Maybe, and returns to Conor. "At least she's not a vegetarian."

Maybe extends her middle finger without looking at him.

"You're not, are you?" He squints at me. "A vegetarian?"

"No." I can't tell if he's seriously concerned about this. "Why?"

As he opens his mouth, Maybe says, "Swear to God, if I hear another sausage joke…"

"We all know you put out for a seven-inch zucchini." He arches a brow.

"Ten inches." Jarret traces the hem of her shorts.

"Whenever I give it to her, she gushes all over it. Guess you could call her a non-dairy creamer."

Conor bursts into laughter, and I press my fingers against my smile.

Maybe twists on his lap to face him. "Have you had that one holstered a while?"

"Maybe." He circles an arm around her waist and pulls her to lean back against his chest. His mouth dips to her neck, and she instantly liquefies beneath his nuzzling bites. I think I even hear a moan.

These people are so obnoxiously hot for each other it makes me squirm in the chair. If I sit here much longer, I might blush, which is ridiculous considering the things I've done for money.

"No one around here's going to buy what you're used to selling." Jake rubs his whiskers, scrutinizing me from head to toe. "What else can you do?"

"Like...other skills?"

"Yes, *other* skills. You're not staying here unless you pull your weight like everyone else."

Sex is one way to a cowboy's heart, but it's not the only way.

"I can cook." I push my shoulders back. "Native American cuisine mostly, but I can grill and—"

"You're hired." Jarret claps a hand on his thigh. "We eat breakfast at six."

"Really?" My cheeks lift. "You want me to prepare your meals?"

"We don't have the funds to hire a chef." Jake leans back, a hint of boredom in his tone.

"But we need one," Conor says. "Desperately."

"I'll gladly cook in exchange for food and a bed." I shift to the edge of the chair and give Jake strong eye contact. "And shooting practice."

"So you can kill the bastard who raised me." He taps

a finger on his knee.

"Yes."

He heard my story, and if I read his reactions correctly, he sympathizes with my need for revenge.

"All right." His attention slips to the dark landscape behind me, and a grim twist steals across his lips.

I follow his line of sight over my shoulder, anticipating Lorne's presence, but no one's there.

"I'm going to check on him." I stand, searching the field.

*Where did he go?*

"He's probably in the stable." Jarret rises and adjusts his hat. "I'll go."

"I don't know where I'm sleeping, and..." An inexplainable urge to see if Lorne's okay pulls at me. "I want to talk to him."

After a moment of consideration, Jarret nods. "I'll walk with you."

He turns back to Maybe and puts his mouth at her ear, whispering something I can't hear. Whatever he says causes her legs to squeeze together, and her fingernails dig into his arms.

He should just fuck her already and get it over with.

I step off the porch and wait with my back to them.

The all-watching eye of the moon shines its glow over the sleeping countryside, casting the tall grass in a shimmering hue of silver. Somewhere in the distance, an owl calls for its mate.

My ancestors believed that all nature is alive with spirit. Animals, plants, rocks, water, humans—everything has a soul, and we're all connected in one unified whole.

My grandmother taught me the old ways, but I was thirteen when she died. I've forgotten many of the stories. The teaching that sticks with me the most is to always pay attention. Listen to the wind. Listen to the silence. Listen to my gut. The universe speaks, and it *knows*.

Right now it's telling me to help Lorne find his way. To lead him to his soul. In turn, he'll protect me so I can walk the earth unharmed.

Footsteps sound behind me, and Jarret strides past. "Don't wander around alone. Not until this shit with John is over. Understood?"

"Yes." I hurry after him, matching his long-legged gait. "Where's Lorne been sleeping?"

"If he slept last night, it was in his truck. He spent the first night out there." He gestures at a bare spot in the field between the clumps of trees.

"Outside?" My stomach cramps with guilt. "Why didn't he kick me out of his bed?"

"He said the house felt like a prison and ran off with a sleeping bag." His voice roughens. "We tried to stop him."

"He needs time." I pick along the overgrown terrain, thinking back to the men I've met over the years. "A lot of guys come out of prison and isolate themselves from everyone. Doesn't take long before they're drinking too much and using medication to numb the pain."

"He won't drink. Not after his dad drowned in a bottle and beat on Conor."

John used to talk about Dalton's self-destruction with disgust in his voice. I don't know if Dalton knew John killed his wife, but whatever happened between them left a fissure of hatred.

As we approach the stable, deep, somber vocals croon from within. Jarret opens the door for me, and a familiar cover song strums from the stereo on a nearby shelf.

*Hurt* by Johnny Cash isn't exactly an uplifting song. I scan the space, searching for signs of Lorne as the bitter, self-loathing lyrics fill me with dread.

# Booted

Beyond the farthest stall, a boot catches my eye, the rest of the man out of view behind the half wall. I nudge Jarret and point.

Heading in that direction, I pass the stereo and turn off the depressing song.

"I was listening to that." Lorne's growl drifts from around the corner.

"It's a great song." I glance at Jarret, grimacing. "If you're thinking about killing yourself."

Lorne's scathing laugh shudders the air.

As I pass the rows of horses, I do a double-take at the cow cuddled up in her own stall. Her pristine white hair is neatly brushed, her bedding fresh and halter made with fine leather, as if she's as pampered and loved as the purebred stallions.

"Keeping livestock as pets?" I raise an eyebrow at Jarret.

"That's Chicken." An affectionate grin lights up his face. "She's family."

A cattle rancher with a pet cow? That's unexpected, but so is the warmth spreading through my chest. Maybe John's sons aren't a chip off the old block. One can only hope.

I reach the end of the walkway and stop beside Lorne's boot.

He sprawls on the ground with his back against the wall, one leg bent, the other stretched out before him. Chin down and hat tipped low on his brow, he hides his face from view.

His arm hangs over his bent knee, and an unopened bottle of whiskey sits between his spread legs.

"What are you doing, Lorne?" Jarret crouches beside him. "You don't drink."

Lorne grips the neck of the bottle and moves it out of reach.

Jarret's gaze follows the liquor. "Talk to me."

Lorne unscrews the cap.

"Give it here." Jarret holds out a hand. "Unless you're aiming to turn into your—"

"If you mention his name, I'll break your fucking face." Every muscle in Lorne's body goes rigid, his voice cutting. "Get out."

He hasn't cooled off. If anything, he's even more keyed up, and his irritability is rubbing off, given the flex of Jarret's hands. Two raging bulls in a small space are guaranteed to lock horns.

"Christ, you're a stubborn fuck." Jarret jumps to his feet. "If this is how you want—"

"Jarret." I grip his shirt and gesture toward the exit. "Outside."

"Or what? You gonna shoot me with an unloaded gun?"

"Nope. The one I aim at you will be loaded." I walk to the door.

Thankfully, he follows. I guess he's smart enough to realize his anger isn't helping.

The moment we step outside, he clutches the back of his neck.

"I don't know what to do. That guy..." He thrusts a finger at the door. "That's not Lorne. That's not the brother I grew up with."

"Yes, he is. Stop making fists and screaming for his attention. You're acting like a butt-hurt baby."

"The fuck I am."

"You waited eight years for his return. He's finally here, and you still have to wait." I soften my voice. "I can't imagine how much that stings, but he needs you to be patient."

"I only have patience when I'm not breathing," he mutters.

"Not true. I was in there when you helped Maybe pack up her apartment."

They thought I was asleep, but I heard them talking about their separation.

"You waited for her for eighteen months." I give him a gentle smile. "And you'll keep waiting for Lorne because that's what he needs."

His stark eyes tick between the estate and the stable before resting on me. "I won't leave him in there alone all night."

"I'll be with him."

His gaze dips to my chest and bounces away. In the distance, two silhouettes float across the field, heading toward us.

I squint. "Is that—?"

"Jake and Conor. I'll head them off so you can..." He motions at the door. "Be alone with him." He strides off toward his brother.

He thinks I'm going to offer my body to Lorne. Because that's all I'm good for. Maybe the latter is true, but Jarret doesn't know I already tried and was rejected.

I pull in a steady breath and return to the man and his whiskey.

# 7
## Raina

Lorne hasn't moved from his slouch against the wall. It's more of a non-slouch with the amount of surly tension and developed muscle vibrating along his frame. He lifts his head, and his gaze rams into me with enough animosity to make me second guess why I'm here.

The bottle of whiskey waits beside him, his fingers twisting the cap off, on, off, on. The universe might be telling me we can help each other, but all bets are off if he turns into a drunk.

"You don't want that." I kneel in the *V* of his spread legs and sit back on the heels of my boots.

"You have no idea what I want."

"I know what you *don't* want."

He bumps up the brim of his hat and shoots me a withering look.

"You don't want the nightmares." I fold my hands on my lap and meet his glare head on. "Or the memories. The constant itch to look over your shoulder. The pain."

His eyes flash.

I lean in. "The things you carry today will strengthen you tomorrow."

"Don't preach your hippie bullshit to me."

"I'm a grown-ass woman, and I'll preach whatever the fuck I want to whomever I want."

The muscles in his face tighten, and his entire body goes motionless, breathless. I brace for a mean insult, a whip of rage. Men like him don't respond kindly to defiant women.

"Damn," he whispers, and the tension leaks from his shoulders.

"What?"

"You're so extraordinarily beautiful it pisses me off."

A startled thrill jolts through me. "That's the strangest compliment I've ever heard."

"It's the only one you'll get from me." He shoves the hat back down on his forehead. "Fuck niceties and social pretense."

That's the kind of attitude that's bred within the concrete walls of a heartless, oppressive system, where men are caged and deprived of love, respect, decency, and humanity.

"It's okay, you know." I tilt my head. "To be uncomfortable around people."

His nostrils pulse.

"You won't be able to avoid interaction forever," I say. "But I can promise you one thing."

His deep green eyes find mine.

"You'll survive it." I bend over my lap, resting elbows on my thighs with my head down. "No matter how uneasy it makes you feel."

I don't know if I'm saying the right things, if I'm getting through to him or helping him at all. I have only his silence and what it's telling me.

My grandmother used to say, *Your tongue will keep you deaf.* Maybe I'm talking too much?

I fall still, gaze on my lap, prepared to listen. Or wait him out for however long it takes.

Minutes whisper by, and neither of us moves or speaks. At least he isn't drinking, the whiskey seemingly forgotten at his side.

I let my eyes close, tracking the sound of his breaths. As I lose myself in the entrancing rhythm, something stirs my hair. The current of movement races up the strands and tingles my scalp.

My eyes open, and my breath catches.

He's touching me, his fingers sifting through the long black curtain that drapes my arm.

I don't twitch or blink, afraid he'll stop. But when my gaze lifts to his, he withdraws his hand.

"You can touch me, Lorne. If I don't like it, I'll tell you. That's what people do."

"I'm not like them."

Them? The men I've bedded? Society as a whole?

"No, you're not," I say. "The average man hasn't watched the brutal rape of his sister or spent his adult life behind bars for a crime he committed out of love and protection. No one has felt what you felt, perceived, experienced, or examined the things you have. No one will ever know you or truly understand, until they run their fingers through your soul. But you need to let them. Someday, you'll let someone in."

He meets my eyes, his expression guarded, giving nothing away.

I'm running my mouth again, and who am I to give advice about letting someone in? My heart is an island, completely disconnected from the world and anything that might hurt it. I know how to seduce. I know how to fuck. I know how to redirect the focus, the pleasure, and all thought to anyone's emotional damage but my own.

His eyes shift to the stall behind me. I glance back at the white and brown dappled palomino stallion they call Captain Undies.

When I stayed here with John, his sons took Lorne's horse out every day. Captain hasn't been neglected, but I imagine he misses Lorne.

"Have you ridden him?" I ask.

A blank wall crashes over his face.

That would be a *no*.

I stand and head into the tack room. Loading my arms with gear, I walk back to Captain's stall, lead him into the walkway, and saddle him.

"What are you doing?" Lorne's voice scuffs with disinterest.

"John used to make me tack his horse, the lazy cunt. But he never let me ride."

He stares at me, emotionless.

I shrug. "I was his whore. Nothing more."

His eyes harden before lowering to the dream catcher necklace on his wrist. "You're not taking Captain out."

"Nope." I cinch the straps and adjust the noseband. "You are."

"Not tonight."

"You hear that, Captain?" I glide a hand along the horse's strong neck. "Lorne would rather pout than give you a proper run. Maybe it's time to find a new friend. A man who's willing to dip into his soul and remember what calls to him. The wind in his face, the freedom on your back, the feel of your strength between his legs, the sound of your loyal heartbeat—your gifts should be appreciated."

"You're fucking nuts." Lorne rises and steps around me, pulling on the buckles and checking my work.

# Booted

I angle away, hiding my smile.

He's not giving in. He's going to take Captain for a ride because deep down, he wants to. Badly. He just couldn't see that through his fog of despondency.

"Hop on." He pats the saddle.

"What?" My gaze flies to his, and my heart skips.

"I won't repeat myself."

I touch Captain's mane, stroking the coarse hair. Oh, how I've ached to ride. I had lessons when I was little, when my mom was sober. It was so long ago I don't even remember how to mount a horse.

But this isn't for me. It's about Lorne and getting him back in the saddle again, figuratively and literally.

"You'll ride with me?" I ask.

"Can't leave you alone with John on the loose."

Right. I scan the saddle gear and reach for the pommel. Hooking a boot in the stirrup, I attempt a climb that leaves me clinging ungracefully to Captain's side.

Upper body strength would be great right now. And jeans. Every time I try to throw a leg over, my borrowed dress slips into flashing territory.

"You might want to look away." I grapple for a handhold, certain my panties are on full display.

Strong hands grip my hips and launch me upward. The momentum nearly sends me off the other side, but he stays with me, swinging into the saddle and pinning my back against his chest.

A thick forearm hooks around my waist. Brawny thighs hug tightly to the outsides of mine. He adjusts me where he wants me. No hesitancy in his touch. No uncertainty. His movements are assertive, confident, like he's ridden with a woman hundreds of times.

"Thank you." I gasp, trying to catch my breath.

He gathers the reins and steers Captain out of the stable.

69

My pulse shivers. My nerve endings stir, and my core floods with a rush of warmth. My fevered elation has nothing to do with the horse ride and everything to do with the hard chest rubbing against my back.

My body is an alien, buzzing and tightening in a state of war. Lorne is just a man. He has a deep voice, masculine scent, abundance of muscle mass, and a cock between his legs. Who cares? I've traversed the male landscape more times than I care to remember.

So why am I gulping for air and wriggling restlessly in the cage of his arms? The initial delight in touching an attractive guy should've gone stale by now. Now would be the time I start yearning for escape.

The faster I get them off, the quicker they go away.

But Lorne isn't a job. He isn't John Holsten. He's the first man who's ever held me without stripping off my clothes.

"How many girlfriends did you have in high school?" I rest my hands on his knees.

"None."

I know he went to prison at a young age, but sweet Lord, he's so wildly, overwhelmingly good-looking he couldn't possibly be a virgin. Could he?

I lick my lips. "Are you—?"

"No."

"Ah. So you played the field?"

"I had options when I was young."

"You're still young, and you still have options. The fine women of Sandbank would climb over one another to be with you."

A harsh breath hits my neck. "Lay off the goddamn pep talks." He drives a boot into Captain's side with unnecessary force. "Your fucking voice gives me a headache."

My spine snaps straight, and I shove his arm away

from my waist. "I know you're going through some adjustments, but that doesn't give you a pass to disrespect me. I tolerated a lot of cruelty the last couple of years, but no more. Do you hear me, Lorne? I'm done with it."

We rock together in stiff silence, floating across a tenebrous landscape. After several bristling seconds, he releases a low-pitch whistle and brings the horse to a stop.

We're out of view of the estate, the stable, or any hint of civilization. He could strangle the air from my body, and no one would hear me scream. There's no one left in my life who would care.

His right hand comes around me, slowly lifting across my chest to rest on the left side of my face. My pounding heartbeat grows loud in my ears as he uses the featherlight touch to guide my head ever-so-softly to look at him. I'm too shocked by the tenderness to fight the pull.

Dense, black lashes fringe seductive green eyes. Slack lips, unlocked jaw, he looks calm. Innocuous.

His thumb falls against my cheekbone, ghosting across my skin as his cruel, gorgeous mouth drifts lower, closer, inches from mine.

"I'm sorry." His breath caresses my lips.

Fucking damn, he's potent. The intoxicating scent of him, the reserved beauty in his face, the strength of his heart that shines so clearly in his tortured eyes, and his touch...

The universe must hate me, because that delicate, complicated, barely-there pressure of his fingers feels like a fist slamming between the rungs of my ribs.

In that candid moment of connectedness, something passes between us. A soulful greeting? A peek behind our defenses? A what-if? Whatever it is, it shakes something loose inside me while reinforcing my number one rule.

They can have my body, but everything else is off-limits.

I offer him a nod, accepting his apology. With a quick shift of my hips, I face forward, escaping his touch. And his eyes.

Vibrant, melty, poisonous eyes. I'm angled away, but I can still see them, still feel them luring me in with filthy promises.

I don't even like sex. Or men, in general. I offered myself to him, because I don't want to be in his debt. I stole his money. Now I'll be eating his food and sleeping in his house. That makes me dependent, and dependency makes me uneasy.

*He* makes me uneasy.

He leans against my back and rests a hand on the saddle horn, leaving no space between my bottom and the swollen, steely length of him trapped against his thigh.

I bite down on my cheek, my throat an arid desert.

His mouth skims my ear. "You wear a fearless mask, but I hear you, Raina. I feel your fear."

"I feel your erection." I turn my neck, my lips a hairbreadth from his. "Are you reconsidering my offer?"

His jaw stiffens. "You use sex like a weapon, wedging it between you and anyone who might *run their fingers through your soul.*"

My head jerks back at the verbal slap, and I quickly look away, grasping for a subject change. "When was the last time you slept?"

"Prison."

Three days ago.

I stole his bed the first night and ran off the second night. "Because of me?"

"Because I can't sleep." He makes a clicking sound with his cheek, and the horse lurches into motion.

"Do you want to talk about it? I'll listen—"

"No."

# Booted

For the next thirty minutes, Captain carries us through the dark at a lazy pace. My chest bounces uncomfortably, my boobs in desperate need of a bra. But I don't own one. So I center myself in the tempo of chuffing snorts and the stretch of the horse's powerful muscles.

It's so tranquil here. A light breeze, an explosion of stars, the atmosphere flows with energy and life.

Behind me, Lorne's as quiet as a statue. But I'm viscerally aware of the muscled bar of his arm across my abdomen, the contraction of his thighs against mine, the strength in his fingers around the reins, and the warm massage of his breaths along my neck.

I'm so distracted by him I don't realize where he's taken us until he stops beside an unlit, one-story building.

"What is this?" I search the unfamiliar landscape of sparse trees. "Where are we?"

"The ravine."

My breath catches. "How? It doesn't look—"

"Jarret and Jake filled it in." His voice creeps over my shoulder, cold and distant. "Jake built Conor's veterinary clinic right on top." He motions at the building.

She works here? Where she was raped?

"Doesn't that unnerve her?" I ask.

"I guess she doesn't believe in ghosts."

"Ghosts?"

He huffs a sound of annoyance. "They buried the bodies in the ravine."

"Oh." A chill spreads over my scalp. "I didn't know."

"Neither does John, and it'll remain that way."

He doesn't move to dismount or inch Captain closer to the place that altered his life. We sit there for so long I wonder if I've lost him to the past.

Does he wish the ravine wasn't filled in so he could visit it a final time? Is he reliving Conor's attack? His hunt

73

for her rapist? Or the catastrophic moment when he gunned down the wrong man?

"Lorne?"

"Quiet," he snaps.

I have so many questions scraping along my tongue, but I trap them behind my lips and close my eyes.

Until his fingers drift through my hair.

I fix my stare on the building and go unnaturally still.

His touch is airy at first, floating through the stick-straight strands like a suggestion. Then his exploration curls into a soothing brush, sinking midway into the length and raking to the end, where it tickles my elbows.

Over and over, he strokes. Neither rough nor hesitant, his movements seem to be absentminded. Except whenever his fingers graze my arm, they linger, feeling my skin through the veil of my hair.

After a while, he abandons my hair altogether to trace the shape of my bicep.

With the pad of one finger, he roams the curve of my shoulder, under the strap of the dress, and back to my upper arm. The slow, methodical caress shoots delicious shivers up my spine.

His breathing accelerates, and mine follows. He sways closer, and I relax against his chest. The heat of his exhales quickens my pulse. My blood warms. My eyes grow heavy, and an involuntary clench quivers forgotten muscles between my legs.

I've been touched and kissed and fucked in every way under the sun, but never like this. Never with this much concentration on such a chaste part of my body.

Sliding my hair out of the way, he continues the diabolical assault. He stays on my arm, never dipping past my elbow or extending toward my chest and neck. It's the weirdest and best thing I've ever experienced.

# Booted

It feels safe.

His groin presses so tightly against my backside I know he isn't aroused. He's giving me this...this nonsexual gift, and that alone rocks my world off its axis. He's gone eight years without the touch of a woman, yet he's doing the touching, the giving, without taking anything in return.

It makes me uneasy, suspicious, and my stomach hardens inside a fist of dread.

I must've tensed, because he pulls his hand away.

"We should get back." He straightens and grips the reins. "Yah!"

His sharp command launches Captain into a canter. I clutch Lorne's legs for balance, marveling in the hard feel of his thighs through the denim. A tremor moves through him, his breathing deep and erratic. He feels like a livewire, strung taut and amped up.

"Why did you do that?" At his silence, I clarify. "If you don't want to have sex, why did you touch me?"

"You didn't tell me to stop."

"But you didn't get anything out of it."

"Of course I did."

I grind my teeth. "If you tell me that giving a woman—"

"It calmed me." He tightens his arm around my waist and leans over my shoulder. "Touching your skin, your hair... It quieted my mind."

My ribs expand. "After everything that happened all those years ago, I know you feel things about it. If you don't want to tell me about the ravine, will you share one thing you were thinking about back there?"

"Colors."

"What?"

"The colors of the land and the sky and all the little things I never noticed before."

I blink at the surroundings. All I see is shadows and

darkness and obscure, very non-colorful objects and bulges. "I don't understand."

"I haven't touched a tree in eight years. I used to pick wildflowers in the field and put them in Conor's hair. Back then, I didn't appreciate the hues of the petals. I just liked the way they made her smile. But now, I'm just... I'm overwhelmed by the abundance of color."

That's so tragically beautiful it makes my heart sigh. I caress a hand along his thigh, lost in the enigma of this complicated man.

We ride the rest of the way in silence. Rather than returning to the stable, he drops me off at the back porch of the estate and helps me dismount.

"If you need something to sleep in," he says, swinging back into the saddle, "there are clothes in my room. Just dig through the boxes."

"Are you not coming back?"

"No."

"Lorne, I don't feel right about—"

"Lock the door."

Captain stomps a hoof, and Lorne rocks with the movement.

"Go on." He runs the reins through the curl of his hand.

He can sleep where he wants. That's not my call, even if it makes me feel bad. So I head inside, close the door behind me, and find his gaze through the glass.

He doesn't move, his eyes watchful and stern, waiting.

I turn the lock.

Cupping a hand over the top of his hat, he bows his head in acknowledgment. Then he kicks Captain into a gallop and vanishes around the corner.

He has a protective heart. Vigilant and, on rare occasions, chivalrous. But also lethal.

# Booted

The mean glint in his eyes clashes with the gentlemanly boots and hat. He harbors a darkness that doesn't fit quite right in leather so respectfully worn.

When he opens his mouth, it's with a sexy drawl, and the skin on his hands is softer than my baby sister's. His bearing radiates confidence, and his eye contact never wavers. It's as if he knows the effect he has on women and uses that as bait to lure and trap.

I could never trust a man so perfect. As far as I'm concerned, the more handsome the picture, the greater the danger.

Good thing I know how to deal with his kind.

I wander through the sprawling estate, its occupants shut behind bedroom doors. Hopefully, they're working off some of that noxious sexual tension.

In Lorne's suite, I shower, pull on one of his oversized t-shirts, and make my way to the kitchen to take an inventory. I have five ranchers to feed at the crack of dawn.

Last time I was here, I started an herb garden out back and foraged an abundance of native ingredients from the property. Things I dried, canned, and stored. When John learned that I love to cook, he banned me from the kitchen. He was afraid it would distract me from my job as his whore.

I rifle through the pantry, digging way into the back, searching for... *Yes!* Airtight cannisters of herbs and spices, jars of roots, everything I left behind is still here.

As my mind sifts through family recipes, my insides tremble with excitement. I have a purpose, a legitimate job, and a real chance at killing John Holsten.

Humans can go without sleep for seventy-two hours and still function. After that, things start to misfire, and the senses float in a clumsy, intoxicated state, similar to drunkenness. It's an exhilarating form of escape without chemicals or alcohol.

The downside is once I reach this level of sleep-deprivation, I'm too wired to close my eyes and let go. Especially with the hot currents of hunger thrumming through my body.

Stripped down to my briefs, I lie on a sleeping bag in the field behind the house. The summer night billows out around me like a giant tent of rustling grass, old trees, and glittering stars.

For the past hour, I've tried to tune into my childhood surroundings, but my thoughts are elsewhere, suspended in a fog of seductive whispers.

The soft, melodic voice in my head belongs to a Native American goddess, one I have no business fantasizing about. I feel her small hands on my legs, the erotic curve of her spine against my chest, and her purring, insightful words in my bloodstream.

The only reason she's under my skin is because I haven't been around a woman in years. Doesn't help that she's a goddamn knockout. Silky black hair, plump tits, tight round ass, satiny bronze legs, exotic features—she's a perfect ten on top, bottom, and everywhere in between.

I told her I didn't have to pay for sex, but she's so devastatingly gorgeous I'd empty my savings account to tap that.

Why am I not in there right now nailing her against the wall? She's convenient. Experienced. Willing. Hell, she *wants* to be used for sex.

Because she's messed up. Probably more mentally fucked than I am.

I stretch out on my back, clasp my hands behind my head, and sink into the vast starlit sky.

There are windows in prison, narrow gaps of heavy glass where an inmate can view the stars that are banked in the sky over razor wire fences. Indulging in that luxury, however, exposes his back to anyone who wants to take out some aggression.

A shudder ripples through me, and I close my eyes. I don't know how long I lie there, unable to fall asleep. I'm about to give up when something traipses through the grass in the distance.

I strain my hearing, my senses on high-alert.

Dirt scrapes beneath tripping steps, followed by a huff of breath. If someone wanted to get a jump on me, they wouldn't be making this much racket.

Jake and Jarret have distinct rhythms in their gaits. I can pick out the sound of their boots in a crowd. Conor's pace has a swiftness to it, a determination. I don't know Maybe, but I'd bet my best hat Jarret wouldn't let her loose in the middle of the night.

The approaching footsteps are light and haphazard, moseying across the terrain with irritating nonchalance before pausing within reach of my head.

I don't bother opening my eyes. "I told you not to wander around alone."

"How did you know it was me?" Raina inches closer, kicking up dirt beside my face.

"You're a pest, buzzing around and grating on nerves."

"You say the sweetest things," she deadpans.

"Why are you here?"

"I let the universe guide me."

I crack open an eye.

She stands over me, wearing one of my flannel shirts, nipples poking beneath the cotton, a thermos in one hand, and miles and miles and miles of tanned legs. If I shift a couple inches closer, I'd see under the hem and find out if she's as bare as her thighs.

My groin tightens, a reaction I can't hide as her dark gaze travels across my briefs. She continues her perusal, openly checking out my legs, my abs, my chest.

If I were modest before prison, I lost all traces of that by the time I was released. Nudity doesn't affect me, but the way she's looking at my body, eyes hooded and mouth parted, leaves a very hard, painful response between my legs.

"Hmm. No tattoos." She holds out the thermos. "I brought you tea."

"I don't want tattoos. Or caffeine."

"It's decaf. An old family recipe for insomnia."

I keep my hands folded beneath the back of my head.

She twists off the cap and sits beside my hip with her legs crossed. Tucking her bare feet under her thighs and knees wide open, she gives me a straight shot of the pink fabric covering her pussy.

I know for a fact she ran from John's house without undergarments.

"Where did you get those?" I direct my eyes at her panties, wondering if they belong to Maybe.

She glances down but doesn't move to cover herself.

"When I drove your truck into town yesterday, I stopped at Walmart and…" She pours the tea into the cup-sized thermos cap and shrugs. "I stole them."

*Little fucking thief.*

I narrow my eyes. "Did the universe guide you then, too?"

"Don't be a dick."

"I'm serious. Stealing seems to be a habit of yours."

"I only do it when I'm desperate. Yesterday was a desperate day."

"And the other times?" I soften my tone, removing all traces of judgment. "Did the universe guide you to sell your body?"

"No." She stares at her hands. "There was incessant pull to leave my sister's life up to fate. But I couldn't accept that. In the end, the universe got what it wanted." She hovers the tea beside my face. "Drink."

"No, thanks." I'm not ready to change the subject. "You jump down my throat for disrespecting you, yet you disrespect yourself by allowing men to use you."

"I *allowed* it. That's the difference. *I* made the choice to let them use my body. What I won't do is allow you to attack my character."

I don't care what mental gymnastics she undergoes to rationalize her decisions. She won't sell her body again. Not while I'm breathing.

"You've been out here for two hours," she says. "Have you slept at all?"

I grit my teeth. "If I drink that, you're going to march your ass back inside."

"That was the plan, because let's be honest. You're not a lot of fun to be around."

I sit up and snatch the cup from her grasp. Bringing it to my lips, I sip slowly, letting the warm, sweet, earthy taste of herbs roll over my tongue. It's not bad.

I gulp the rest and hold out the cup. "It'll help me sleep?"

"Yep." She pours a refill. "It's been passed down through my family for generations."

"What's in it?" I tip back the cup and finish it in a long swallow.

"Damiana leaf, white oak bark, chamomile, lavender, and..." She blinks. "Other herbs."

She hesitated there. Why?

I stare down at the empty cup. "Explain the *other*."

She glances left, right, and mumbles, "Muira puama."

"Say again?"

"Muira—"

"I heard the first time. What is it?"

"A plant."

"And?"

"It treats menstrual disorders." She wings up a brow.

"Horseshit."

"No lie." Her mouth twitches. "It also helps with libido and male sexual performance problems."

A grunt puffs past my lips, and I return the cap to the thermos. "If you think I have issues with that—"

"No, I just thought..." She stares at her hands on her lap. "When a nice girl comes along, it'll give you a little boost. That's all."

"Don't put that crap in my drinks again."

Her eyes catch fire. "I brought you the tea because I wanted you to sleep well. Say *thank you*, Lorne." She rises to her knees, shoves her shoulders back, and hardens her voice. "Say it right now, and you better fucking mean it."

*Jesus.* I didn't tell her to come out here, half-dressed and ten kinds of seductive with her legs and her tits and her goddamn love potion.

Full lips form a pouty curve over her jutting chin. Sharp, high cheekbones underscore the ferocity in her deep brown eyes. I thought she was stunning before, but when she's pissed, she's intoxicating.

And resilient.

Her shields are so thick it's easy to forget the horrors she endured. John let her sister die. She didn't get to say goodbye, didn't get to be there during those final moments. Instead, he kept her in the dark, all the while raping and abusing her repeatedly.

Bruises mark her body, but she keeps the emotional trauma hidden, buried beneath all that free-spirited energy. I know she can't escape the pain. When she's alone with her thoughts, she relives every agonizing detail.

And all she asks is that I thank her for the tea.

"Thank you." I mean it and wish I could give her more.

She nods. Her lashes lift, and her gaze gravitates to mine.

In that shared look, we probe and analyze, trying and failing to read each other's thoughts. She doesn't know me, doesn't want to know me. But she wants *something*.

It's in the lift of her hand as it edges toward my face with uncertainty.

I drop back to my elbows, my entire body stretched taut in the open air. She angles for my jawline, fingers slack and closing the distance with excruciating hesitancy.

# Booted

Laid out beneath her, I have a direct view of the tent pitching my briefs. My insides throb, restless and hot, hard and ravenous. If she goes for my dick, I'll be inside her so fast she'll have to steal another pair of panties.

But she doesn't look at my erection. Her attention fixates on my face.

I wet my lips, silently demanding.

*Do it, baby. Put your hands on me. Stroke me. Grip me hard. Spread your cunt. Ride my cock. Take it. Fuck it.*

She leans in, mouth open, fingers hovering a decision away. The moment she touches my jaw, my arm snaps out. My brain moves slow, too groggy to stop my hand from clamping around her wrist.

What am I doing? Do I want to pull her to me? Push her away? Fuck her into mindless oblivion?

She's here because of John. Less than a week ago, she was chained to a wall and forced to endure *his* hunger and cruelty. She doesn't need mine.

I release her and jerk to the edge of the sleeping bag, white knuckled and wound up. "Go to bed."

Her face closes off, her arms falling to her sides.

"I'll leave the tea." She stands and heads toward the house.

"Raina." I wait for her to glance over her shoulder. "What tribe do you belong to?"

"My maternal grandparents were full-blooded Cherokee." She looks at her feet. "Good night."

I watch her walk the distance. When she slips inside, I stare at the door long after she closes it behind her.

Did she lock the bolt? Jake installed security cameras and motion-activated alarms that encompass a wide perimeter around the estate. Jarret is right across the hall from her, and I'll hear anything or anyone approaching.

She's safe.

But I won't be able to sleep until I check that lock.

By the time I make the trek to the porch, test the door, and jog back, I'm staggering beneath the weight of exhaustion. It hits me quick, dragging down my eyelids as I collapse onto the sleeping bag.

Within seconds, I'm out.

I sleep and wake frequently throughout the night, drenched in a cold sweat and shaking from nightmares. But unlike the past eight years, I fall back under quickly and doze for longer stretches of time.

By morning, I feel more rested than I have since I was a kid.

As the sky pales from black to gray, I pull on my clothes and boots, pack up the sleeping bag, and head inside.

The din of chatter and scent of pork grease lures me to the kitchen. Raina stands at the sink with her back to me as Jake putters around her, searching the cabinets.

The rest of the family gathers around the table, grabbing at the buffet of food in the center. They fight over biscuits, laughing and swatting at one another, too preoccupied to notice my entrance.

"What are you looking for?" Raina asks Jake, without glancing up from the pan she's scrubbing.

"The blueberry stuff—"

She points to the cabinet behind him and resumes her task.

I guess there hasn't been much reorganization since she lived here last. She seems to know where everything is.

Her hands work vigorously over the skillet, her banging body clad in my old clothes from high school. I was rangy back then, still growing into my height. But my jeans look fucking fantastic on her. They bunch around her ankles, about six inches too long, and hang low and loose on her hips. My God, her ass fills them out, the pockets cupping and squeezing those perky round cheeks.

Her hair falls in black sheets over the t-shirt, which slouches off one shoulder. She knotted the extra length at her midriff, baring a tantalizing sliver of sun-kissed skin. It doesn't get any sexier than that.

My pulse pounds through my body as I set my hat on the counter and drag a hand down my whiskered throat.

"Morning!" Conor spins toward me, a smile stretching across her whole face.

"Mornin'." I tip my head at her. "What's for breakfast?"

"Sausage, eggs, biscuits, berries, fried potatoes, and..." She holds up a slimy green thing. "What's this again?"

"Ramps." Raina doesn't look up from her scrubbing.

"Ramps." Conor's brows lift in a *whatever-that-is* look.

"Where did you find wild leeks?" I ask the back of the woman who has yet to acknowledge me.

"It grows on the hillside." She motions at the window without turning around.

The snippy dismal in her tone rubs me the wrong way.

As everyone settles in to eat, I cross the kitchen and step into her space. Leaning a hip against the counter, I fold my arms and stare down at her.

She rinses the pan and grabs another one.

I wait.

She cleans two more before slamming her hands down on the edge of the sink.

"What do you want, Lorne?" She glares at the soap bubbles.

"You look riled enough to bite yourself."

Behind me, the table of noisy eaters falls quiet.

She shoots them a dirty look and pushes away from the counter to face me. "How'd you sleep?"

"Fine."

Her eyes narrow, scrutinizing mine for the truth. "Liar."

"I slept *better.*"

"Are you going to train me today?"

Her tone shivers with agitation. Is this about last night? Because I sent her to bed? Does she think something happened between us? Something that could distract her from the reason she's here? If so, she has nothing to worry about.

"I need to run some errands," I say. "But you'll get your training."

She releases a breath. "Okay."

"Thank you for breakfast." I nod at the table. "Join us."

"I already ate." She cocks her head. "You have a lot of old jeans in your room that are way too small for you. Do you mind if I cut some of them into shorts?"

"Do whatever you want with them."

"Thanks." She steps back and strides out of the kitchen.

My gaze follows her out, lingering long after she slips around the corner.

Until Conor clears her voice.

I join them at the table and fill my plate with more food than I've seen in years.

"How was last night?" Jake bites down on a sausage link, eyes glimmering.

"Fine."

"On a scale of one to ten." He reclines in the chair. "How fine?"

Jarret drags a hand over his mouth, but I don't miss

his grimace.

They think I had sex with Raina. Why wouldn't they? I just got out of prison and spent the evening with a beautiful woman.

"Leave him alone." Conor points a finger at them. "Both of you. This is our first breakfast together and—"

"No, actually... Let's do this." I drop my fork on the plate, rest my forearms on the table, and stare at Jake. "Say what's on your mind."

"All right." He taps a finger on the armrest. "I want to know what you did with her. Seeing how she's a professional, I'm just curious. I want details."

"Christ." Jarret pinches the bridge of his nose and groans. "I don't want *any* details."

Jarret and I lost our virginities around the same time. We learned from each other by swapping stories, swapping *girls*, and exchanging kinky ideas. There was nothing we wouldn't talk about.

Times have changed.

"What's your problem?" Jake asks his brother.

"She fucked our old man." Jarret shakes with an over-dramatic shiver. "It's weird."

I lean forward and meet his eyes. "Your fiancé fucked my half-brother. Think about that. She was married to a man who shares my last name. A man you killed. *That* is fucking weird."

"Here we go." Maybe stands with her dishes and carries them to the sink. "I wondered how long it would take before that was brought up."

Conor glares at me. "Lorne doesn't mean to be rude."

"Yes, I do."

"That's okay, because you know what?" Maybe charges back to the table. "This needs to be aired."

Her hands tangle in the mass of blond curls around

her shoulders as she bursts into a tirade about her missing husband.

She blows out the whole sordid tale, one I already heard from Jarret. Except this time, I'm given a different perspective. An emotional frame of reference from a woman who felt deep guilt for hiding secrets from my family—the biggest one being the brother that Conor and I didn't know we had.

As she paces the kitchen and explains her side of the story, she doesn't make excuses or defend herself. But it's clear in her voice that she needed those eighteen months away from Jarret to come to terms with the decisions she made. The woman before me now is stronger, more confident than the one I met in prison two years ago.

She stops beside me and bends into my personal space. "You're going to warm up to me."

"I warmed up to Wyatt Longley. Then I gunned him down in a field."

"Lorne," Conor scolds.

"There's a soft center in you somewhere." Maybe straightens. "You'll let me see it someday."

I grunt. "Don't hold your breath."

She holds her breath. Literally. With her fists on her hips, she clamps her lips together and puffs out her cheeks.

Seconds tick by, and she doesn't move, doesn't breathe.

"Maybe, stop." Jarret leans forward, his gaze glued on her. "You're going to pass out."

She shakes her head, face turning red and eyes bulging as she watches me.

Adorable? I'm thinking it. Crazy? Oh, yeah. She's way off her mental reservation.

Aren't we all?

My lips tug at the corner, bouncing my cheek.

# Booted

She gasps, gulping for air. "Ha! A smile! Told you!"

"Where did you find this?" I ask Jarret, thrusting a thumb at her.

"She found me." The pussy-whipped motherfucker stares at her with throbbing, heart-shaped eyes.

"And you didn't let me go." Her entire demeanor turns to mush as she circles the table and plants a kiss on his open mouth.

He tries to deepen it, and his hand slides to her ass.

"Hold your horses, cowboy." She dances out of his grasp and heads toward the mudroom, drawling in a hillbilly accent. "I gotta get them critters some vittles up yonder and fix the *dern* fences down by the crick."

"I'll be *dreckly* behind ya, sugar," Jarret hollers after her. Then he looks at me, taking in my arched eyebrow. "What? She thinks I'm a redneck."

"You sound like one."

"It turns her on."

"You guys are sick." Conor laughs and rises from the table. She makes her way to my side and hugs my shoulders. "I missed you, big brother. So damn much."

"You, too." I squeeze her arm, marveling at the colorful murals of ink.

"Have you been to the ravine yet?"

"Went last night."

"Okay." With a sigh, she steps back. "If you're out there today, stop by and see me."

"It'll take me a few days to get back into the swing of things, but I'll check out your clinic soon." Eight years slams into me, knocking the air from my lungs. "My sister's a doctor."

"A damn good one, too." Jake stands and grips her hand. "I'll walk you out."

Jarret and I dig into our food as Jake leads Conor out the back door. Through the window, I watch him kiss

91

her. She moves to leave, and he pulls her back to kiss her again.

"How's she doing?" I ask Jarret.

"She has good days and bad days, but the good far outweighs the bad." He glances over his shoulder, watching as she leaves Jake standing on the porch. "He's helped her a lot, Lorne. He gets her in a way no one else does."

"I know."

To think, Raina's been through the same hell. Conor was raped by two men in one night. Raina was raped for two years. She might not see it that way, but it wasn't consensual. John forced her by threatening her family.

Conor was abused by our dad, and Raina was abused by the other man who raised us. I'm indebted to Jake for helping my sister when I couldn't. But is it my responsibility to help Raina? I can train her to shoot a gun and defend herself. Beyond that, I wouldn't know where to begin.

The back door opens and shuts, and Jake returns to the table. "What's wrong?"

I meet his eyes and look at Jarret to find him watching me.

"I didn't fuck her." I sit back and rub a hand against my thigh. "You know what your dad did to her."

"Yeah." Jake scowls at his plate. "She filled in the blanks last night. Her sister..." His jaw clenches. "That's fucking brutal."

"Then you understand what she's dealing with."

Jake nods. "I support whatever you decide to do with her and John Holsten."

"Same," Jarret says.

A weight I didn't know I was carrying falls off my shoulders. "Where are my guns?"

"Locked up in my safe," Jarret says. "You

remember the combination?"

"Yeah."

My attention drifts back to Conor, and a sudden gnawing urge tugs at me to run after her.

I move before my brain forms the words I want to say. I stride out of the house, off the back porch, and cross the field with quick, determined strides.

In the distance, her red hair gleams in the sunlight, flickering like the flames in my soul that are reserved only for her.

"Conor!" I quicken my gait until she pivots a few feet away.

As her green eyes search mine, affection and love glistens along her lower lashes.

Our relationship has taken some significant hits, but we'll never stop fighting for this bond between us. If there's one thing I can count on, it's the certainty that none of us will ever allow our family to disintegrate into a dysfunctional mess.

"I'm sorry." In two long strides, I erase the gap, with my hands twitching at my sides. "I'm sorry for abandoning you and leaving you with Dalton and being such an anti-social dick the past few—"

She throws herself into my arms and buries her face in my neck. "You're forgiven a thousand times over. God, I missed you, Lorne. It's just good to have you home again."

When she leans back, her smile penetrates my insides and soothes my blood. Her happiness forms a sphere of energy around her, radiating outward, like a tiny world of its own.

"Conor, listen." I rest a hand against her face. "I don't know when I'll get back to the way things were, if it'll be tomorrow or next week, or if I'll ever be the person you remember. Sometimes, it feels like I'm starting over."

"It's okay. Starting over is good. As long as you do it

with us."

I close my eyes and absorb her positivity, letting it recharge my neurons until they rekindle and spark.

"I love you," she says, drawing my gaze to hers. "Dammit, Lorne. I just... I really missed my big brother."

"I love you, too." I pull her against me and kiss her hair. "More than you know."

"What can I do to help you?"

*I don't know.*

"I need time." I grip the back of her head and put my face in hers. "No matter what, I'm not going anywhere. I'll never abandon you again."

"I know." Her eyes brim with tears, her smile glowing with trust.

"Go on." I release her and step back. "My brilliant sister is a big fancy doctor now, and she has critters to save."

"That's right." She walks backward. "I'm the smartest one in the family."

"Let's not get carried away."

She flips me off, grinning, and turns back to the trail. I watch her go until she vanishes beyond the hill. Then I return to the kitchen, where Jarret and Jake are discussing ranch business.

After breakfast, we clear the dishes. The guys head to the field, and I make my way to the suite that now belongs to me.

Raina sits on the bed, surrounded by denim and armed with a pair of scissors.

"Are you going to stab me with those?" I step into the room and close the door.

"We'll see how my training goes."

She doesn't sound as curt as she did in the kitchen, but something's wedged up her ass.

I stride through the room, snatch the scissors from

her hand, and toss them aside. "What's with the sour mood?"

"Your asshole reflex must be contagious."

"Don't put this on me. Take accountability for your own attitude and actions."

She sniffs and leans back. Then her shoulders sag. "You're right."

When she doesn't elaborate, I bend down and stare at her from an inch away, with my hands braced on the mattress on either side of her hips.

I want to hear what she's thinking, feeling. Because I love talking to her. She's more like me than anyone I know. It's the wildness in her, the uncultivated way she views the world.

She isn't bound by social constructs and doesn't exert energy on outward appearances. Everything that matters to her resides in the space between the earth and her soul.

She's guided by feelings and instinct where I'm led by cool logic, but we share the same desire for the right result in the end.

Peering up at me with deep brown eyes, she scrapes her teeth across her bottom lip and sighs. "I got a little twisted up in my head when I went to bed. You're just so...ugh! One minute I think you like me. The next you hate me. It shouldn't matter. I shouldn't *care,* but I made the decision to stay here and work on a plan that involves you. After you pushed me away last night, I thought..."

"I wouldn't help."

She lifts a shoulder. "You send a lot of mixed signals."

"Come with me." I push off the bed and stride out of the room.

Raina

9

My insides quiver with curiosity as I follow Lorne down the hall and into Jarret's room. He slips into the walk-in closet and spins the combination lock on the floor-to-ceiling safe.

When it opens, he removes a shotgun and a pistol and checks them both for bullets.

I bite the inside of my cheek. He's not supposed to handle firearms, even if they're empty.

The moment I have that thought, he thrusts the biggest gun into my arms.

Surprised by the heavy weight, I adjust my grip, jostling it in an attempt to properly hold it.

He grabs the barrel and shoves it downward, his voice smacking like a hammer. "Never point a gun at my fucking face."

"I just watched you check the chamber—"

"*Always* treat every gun like it's loaded."

My neck stiffens. I treated John's gun as loaded, and we know how that turned out.

Gathering several boxes of ammunition, he locks the safe and lumbers back to his suite. "Keep your finger off the trigger unless you're ready to shoot."

I jerk my hand away from the trigger guard and aim the shotgun down, gripping it awkwardly as I trail behind him.

He recites a dozen other safety rules in a rumbling, emotionless voice.

*Be aware of my target and what's behind it. Understand the mechanical characteristics of the gun I'm using. Don't depend on the gun's safety to keep it from firing...*

As he drones on, I realize my training has begun.

In the bedroom, he crouches on the floor and breaks down both weapons into a panoply of metal parts. Then he reassembles them in a blur of motion, his huge hands moving with confidence as he explains how to fit each piece back together.

"Your turn." He takes them apart again.

"I'll never remember all that."

"Then by all means, go back to doing what you're good at." He gives my body a deliberate up and down glower of judgment.

"You're a cocksucker, you know that?"

"No, darlin'. That is one thing I am not." He tosses off his hat and reaches behind him to yank his shirt over his head, baring the sculpted monolith of his torso. "I want those guns back together by the time I'm out of the shower."

The only guns holding my attention are the ones bulging and flexing from his shoulders. He's an eight-pack man with a sparse smattering of hair across square pecs that look hard enough to bounce bullets.

One would think with all that bulk that he'd be plodding around with stiff, lead-footed movements. But as he rises from his crouch, his hand falls to his belt buckle and the line of his body flows upward in a loose, sinuous roll of hips and abs.

It's an alluring crunch of upper body strength with the nimble sensuality of a male stripper.

His boots come together as he straightens. His chin dips down, and hell to the damn... The bunching of denim around his fly creates an enticing bulge, one that's undeniably filled to the extent of its seams.

I openly gawk as he ambles away, toeing off his boots and removing his belt. Surely, he's not going to...

Yep. He shoves down his jeans and briefs, kicks them aside, and strolls to the master bathroom unabashedly nude.

The bricks of his glutes tighten with his strides, and sinews bunch and play along the valley of his spine. There's no loose skin anywhere. Every inch of him is taut, hard, and honed like the sharpest blade.

Maybe he's trying to torment me, but I don't think that's it. I've heard stories about the loss of privacy and inhibition in prison. Clothes are stripped. Showers are open. Shyness is simply not accommodated.

He disappears into the bathroom, leaving the door ajar. The shower turns on, and a moment later, steam wafts from within.

I imagine him standing under the spray, his head tilted back, and a soapy hand working over his cock. Is he long? Thick? Swollen with arousal?

Men rarely live up to the fantasy, but the fantasy's all I need. My pussy clenches, stirring from dormancy in waves of heat.

I'm tempted to lie back and finger myself to orgasm. When was the last time I did that? Not when I lived in Texas. John fucked my libido into extinction.

The last time I felt any sexual urges was when I first

moved here and caught a glimpse of Jake and Jarret. What would Lorne say if I told him I touched myself while thinking about his brothers?

Well, they're not the ones I'm thinking about now, and that's dangerous in itself. Lorne might be a damn fine sight to look at, but he's meaner than a snake. Sometimes, I wonder if he treats people like shit just for the hell of it.

That's the real reason for my mood this morning. He pushed me away last night when all I did was try to be nice.

He hurt my feelings.

I know better than to give him that power over me. Feelings aren't part of our arrangement. I won't tolerate him disrespecting me, and I'll continue to stand up to him at every turn. But I can't let him get to me.

Indifference is the only way to deal with Lorne Cassidy.

He wants his guns put together, and I'll try to do that. Only because it's part of my training. I'll learn everything there is to learn about a firearm so that the next time I shoot John Holsten, I won't fail.

Turning my attention to the scattered parts, I throw myself into the task.

Too soon, the shower shuts off, and Lorne rolls out in a mist of condensation with a towel wrapped around his trim hips.

I succeeded in sliding the bolt thingy into the hole where the barrel's supposed to go, but I might've messed up the order of operations. If he shows me again, I'll get the hang of it.

He glances at my work, and his lip curls back. "Did you even try?"

"Yes, of course. I—"

"Fucking worthless." He snags his jeans from the floor.

A hot ember lodges in my throat, but I swallow it

down. "You need to have a little patience with me."

"That *was* me being patient. I gave you a simple task and clearly expected too much north of your ears."

"Oh..." I laugh with mirthless disbelief and drop the gun parts. "No. No, you will not talk to me that way." I slowly rise to my feet, my voice shaking on the edge of explosion. "Apologize. Right now."

He turns his back and collects his clothes, dismissing me.

I can't make him retract his insult, but I don't have to stand here and look at him.

Pivoting toward the door, I walk out with more calm than I feel.

"Raina." His footsteps follow as heavy as his voice. "Get back here."

I pick up my pace and make it to the hall before his fist captures my hair and yanks me back against his chest.

"Where are you going?" He breathes at my ear.

"Let go." I claw at his grip, unable to budge the steel vise of his fingers.

His other arm clamps around my waist, and panic jolts through me. But I force myself to go still so he can focus on my words.

"Bully me all you want, Lorne. You'll be the one walking like John Wayne for the rest of your life. Don't forget I prepare your food, and I swear on all that is holy your next meal will grow warts on your asshole and spread a rash to your balls. Everything below your belt will be so painful to look at you won't just want your dick to fall off. You'll take a knife to it in horrified desperation."

"Christ." He releases a sharp breath, and his hold on me disappears.

I lurch forward, burning the breeze in my hurry down the hall. I don't look back until I reach the foyer.

He stands where I left him, arms at his sides, towel

hanging precariously on his hips, and gaze pinned on mine. His stunned face looks like that of a coldblooded predator, but there's definitely shock there, etched in the terrible beauty of his scowl.

I continue through the house and out the back door. The summer heat sucks the air from my lungs, and I squint against the unforgiving sun, wishing I owned sunglasses.

At least he didn't follow me.

Weapons training will have to wait until I can stomach the thought of looking at him again.

I have plenty of distractions, such as an herb garden to revive, berries to forage in the grove across the field, and meals to plan.

I spend the rest of the day doing just that. I don't know where Lorne went, and thankfully, I don't see him again until dinner.

The smoky aroma of barbecued meat permeates the kitchen as I set out the brisket, fried hominy, and warm bean bread. These were some of my favorite foods as a child. I doubt I prepared them as well as my grandmother did, but everything smells delicious.

The door to the mudroom opens, followed by the clomp of boots. One by one, the ranchers find their way to the table, leaving a trail of dirt on the floor I just cleaned.

I didn't sign up to be their maid, but I can't stand a dirty kitchen. Some ground rules might be in order.

Lorne is the last to enter, his jeans carrying fewer stains than the others. His eyes dart directly to mine, and I busy myself with the pans in the sink.

"This looks amazing, Raina." Maybe lifts a spoonful of hominy to her nose and inhales.

"Thank you." My stomach rumbles.

I haven't eaten since breakfast, and I don't know the protocol. What's my role here? John never ate his meals with me.

# Booted

"Oh my God, this is delicious," Conor says around a mouth full of brisket.

"How was your day?" Jake settles in beside her and runs his knuckles along her cheek.

"I treated a horse with desmitis. The poor thing."

As she launches into her medical care, Lorne pulls out the chair next to his and finds my eyes.

*Sit*, he mouths.

I'd rather not sit by him, but it's the only seat left. I can act like a child and refuse. Or I can do the mature thing.

As I lower beside him, Conor points her fork at him and asks, "What did you do today?"

He kicks back in the seat, all swagger and sex appeal. "I bought a cell phone, renewed my driver's license, worked out, and was put in my place by a very scary woman." His eyes drift to me.

A tide of heat rises up my neck, and not just because I'm imagining him working out.

"Why were you put in your place?" Jake glances between Lorne and me, his expression indecipherable.

"I showed my ass," Lorne says matter-of-factly.

"In the metaphoric sense?" Conor lifts a brow.

"In every sense." He stretches a leg beneath the table, his fathomless green eyes fastened to mine.

It's not an apology, and I'm not willing to let it go just yet. "Was there a lesson learned?"

He stares down at the food he hasn't touched on his plate, his lips twisting into a cocky smirk. "Don't piss off the woman who prepares your meals."

Around the table, mouths freeze in mid-chew.

"The food is safe." I pick up my fork and demonstrate by taking a hearty bite of barbecued brisket.

A communal sigh of relief ripples through the room, and the conversation steers onto safe topics, like this year's cattle stock.

After dinner, Lorne sticks around to help me tidy up. The family is good about loading the dishwasher and offering to pitch in. They've been fending for themselves their whole lives. But I chase them away to clean up the mess I made while cooking.

"I have a few more errands to run tonight." Lorne leans against the counter beside me. "You'll be riding along."

"Why?" I toss down the towel and turn toward him.

"We both need clothes."

"You want to take me shopping?" I can't picture it. "I don't have money. Besides, the stores will be closed."

"You're earning your keep, and I have a friend who owns a shop." He strides away. "We leave in ten."

"I need to take a shower."

"I'll be in the truck." He prowls out of the kitchen.

I growl under my breath and head to the bathroom.

Twenty minutes later, I stroll out to his pickup. I skipped washing my hair in lieu of cutting a pair of his jeans into shorts. And I cut them *short,* right beneath the panty line, giving a new meaning to *boyfriend jeans.*

His gaze flies straight to my legs as I climb in beside him.

"You can't go out in public like that." He rests an arm on the steering wheel, his expression tense.

"I can, and I will." I latch the seat belt.

"You look like a buckle bunny."

"If you don't lay off, you'll be shopping alone." I adjust the knot of the flannel top to sit higher so my entire midriff is bared.

With a grunt, he starts the engine and hits the road.

The moon hovers over the tops of the trees and follows us into town. He takes the main drag through Sandbank and pulls into the driveway of a modest colonial home with a columned front porch and evenly placed windows.

A familiar SUV sits in front of the single garage, with a light bar mounted on the roof.

"What are we doing here?" Roiling heat ignites in my belly.

"Stay in the truck." He climbs out and stalks to the front door.

After two curt knocks, the porch light illuminates, and Sheriff Fletcher steps out.

I sink into the shadows of the cab, my pulse thundering.

John Holsten and the sheriff of Sandbank are thick as thieves, their corruption so intertwined I wouldn't be surprised if John was shacked up here right now, waiting for me to wander into town alone.

My spine chills as I lock the doors and nervously scan the sleepy street.

Fletcher tips his hat at Lorne, and Lorne gives him a nod in greeting. They exchange words, a conversation I can't hear, while assuming the same dominant postures—boots planted in wide stances, hands resting on belt buckles, shoulders back, and eyes stony.

Lorne motions at the truck, and the sheriff's greasy gaze slithers to mine. My breath stutters.

What is Lorne doing? Why the fuck are they staring at me?

Five minutes pass. Then ten. Lorne does most of the talking. Neither of them shows any signs of hostility, but the strain on Fletcher's face confesses his growing agitation.

The confrontation ends with a jerky nod from the sheriff. He remains motionless and watchful as Lorne steps off the porch, unlocks the truck, and slides in beside me.

"What was that?" I grip the armrest, trembling on pins and needles.

"A prayer meetin'." With a straight face, he pulls onto the road.

"Was that a joke? Because I'm not laughing. That man is a rat with a badge. Did you know he and John went to school together?"

He stops at a red light and squints at me. "No."

"They've been good ol' pals since before John met his wife."

"What are you saying?"

"I'm saying Sheriff Fletcher had a hand in the deaths of Julep and your mother."

He searches my face. "You believe that."

"I believe it's possible that a small-town sheriff shows up at the scene of a car wreck, messes with evidence, and makes it look like an accident. All the while, his best bud is sitting on oil-rich land with the promise of sharing some of that wealth."

His nostrils flare. "Motherfuck."

The light turns green, and he punches the gas.

"What did you say to him?" I ask.

"Told him I had what John was looking for."

My hands ball on my lap.

He glances at my fists and returns to the road. "I went there with a warning, Raina. If John steps foot in Sandbank, Fletcher will contact me."

"Or?"

"Or he'll spend the rest of his life behind bars."

"He'll take your family down with him."

"Not if he wants his wife to live." His hand clenches on the steering wheel. "If there's one thing Fletcher loves more than money, it's his high school sweetheart."

My blood shivers. Lorne threatened the sheriff's wife, and I have no doubt he'd follow through on that threat if something happened to his family.

He drives the truck down Main Street, the traffic scarce this time of night. Sandbank is enclosed on all sides by farmland and cattle ranges. The closest highway sits on the outskirts of town.

He heads in that direction and stops at the intersection that marks the city limit. A few miles up ahead lies the freeway. A huge tractor supply warehouse spreads out on my right. Anyone and everyone coming into Sandbank passes through here.

"Is there always a security guard on duty?" I point at the marked car parked in the shadowed corner of the warehouse lot.

"As long as I can remember. Old Cal doesn't trust his security cameras. He's been robbed and vandalized too many times over the years."

Movement shifts beside the security car, drawing my eyes to the young man standing near the building. He lifts a cigarette to his mouth, his tall frame clad in a drab security uniform.

I have an idea. It's a long shot but worth the try.

"Pull into that parking lot." I brush my hair over my shoulders. "I want to talk to that guy."

"Talk to him about what?" His lips form a flat line.

"If what you said is true, Cal's security guards see every car coming and going out of Sandbank. I'm going to ask that one to keep a look out for us."

He barks a sound of disdain. "Waste of time."

"If you're so certain, give me a chance to prove you right."

He rolls his lips between his teeth. Then he turns into the empty lot.

"Right here is fine." I point at the first parking spot.

On the opposite end of the blacktop, the security guard lowers into his car, swallowed by the darkness within.

"Give me the number for your cell phone." I search the cab for something to write it on.

He removes a wrinkled receipt from the glove box, jots down the number, and hands it to me, with annoyance written across his face. "Try not to get yourself abducted."

Lorne might be a class-A prick, but I know he won't take his eyes off me between here and that car. Besides, John Holsten would be a fool to show up with Lorne's truck sitting here.

I hop out and stuff the paper in my pocket. Hair swaying around my shoulders and boots clicking on the pavement, I glide across the lot with a subtle sway in my hips.

When I approach the passenger door of the security car, the window immediately rolls down. I lean in and fold my arms on the frame, giving the early-twenties security guard an unhindered view of cleavage.

Blue eyes zero in, hooded and captivated.

"Holy hell," he whispers. "Where did you come from? Because one thing's for certain, you ain't from around here."

"Evening, handsome." I trap my bottom lip between my teeth and let it slowly slide free. "Want some company?"

"I could never turn down a pretty thing like you." His gaze jumps to Lorne's truck, to the cameras on the building, and back to me. "But I'm not supposed to let people on the property."

"Aww, shoot." I straighten and hook a thumb beneath the waistband of the cut-offs, inching them so low it leaves little to the imagination. "I'm in a bit of a predicament and could really use some help from a strong, strapping man like yourself."

The sounds of his breaths grow deeper, faster. A

# Booted

moment later, the door unlocks with a victorious click. I climb into the car.

# 10

## Lorne

The moment Raina disappears inside the dark car, my stomach knots. Restlessness grips my legs. My body temperature rises, and I feel like my insides are shaking.

My anxiousness is completely unwarranted. The security guard is such a skinny little twat she could swat the air and knock him over.

But I don't like it. I hate that she's alone with him. I hate that I hate it.

Twisting the dream catcher pendant on my wrist, I probe the surrounding fields and vacant roads. My foot bounces, and I squeeze the back of my neck, unraveling by the second.

Blowing out a series of short breaths, I try to gain control and ignore the car that obscures her. But my gaze crosses the lot without my permission, straining to make out the dark interior.

What the almighty fuck is she doing in there? She wouldn't have sex with him. Not for something as menial as keeping a lookout for John Holsten.

But there are other things she could offer in exchange for the guard's cooperation.

A growl rips from my throat, and I reach for the handle to shove the door open.

Across the lot, Raina emerges from the car, hits the door closed with her hip, and struts her ass back to the truck.

Her glossy black hair shines beneath the glow of the lighting poles. Her tits jiggle in the gap of the flannel shirt, and her long legs carry her with a seductive, defiant air.

She's breathtaking, spellbinding, built head to toe from earth, wind, and handcrafted sin.

She slides into the truck and buckles up, her expression closed off and shoulders tight. "Where to next?"

"What happened?" I bow across the seat, grinding my jaw with built-up tension.

"It's all good. He'll call—"

"What did you do?"

Her gaze flicks upward, as if seeking patience. Then she claps those huge brown eyes on me. "I let him feel me up."

My vision clouds, and my hands clench into burning fists. "Over or under the shirt?"

"Under." She juts her chin.

I seethe. I growl. I harden in places I shouldn't, as violent boiling outrage steams from every pore in my body. I want to grab her throat, maul her mouth, and wail on her ass until it's red and swollen.

How could she so flippantly let a man grope her? After the brutality she suffered with John, shouldn't she be running in the other direction?

How does she not understand why something like this would piss me off?

# Booted

Fuck, I don't even understand it. I'm tempted to shove her out of the truck and drive to the nearest liquor store. I need a drink and some goddamn peace.

A ringing phone breaks through my haze, and I follow her line of sight to the device on the seat between us.

"That's Ford." She glances at the car on the other side of the lot.

*Ford* is the little boob-grabbing fuck?

I crack my neck, my thoughts swimming in blood. "That's not a name. It's a goddamn truck."

"Do you mind?" She points at the chirping phone and snatches it without waiting for my answer.

"Hello?" A smile curls her demon lips. "Yeah, it's me." She tilts her head, listening, then releases a husky laugh. "You, too, honey. Now don't forget to tell your boys to keep an eye out—"

I yank the phone from her hand and press it to my ear. "You're dead, motherfucker."

The silence on the other end yanks my attention to the car fifty yards away.

"Who is this?" Ford's voice wobbles.

"Lorne Cassidy."

"Oh, shit..." He gasps, and something thumps on the other end. "Fuck!"

Of course, he knows me. My trial was the biggest news story in Sandbank history.

He disconnects the call. A second later, he flicks on his headlights and races out of the lot, fishtailing as he swerves onto the road and out of sight.

"He can run." I drop the phone and flex my hands. "But I'll catch that dumbass son of a bitch."

"Yeah, you do that. Right after I rip off your dumbass balls and slap your dumbass face with them." She stomps her foot. "Dammit, Lorne. He was going to help us."

I stab a finger in the direction of the car. "You let him grope you!"

"They're just boobs." She throws her arms in the air and lets them drop. "I don't get you."

Christ, her fucking mouth... I want to shove my cock between those shameless, taunting lips and shut her the fuck up.

I twist toward her, giving her the full force of my eyes. "Don't *ever* do that again."

"Let me get this straight." She sits taller. "You don't want to touch me, and no one else can touch me, either."

"Sounds like you get me just fine."

"You don't own me."

"No, but while you're living under my roof, you'll abide by my rules."

"Okay, *Dad*."

My hand flies to her throat, and I wrench her face to mine. "I assure you there isn't a fatherly thought going through my head."

She swallows against my palm, and fear blazes in her eyes. She trembles with it, but instead of pulling back or clawing at my grip, she leans closer. Not in submission, but in brazen contempt.

"Do it." She bares her teeth and digs her nails into the denim on my thigh. "Choke me, if it makes you feel like a man."

Fucking hell, she turns me on. I can make a homicidal inmate walk the other way with just a look. But this wisp of a woman seems to welcome my fury. I know she fears me, yet she never cowers.

I release her. Her fingers fly to her neck, and her eyes... If looks could kill, I'd be laid out in a pile of eviscerated organs.

We make a toxic pair, she and I. The sooner I get her

trained and out of my life, the better. Because if she stays around much longer, I *will* fuck her, and it won't be decent or reconcilable. I'll punish her with every feral breath in my body while destroying every orifice in hers. I don't think either of us would survive it.

She crosses her arms. "You're such a—"

"Find something to listen to." I toss my phone at her and shove the truck into drive.

If I know her as well as I think I do, she's burning to tell me all the ways I'm a miserable fuck. Hell knows, I don't need the reminder.

She scowls at the phone in her hand, her thumb slapping angrily against the screen. After a few more swipes, a snappy beat stomps through the speakers of the truck.

She's playing *Cowboy Casanova* by Carrie Underwood, and given the smirk on her face, she selected the man-bashing song for me.

As I veer onto the road, she sets the phone on the seat and angles toward the passenger window.

Our last stop sits on the outer edge of town, nestled in a long one-story group of buildings. I park in front of one of several adjacent retail shops and shut off the engine.

The lot is empty, all the stores closed for the evening. After spending the day running errands and dealing with people, my patience is shot.

Society is a steaming pile of self-centered fucks. I couldn't help but laugh at their common miseries as they huffed in the long line at the drivers license bureau, honked and road raged at other drivers, and sneered at crying children.

When I saw a baby in the phone store today, I couldn't stop staring. I don't care if I looked like a pedophile. She was just so damn beautiful and innocent with those big tears in her eyes. Meanwhile, the assholes in line glared and winced.

I can't stomach the thought of being around more assholes.

So here I am, sitting in front of a glass door with a sign that scrawls *Cora's Clothier* in curly letters.

In high school, Cora said she would open her own shop in this very location. I'm not surprised she made it happen.

When I called her a couple of hours ago, she was more than happy to let me in after-hours.

I scrutinize the shadows beneath the awnings, the residential homes along the street, and the unlit windows of the closed shops. If John hired someone to collect Raina, now would be the time to attack.

I'm not packing a gun, but I always carry a hunting knife in my boot. It's the same knife that cut Jarret and I out of our restraints the night Conor was brutalized. It saved our lives, and I trust it to save me again.

Raina stirs beside me, her eyes sweeping over the sign on the door. "Who's Cora?"

The last girl I fucked. I took her to prom. Then I drove her to a field and took her in the bed of my truck. I ripped her fancy dress in my urgency, but she didn't care. She's a seamstress, after all, and by the dreamy look on her face that night, she was fixing to chase me for a lifetime of more.

I liked her well enough. Hell, she could've been the one I married. But life had different plans for me.

"She's an old friend." I exit the truck and pocket the phone. "Slide out on my side."

Raina's chest hitches, and her gaze darts over the pitch-black surroundings.

"Don't rush on my account." I drop my hands to my hips.

# Booted

After another moment of indecision, she scoots across the seat and climbs out.

"Do *not* leave my side." With a hand on her stiff elbow, I lead her into the shop and lock the bolt behind me.

A bell rings overhead, followed by the pad of soft footsteps. A tall, willowy blonde emerges from the back, and my breath snags. Lord help me over the fence, she's even prettier than I remember.

My hand falls from Raina's arm, my skin tight and hot.

Cora's huge smile spirals through the space between us, and she squeals with delight. Weaving around circular racks of clothing, she hurries toward me and tackles me in a hug.

"Welcome home, baby." She leans back, her guileless gray eyes full of sweetness and laughter. "I'm so glad you called."

"Thanks for seeing me after hours."

"Anytime." She cups my face and slides her hands down my neck and over my shoulders. "My stars and garters, look at you! I mean... Wow. You're quite the looker, Lorne Cassidy. You always were, but the years have been very, very kind."

The years have been lonely and cruel, but I don't bother correcting her.

"And who's this lovely lady?" She turns toward the simmering woman at my side.

"Raina Benally." Raina gives her a stiff wave and an even stiffer smile.

"Raina's a friend of the family," I say. "She's staying with us for a while and needs some clothes fit for the ranch."

"Excellent." Cora claps her hands together. "I'll hook you both up."

"How's business?" I stroll through the shop, keeping an eye on Raina while searching for exterior doors.

"It's been a tough eight years," she says. "My passion is tailoring and shopping for new clothing lines, but most of my time goes to building my brand and bringing in dedicated clientele. Self-employment means long hours and no personal life." She holds up her ringless left hand. "Still not married. Guess I haven't found a man willing to put up with my ambitions." Her gaze lowers to a garment rack, and she fidgets with the hangers, mumbling, "Or maybe I've been waiting for the right one to come home."

I catch her meaning loud and clear and wouldn't mind giving it a go with her again. At a minimum, I'd enjoy sinking into her soft cunt. As the idea settles through me, I brace for a roaring fire to spark in my belly.

Nothing ignites, and my gaze shoots to Raina.

She stands off to the side, a hand on her cocked hip, and her expression pinched as if she swallowed a lemon. Just the sight of her dries my mouth. She's an addictive drink of legs and attitude, with a kick of heat and vinegar.

That's when I feel it, low and angry beneath my belt. A twisting, thrashing, burning inferno of frustration.

I roll back my shoulders and turn to Cora. "You keep the back door locked?"

"When I remember." She laughs. "It's quiet around here."

"Mind if I check it? I don't want someone slipping in and catching you unaware while you're here alone at night."

"Oh." Her cheeks flush. "Yes. Please, do. It's right through there."

I follow the point of her finger through the cramped space and spot the door beyond a row of shelving units. Heading that way, I mark Raina's location.

# Booted

The bolt on the door looks old and easy to kick in. There's no overhead bell like the front entrance. Nothing to alert me if someone breaks in.

I glance at Raina's bristling posture and search the space around the door, honing in on the trashcan. Empty cans of energy drinks fill it to the rim. No wonder Cora's so bubbly and energetic. She's hyped up on caffeine.

As I line up the cans in front of the door to create a makeshift alarm, my thoughts descend to the swelling hunger between my legs.

I've only been out of prison for a few days, but I can't ignore this restless ache much longer.

I need to get laid.

## Raina

I lean against a display table of western apparel, wishing I was anywhere but here. I don't need a degree in human sexuality to tune into the leg-humping vibes between Lorne and Cora. Their lingering eye contact, the ease in which she touches him, and the undercurrent of intimate history is enough to make my stomach collapse.

The beautiful, bouncy, animated seamstress is everything I'm not. She glows with sheltered innocence and passes out Disney smiles like it's her only mission in life. She's blonde and fair and bursting with musical light.

Meanwhile, I'm tempted to retreat into the shadows with my black cloud of *fuck this*.

I have a mission, too. It's to kill the man who tortured me and let my sister die. I guess that makes me the bitter, vindictive villain. Hopefully, not the kind that perishes in the flames of her own stupidity.

In the back of the store, Lorne lumbers around the door, setting up some kind of booby trap. At least he's dependable. I can rely on him to keep me alive and insult me every time he opens his mouth.

"Look at him, being all protective." Cora rests a hand against her breastbone. "I always knew he had a heart made of honey."

Oh, his heart is honey, all right. Honey that crystallized and hardened in a cold dark corner for eight years.

"Should we get started?" I gesture at the racks of clothes.

"For sure!" She flutters around, gathering denim and cotton while carrying on about this season's fashion.

When Lorne emerges from the back, she directs him to the dressing room.

"Remove your shirt and…" She sweeps her gaze down his torso. "Whatever else. I'm gonna grab a tape measure."

Does she really need to measure him? *Just ask his size.*

I release a breath, irked by my dreadful mood.

The measuring and flirting and half-naked touching—this is happening. I just need to deal with it.

Lorne snaps his fingers, drawing my attention to his wide stance in the dressing room.

"Stay where I can see you," he growls, too low for Cora to hear.

I give him a middle-finger salute and a saccharine smile. Then I step as far away as I can while remaining in his line of sight. There, I focus on the front door, because that's a safer view than the asshole stripping in my periphery.

Footsteps sound behind me and stumble to a stop.

"Oh sweet lord baby Jesus," Cora whispers over my shoulder. "That's more man than I have ever… Well, I *have* seen him. All of him, if you know what I mean."

# Booted

On the other side of the store, Lorne folds up his clothes, his mouthwatering body clad in tight-fitting briefs.

My pulse responds with a punch of eagerness, as if this were the first time I ogled his obscenely perfect physique.

Evidently, this isn't a first for Cora, either.

I give her a narrowed look, which she interprets as a question.

"Prom night." She sighs blissfully, her voice achingly quiet. "God, he looked downright lickable in a tux. And out of it. I thought he was the one, you know. Then he got arrested."

I've never been to prom. Never been with a guy who didn't pay by the hour. I've certainly never referred to anyone as *the one*. But if I did, I wouldn't have let him go.

"Did you visit him in prison?" I glance at Lorne, confirming he's out of hearing range.

"No, I..." She swallows. "It was too hard."

Too hard for *her*? If she loved him, she would've carried her fragile little heart to the Big Mac and supported him every grueling day he was imprisoned there.

I'm all for Lorne finding a nice girl, but this one isn't right for him.

I also might be a tad bit jealous.

So I do the responsible thing and unleash my inner bitch. "It's too bad what happened to him."

"What?"

"You didn't hear?" I edge close and whisper at her ear, "He contracted a sexually-transmitted illness in prison. The debilitating kind."

The blood drains from her cheeks. "How debilitating?"

"It made him sterile." I scrunch my face in horror. "I feel terrible for him."

"What is it? Like HIV or something?"

Can HIV cause male infertility? I'm not sure, but I roll with it. "Yeah."

"How did he get that in pris...?" Her eyes widen. "Lord love a duck, that stuff really happens in there?"

Not as often as people think.

I nod. "All the time."

"That's awful." She touches her throat and stares at him wistfully. "He would've made such pretty babies."

Ain't that the God's honest truth.

"Well..." She straightens. "Since I chose my career over childbearing, I'm beginning to think he was returned to me for a reason." Her gaze wanders to the half-naked cowboy across the room. "He can put his shoes under my bed any day of the week and twice on Sunday."

I chew the inside of my cheek. "He's contagious."

She waves a hand between us, brushing away my words. "That's what condoms are for, sweetie."

A fist clenches in my gut as she strides away with her tape measure, swinging hips, and no doubt a beautiful, genuine smile decorating her pretty face.

Lorne lifts off his hat and sets it aside as she approaches. His green eyes find mine briefly before settling on her.

"Arms up." She turns him toward the mirror with his back to me. "I'm just gonna take some measurements."

His arms lift, flexing the tendons along his sides. Then the touching begins.

Her hands glide up and down the length of his torso, measuring, caressing, and lingering on the rounded line of his tight ass.

I can't see his groin, but I know he's responding. The layers of muscle in his back heave and squeeze with his breaths. His eyes capture mine in the mirror, and his nostrils pulse to accommodate the force of air from his lungs.

My chest clamps, and everything inside me coils to lash out. He doesn't want anyone to touch me, yet he's basking in his double standard with his reflection staring right at me.

Maybe he's trying to hurt me? Because of what I did with the security guard?

I really didn't mean to upset him. I didn't know he cared.

Does he care? It sure as hell doesn't seem that way.

Cora shifts behind him, lifting on tiptoes to whisper at his ear. At his nod, she drops the tape measure and roams her hands around his hips to his abs. And lower.

His eyes close, breaking our connection, and his palm lands on the mirror to support the lean of his body. He groans at whatever she does to his dick, and that's my cue to walk away.

I wrap my arms around my midsection, shaking with the effort to hold in my emotions. I shouldn't feel anything. I'm not here to be coddled or adored. That sort of thing was never in the cards for me.

When I reach the front door, I realize I'm trapped. I might not be thinking clearly, but I'm not stupid enough to go out there alone.

"Raina?" Cora strides toward me, her eyebrows squishing together. "He, uh... He sent me to get you."

Ever the protector. Even when he's getting a hand job.

I suck in a burning breath. "I'll be right there."

"He seems kind of angry. I wouldn't make him wait." She scrutinizes me with suspicion. "Is there something between you two?"

Poison. Acid. Volcanic animosity. It festers and fizzes and spews in every direction whenever we're together.

"Not at all." I brush past her and storm back to the dressing room.

He waits in the doorway, hands on his hips and feet braced apart. How a man can look threatening in underwear is beyond me.

It's the devil in his eyes, blazing at an intensity that evaporates the oxygen from the air.

"I told you not to leave my sight." His harsh whisper booms through me, rattling my teeth.

"I don't want to be the cockblock—"

"Sit." He stabs a finger at the stool in the dressing room.

"Please, don't make me watch—"

He grabs my arm and yanks me into the small room. Closing the door behind him, he brings his mouth to my ear. "You will sit, because the alternative is chains and whips, busted eyes and broken bones, John Holsten raping you, sodomizing you, and Tiana's death going unpunished."

The images crash through me, awakening memories and grief I've tried so hard to lock away. Resistance leaks from my bones, and I slump onto the stool, trembling. Cold. Hollowed out.

"I'm sorry, Raina." He crouches before me and brushes the hair from my face. "I can't risk your safety. I won't."

He rises and opens the door.

"Everything okay?" Cora stands on the other side, her arms loaded with clothes.

"Fine." He takes the bundle from her and steps aside. "I'll change out here while you get started with Raina."

She slips in and shuts the door. "Hey, honey. Are you—?"

"I'm good." I shake out of my stupor and stand.

# Booted

"Okay, um..." She looks me over. "Do you know your sizes?"

I did before I lost weight in John's restraints. "No."

Without asking me to remove my clothes, she takes my measurements and exits the dressing room.

Lorne leans against the adjacent wall, dressed in the clothes he arrived in, cowboy hat tilted down, and arms crossed over his chest.

"Already finished?" She glances at the pile of folded garments beside his boots.

"Everything fits." He lifts a stack of denim and random ruffly things from the rack beside him. "Do you have these in her size? Also, she needs bras and panties."

Her face goes slack, paling slightly.

I shoot him an incredulous look, but his attention wanders across the room, scanning the displays of women's clothing.

What is he doing? I can't keep up with his ever-changing personality.

"Let me check my inventory." Cora takes the clothes from him and turns toward a wall lined with packaged underwear.

"Not those." He gestures at the mannequins in the back dressed in stringy lingerie. "The lacy ones."

"Those are pretty." She glances over her shoulder at me.

Gone is her smile, replaced with a frown of accusations.

I only lied about the illness. The rest surprises me as much as it does her.

When she shuffles away, I curl my finger at him in a come-hither motion.

He prowls toward me and braces his hands on the doorframe above his head.

"Who are you?" I flick up the brim of his hat to see

his eyes.

"The guy you've been mentally undressing for three days," he drawls.

"You are so—!" I press a hand against my forehead and breathe until my heart calms. Then I hold up a finger. "One. You didn't try on those clothes."

"I tried on a pair of jeans. They're all the same size."

"Different brands fit differently."

He gives me a blank look.

"Never mind." I hold up a second finger. "Two. Why are you picking out my clothes? I can't afford any of that. And the granny panties"—I wave a hand at the wall—"will do just fine."

"Which finger are you on? I'm losing count."

"Are you listening to me?"

"I hear you." His bottomless, vibrant green eyes swirl with startling depth. "Every unspoken thought. Every emotion you cover up." His expression softens. "I hear *you*."

My breath slips away. The room fades, and I'm left with a horrible pang in my chest. "Don't do this."

"What?" His gaze dips to my mouth.

"Don't pull me in and push me away. You're jerking me back and forth, and it's cruel, Lorne. I don't deserve this."

"Are you ready to try stuff on?" Cora breezes around the corner, carrying enough clothes to outfit a drag show.

Lorne pushes off the door frame and gives me a look so deep-reaching it lingers long after he stalks to the other side of the store.

Thirty minutes later, I stand near the front door as he and Cora bicker over money. Or rather, Cora bickers while Lorne holds out the cash without saying a word.

Finally, she accepts his payment and leans in for a

hug. "Let me at least take you to dinner. Or drinks?"

"Another time." He pats her arm and steps back, his focus shifting to me. "Ready?"

He already loaded all the bags into the truck and walked the perimeter to check for signs of unwanted company. After we say goodbye, he leads me outside with a hand on my lower back.

On the drive home, *Just A Kiss* by Lady Antebellum plays on the radio. The tires hum along the pavement, and the man behind the wheel vibrates with things left unsaid.

I squirm in the silence. "Lorne..."

He lowers the volume, his gaze fixed on the road. "I didn't want her to touch me."

"Didn't look that way."

He rubs a palm along his thigh and returns it to the wheel. "In my head, it was *your* hands."

I turn toward the window and rest my fingers against my mouth to hide my expression. A scowl? A smile of pleasure? My lips teeter up and down, as volatile as the cowboy at my side.

"Are we being truthful?" I pick at the frayed hem of my cut-offs.

"Always."

"Okay." I breathe in slowly and release. "I told Cora you have an STD."

He catches his bottom lip between his teeth. Biting down on a smile?

I lean back, stunned. "Are you laughing?"

"It didn't deter her."

"No, it didn't. After the half-naked show you gave her, I'm pretty sure she's planning a night in with the girls." I wriggle my fingers. "Couch hockey for one."

He shakes his head, and that time, his smile breaks free. It makes him prettier, sexier, and harder to be mad at.

Wait. Is that a dimple?

I bend closer, and he drags a hand over his mouth, erasing the grin.

"Please tell me you don't have dimples." I sit back.

"Not intentionally."

That *V*-cut, those arms, that ass, those eyes, that dimple... *Damn him.*

"The security guard..." He adjusts his hat. "You didn't tell him you were with me."

"I didn't give him *any* names. I described what John looks like and what he drives. Said he was a dangerous ex-boyfriend." I swallow. "Ford wasn't willing to help me until I made him that offer."

"Guys like that aren't content with a taste, Raina. Considering the kind of men you've been with, I know you know this. He would've thought about it for a day or two and called with more demands. More of *you.*"

"Maybe."

"No maybe about it. You're the hottest woman he'll ever encounter in his miserable life. He's probably beating off right now."

"Was that a compliment? Because you said I wouldn't be getting any more of those."

"It's a fact, Raina."

My skin heats. "You like me."

"I tolerate you." He steers the truck under the archway of the ranch and parks.

"You're the most mercurial man I've ever met. I swear you have a different mood for every hour in the day. How do you deal with the whiplash?"

"I'm not myself." He kills the engine and lifts his gaze to the estate. "Everything feels backwards, like my cell is my true home, and in there is the prison."

"You can't sleep outside in the winter."

He stares at the dash, his eyes losing focus. Then he

blinks. "I'm not adjusting well."

It can take years. Some inmates never acclimate outside of their cells. But Lorne was only down for eight years, and he has the support of a family that loves him.

I clear my throat. "If there's anything I can do…"

The one thing I'm good at is the last thing I want him to take. It was easy to offer my body when I first met him. The time I spent chained to a wall shoved me into a torpid state of detachment.

But my insides are a jumbled mess now, churning between hatred and desire. I can't have sex when my emotions are so close to the surface. It would break me.

He sets his gaze on me. "Your tea helps."

I sigh my relief. "Then I'll make tea."

12

Lorne

Every night, Raina brings me a thermos of tea. It becomes our ritual—her, me, sleeping bag, open field, vast sky, and quiet conversation. Then I send her inside to sleep in safety. Every day, she prepares our meals, cleans the house, and spends the rest of her time with me. I might not be adapting to life outside of prison, but day by day, I'm adjusting to *her*.

When I'm with her, I feel alive. Needed. Motivated. A little less angry, and a whole lot hungry.

Like now.

In an unused pasture with the sun beating down and humidity clinging to our clothes, I lean over her back and inhale the sweet scent of her hair.

Most of her bruises have faded. The surface cuts are healing without infection. The worst of John's destruction dwells too deep inside her for me to examine.

I'm all too familiar with the need to bury demons. I have plenty of my own.

She's safe here, under the watch of cameras and surrounded by me and the others. But right now, I have her all to myself.

There's nothing around for miles, except her tiny denim shorts, full tits, the curve of her backside against my groin, and the gun in her hand. It's a goddamn religious experience.

"Back off." She trains the shotgun on a row of cans and kicks back with her boot, nailing me in the shin. "I mean it."

"You're holding it like a T-Rex." I grip the butt of the gun and tuck it tightly against her. "Your stubby arms have these things called shoulders. Use them."

"There's nothing wrong with my arms. The problem is your stubby dick rubbing against my ass."

It's been four days since our visit to Cora's shop. Four days of spitting, snarling, kicking, and fighting. Sometimes I rile her just to hear the creative ways her poisoned food will rot off my dick.

It feels a lot like foreplay, because let's face it. She loves to talk about my cock.

"You'd focus better," I say, "if you weren't thinking about it all the time."

"Why don't you stand in front of me, and I'll think about it while I shoot it off."

I nudge up my hat and grin at her.

Her eyes hone in on my cheek, and she laughs through a groan. "That dimple, though!"

It's her weakness. My discovery of that has given me every reason to smile.

"Loosen your arms." I glide a hand along her elbow, adjusting, caressing. "Just like that."

Her breath shivers, and goosebumps pebble her skin. "Lorne."

"Raina."

"You're distracting me." She fidgets with her ear plugs.

"See that coffee can? It's John Holsten's hollow heart." I drift into her space, touching her with my hips, my chest, my arms. Then my lips, just barely against her neck. "When you shoot him, you'll have distractions all around you, and he'll be on the move. Shoot him in the chest."

Her jaw locks. Her finger slides to the trigger, and determination tapers her eyes.

I pop in my own ear plugs and maintain my hovering proximity.

She inhales and squeezes on her exhale, just like I taught her.

Gunfire booms through me, and the shot goes wide, missing the can by a foot.

"Fucking fuck!" She flicks on the safety, sets the gun down, and yanks out her ear protection. "I'm only hitting like one in ten!"

"That's why we're practicing."

"I'm terrible."

"You'll learn."

"Not while you're all up on me." She storms off toward a cluster of trees, where Captain waits in the shade.

We've been out here for hours. She's tired. Frustrated. I should let her cool off, but my boots are already chasing. My pulse quickens. My hands flex, the instinct to hunt firing beneath my skin.

I catch her around the waist and lift her off the ground.

Her elbows rear back, bouncing off my ribs as she thrashes and kicks the air. "Put me down!"

Swinging her toward the closest tree, I spin her in my arms and press her back against the huge trunk.

"If he restrained you like this," I say calmly, "how

would you escape?"

She goes ballistic, clawing and bucking and seething past clenched teeth. But she only succeeds in knocking off my hat.

"Stop." I pin her hips with mine and wrap a hand around her throat, applying slight pressure without blocking her airflow. "Take a deep breath and listen."

She gulps for air, and her arms drop to her sides.

"Your hands are free." My gaze locks onto her bee-stung lips, and a rush of heat gathers beneath my belt. "You're going to strike *calmly* with your thumb or the heel of your hand."

"Where?"

"Target the cartilage right below the bridge of my nose and shove upward."

"The mustache area? Thank you, by the way, for not growing one."

"Yes. And you're welcome."

"Now?"

"Go ahead."

Her hand snaps up, and she opts for the thumb, slamming it above my upper lip and driving upward.

Fuck, that hurts. Even though I expected it, I still drop back, my face forced skyward and my fingers slipping from her throat.

"See what happened there?" I hold my position, one foot behind me and arms out to my sides. "You redirected me and put distance between us."

"Wow. Cool trick."

In a blur, I'm on her. I clap a hand over her mouth and effectively restrain her small body with mine. "That maneuver only gives you a second. A second to scream, run, or prepare to block the next attack. You hesitated, and now you don't have your voice."

Her eyes widen above my hand, her breath hot

against my palm. I release her and step back.

She rubs her cheek, peering up at me beneath long black lashes. "You'll teach me to block?"

"Yes. But your best weapon is your voice. Scream until your vocal chords shatter. Most people suck, but they'll hear you. Someone will come running."

I spend the next couple of hours teaching her basic self-defense. I show her how to escape zip ties and duct tape handcuffs, as well as quick and easy ways to break handholds on her clothing. She listens, asks questions, and obeys without her usual attitude.

She's motivated to live, and I'll make sure she has the tools to do that. But I can't ignore the knot of dread in my stomach. Every time I grab her, spin her, and yank her up against me, that knot coils tighter, thicker.

Over the past four days, I came to the conclusion I could never allow her to hunt down John alone. I would be with her every step of the way.

Except now, I'm coming to terms with a new realization.

I can't let her go after him at all.

She adjusts her ponytail high on her head and faces me with a wide stance.

"Want somma this, big guy?" She pops her neck and balls her tiny fists. "Come at me."

Good God, she's stunning. Gutsy. Full of life. Mine. My charge, my responsibility, my reason for smiling. If another man so much as touches her, he won't survive.

John needs to be dealt with, but not at the risk of putting her in harm's way. I can kill him myself. But if I got caught? I would return to prison for life.

I can't go back there.

I won't.

The idea alone strangles me in a fog of nightmares so crippling my lungs burn beneath the pressure. When I sense her watching me, I empty my expression and shove the hat low on my brow.

"Oh, no." She anchors her hands on her hips and narrows her eyes. "Which Lorne are we now? Broody? Angry? Guilty? Vicious? Definitely not Chummy because..." She pokes a finger at her cheek and makes a twisting motion. "No dimple."

"I need to head back." I grab the shotgun and pack up the ammo.

"We're finished for the day?"

"I'm not keeping up with the ranch work and—"

"Hey." She crouches beside me and touches my shoulder. "Talk to me."

I shrug off her hand and carry the supplies to the horse.

She hurries after me. "Are we being truthful?"

"Always."

She plucks the ammo from my grip and stows it in the saddlebag. Then she clutches my arm, stopping me from mounting. "How did you learn to fight like that?"

"Jarret and Jake. We started beating on one another the moment we could walk."

She nods, purses her lips. Then she tilts her head, squinting at me. "You fought in prison, too."

"When I needed to." My neck stiffens, and I shift back to Captain, checking the saddle straps.

"Tell me about it."

"No." I lift a boot to the stirrup.

She clamps a firm hand on my knee. "Living in that head of yours must be lonely." She nudges up my hat. "I'm right here, Lorne, seeing you, *wanting* to hear you."

"You don't want to hear this." I lower my boot to the ground.

"I have a scary imagination, most of it born in real life experience. I'm picturing the very worst. Trapped in a

# Booted

compound with violent men. Broken, bloody, raped..."

I expel a harsh "Fuck" and drop my forearms on the saddle, head down, and eyes on the horizon.

She steps beside me and rests her arms on the saddle, mirroring my pose.

"It's segregated by races. Then by authority. Influence. Power." I glance at her sidelong. "The pecking order is established immediately. New guys come in. You either make them your bitch or you become one."

Standing side by side, we watch the breeze ripple the grasses. She steals peeks at me. I study her out of the corner of my eye.

She fucked men I was imprisoned with. Inmates who could've been my friends. Or my enemies. I see the faces of the ones released before me and know their crimes. Most would've killed to spend an hour with her. Many could've killed *her* after they got off.

I could demand she give me names and details, but nothing good would come from that.

"They know when the guards aren't looking, where to attack, and how much they can get away with." I scratch the stubble on my throat. "I was attacked a lot the first month. I went in too skinny, too young, and woke every day convinced it would be my last. Then I was ambushed in the bathroom."

Pain stabs behind my eyes. The memories. The fear. The absolute hopelessness.

I crave a bottle of whiskey and the escape it would give me.

Her hand slides up my spine, gentle and supportive.

I slowly release a breath. "There were five of them. Before I could blink, I was on my knees with my face in the urinal. Hands restrained my arms while more pulled down my pants. I knew if they fucked me, my status would be established, and it would happen again and again."

Her fingers curl around my shoulder, digging in.

"A switch flipped," I say. "The same kill switch that shut down my brain the night I shot Wyatt Longley. Instinct took over. The mindless, uncontrollable impulse to hunt, destroy, and claim victory over my enemies. It controlled me in that bathroom. I don't know how I fought back. I was just one person, but I was someone else entirely, like a monster clawing its way up the food chain."

"You escaped."

Did I?

My attackers limped away, but so did I. I'm still limping, still looking over my shoulder, still waking every night in a drenched puddle of torment.

I'm a pussy for letting the experience haunt me. I survived. I'm free. But when I close my eyes, I'm right back in that bathroom, fighting for my life.

The ravine, the abuse Conor suffered by my dad, the years I spent in prison, and John Holsten's threat against Raina—these are my demons. They're relentless and deeply embedded, howling at me day and night.

I'm still trying to escape.

Raina stirs at my side. "You have nightmares."

"Yes."

"Is that why you sleep outside instead of in the room with me? Because I can sleep on the couch or—"

"I missed the stars and hate the confinement of the house."

"Thank you for telling me." She rests a hand against my cheek, turning me toward her. She cups my face and draws me closer, resting her brow against mine. "I hear you."

I grip her wrists, my thumbs roving across her silky skin, my entire body attuned to the pain in hers. "I hear you, too. I'm here if you want to talk—"

"I told you what happened to me. I even had a good

cry in your truck. Now I just need it to be over."

She pulls away and swings up into the saddle, her face angled toward the horizon and expression closed off.

The woman jumps at the chance to pick apart my insides, but the instant I turn the spotlight on her, she powers off.

Because she's scared.

She told me her past, but she refuses to share her feelings about it. Doing so would invite me in and expose her innermost weaknesses and fears. Keeping that part of her closed off protects her from the monsters that prey on vulnerability.

Is that what I am to her? A monster? Maybe that's how she perceives all men.

I grasp her thigh, squeezing the muscle hard enough to earn a sexy glare.

"Have you ever had a lover?" I inch my fingers upward, lingering on the crease of velvety skin where the cut-offs meet the bend of her leg.

"Am I talking to Horny Lorne now?" She stares at my hand, her chest rising and falling. "You should wear changeable name tags, so I can follow along."

"Answer the question." I slip under the denim, teasing hidden flesh.

She's so warm. So fucking soft. One touch and I'm instantly hard.

"No." She grabs my forearm and pushes, unable to budge me. "Sex is a job. Nothing more." She leans down, her brown eyes hard and cold. "You want the best orgasm of your life? I'm your girl. But if you expect more than a fuck, look elsewhere."

My muscles tighten. My cock swells, and my chest expands with a deep, resolute breath. I leap into the saddle behind her and yank her tight against me.

"Your words are garbage, but I hear what you're

really saying." With my arms around her, I gather the reins and touch my lips to her ear. "Your body is mine for the taking. Your heart, I have to work for."

She stiffens. "No, I don't want—"

"Let me tell you something about me. If you were my girl, I'd make you feel like my world. Only then would I deserve to make you feel like my slut."

Raina

The next day, I end the training session early after a heated exchange with Lorne. I might've started the verbal sparring match, but dammit, he's a moody, hackle-raising, fight-provoking egomaniac. Who also happens to be infuriatingly gorgeous when he's mad.

We ride back to the estate in a fume of mutual displeasure, rocking together in the saddle, with his arm barred across my waist. When we reach the back porch, I move to jump off, but his grip tightens, holding me against him.

"Let go." I shove at his bulging bicep, dismayed by the impenetrable strength in it.

"You can push me away all you want. I'm just gonna pull harder."

"Why?"

"You know why."

Because I told him I wouldn't give him more than sex. As if I could treat him like a job.

I'm an idiot.

My words kicked him right in his pride. Of course, he's going to flex his mighty manliness and prove he's the one who can bring me to my knees.

But that's not what set off the latest argument.

While I was shooting at—*and missing*—the evasive coffee cans, he started pressing me about my sister, my mother's drug addiction, and the abuse I endured with John Holsten. I don't talk about those things. I don't examine them. But he kept digging, probing, and watching me with those eyes.

So I snapped and hit him with my temper. In Lorne fashion, he roared right back. And here we are.

Twisting in the saddle, I meet his hard gaze. "We're not good together."

"We haven't killed each other."

"We fight constantly."

"We communicate at full volume." He strokes a knuckle along my jaw.

I shiver. "We push each other's buttons."

"We challenge each other." He cups my throat, holding, not squeezing.

"I'm a prostitute."

Now he squeezes. "You had a job, one you will never go back to."

My heart stops, then pounds, stalling my breaths and eating up his words.

I know this isn't a game to him. Not to either of us. He's thinking and saying and doing what feels right. But what's right for him isn't right for me.

I don't do relationships. I have too many ugly, deep-seeded issues, and the big one is out there somewhere, biding his time until he can catch me and make my insides a thousand times uglier.

"I spent two years in John Holsten's bed." I pull

Lorne's hand from my throat, and he allows it. "Don't tell me that doesn't bother you."

"I hate it, because you weren't there willingly. *You* hated it. But I have never brought it up or used it against you. He has nothing to do with this."

"This," I echo.

"Us."

I've never been part of an *us*. It sounds foreign to my ears, and I don't trust it. "The moment I said you couldn't have my heart, you decided you wanted it."

"I didn't say that."

"You didn't *not* say it." My nerve endings tremble and tingle. "Why are we even discussing this? We've only known each other for a week."

"A week in which we've spent nearly every second together." He dismounts the horse and helps me down. "Outside of my family, I've never had this much interaction with another person. I never wanted to." He cups the back of my head and puts his face in mine. "I like this, and I want to see where it's going."

My pulse hammers, and I grip the front of his shirt. His lips are so close, and his warm masculine scent assails my senses as I waffle between pushing him away and pulling him in.

The wind, the silence, my gut—all of it whispers to pull, to give him a chance. But I'm nervous. Scared enough to flee. My gaze drifts toward the house.

He removes his touch and steps out of my reach. The look on his face isn't disappointment, frustration, or any expression he's ever shown me. The looseness around his mouth and softness in his eyes convey patience and understanding.

I'm beginning to think he really does hear me.

"Jake's in the office today." He nods at the house. Whenever I'm cleaning or preparing meals, someone's always nearby, either inside the estate or watching from outside. I hate that they have to babysit me, but I also appreciate it. Between Lorne's training and having a safe place to live, he's given me more stability than I've ever known.

"I'm going to take Captain back to the stable." He runs a hand across the dappled flank of his horse. "Then I'll be on the front porch, working out."

He exercises every day without weights or machines. Or clothes. Stripped down to his briefs, always outside, he conditions his body with crunches, squats, chin lifts, and whatever else he learned to do in a six by eight cell.

In fact, he only goes inside to eat and shower. His massive suite sits unfurnished, unpainted, and lonely. I don't sleep well in there, and I doubt he sleeps any better on the ground.

He needs to move in and make this place his home again.

With a hand resting on his belt buckle and his other hanging at his side, he idly strokes his thumb along the scar on his palm.

Sunlight hits his face at just the right angle to illuminate a faint scattering of freckles across his nose. His sister is covered in them, thanks to their Irish blood, but his freckles didn't appear until the last couple of days. His skin is darker, too. Healthier.

The fresh air and glow of summer suits him.

"Go inside, Raina, before I forgo the workout for a different kind of exercise."

My mouth parts on a faltering breath, and a jolt of warmth quakes through me. I've been attracted to him since day one, but that shallow sentiment is evolving into unchartered territory. I feel greedy for him, possessive, and utterly confused.

# Booted

Thirty minutes ago, I wanted to break his dick on my boot. Now, I'm imagining it in ways I've never craved a man.

I turn toward the house and enter through the mudroom.

Distance from him is smart, even if the ache in my gut doesn't agree.

I slide off my boots, and my attention falls to the trail of dirt that leads to the interior door. My molars slam together as I follow the mess into the kitchen, where it tracks back and forth and around the table.

"Raina?" Jake bellows from another room.

"Yeah, it's me."

As the sound of his footsteps retreat, an idea hits me, and I run after him.

The office sits off the foyer. When I reach the open doorway, I poke my head in.

Jake sits at a huge wooden desk, surrounded by paperwork and computer monitors. He's the finance brain of the cattle operation, but that's not where his attention resides at the moment.

He stares at a large screen filled with a dozen live camera feeds from various locations on the property. Some of them display Conor's clinic. The view of her exam room shows her kneeling beside a blurry dog-sized animal.

"Is that a goat?" I ask.

He glances over his shoulder at me and returns to the screen. "Yeah." After a moment, he sighs and pushes away from the desk, seemingly with great reluctance. "I could stare at her all day. Conor, not the goat."

"Don't let me stop you. I just wanted to see if you had a marker and something to write on."

His stern gaze sweeps over the messy office. "For what?"

"A sign."

A dark eyebrow lifts. Then he ambles over to the closet and removes an old poster of Chris Stapleton. "Use the back of this."

"You sure?"

"I don't know." He hands me a sharpie from the desk drawer. "I haven't seen your sign yet."

With a grin, I stretch out the poster on the floor and write.

*Attention Ranchers.*
*Take off your clothes.*
*And prepare for disappointment. It's not what you think.*
*If you track in dirt, your next meal will be your last.*

I cap the marker and peer up at Jake.

He bursts into laughter. "Are you hanging that in the mudroom?"

"Yup."

I thank him for his help and head out to take my first stance in this family.

The sign goes on the wall with a dirty clothes hamper beneath it. I set out clean shorts on the shelving unit and clear the bottom shelves to store dirty boots. Then I start mopping.

That night, dinner simmers on the stove as I flit around the kitchen, preparing the salad, buttering the bread, and setting the table.

With the volume turned up on the stereo in the living room, I sing along with my favorite song, *Gun Power and Lead* by Miranda Lambert. The brash lyrics grab me where my heart lives. I belt them, loud and out of tune, in an ode to John Holsten, Lorne Cassidy, and any other man who underestimates me.

# Booted

When the song ends, everything's ready, and I stand at the sink with a flutter in my chest.

They'll arrive any minute and gather around the table, laughing and arguing and sharing stories about their day. I look forward to it with an unfamiliar tug of affection.

More than that, I feel dizzy with anticipation of seeing Lorne.

I had plenty to do this afternoon, none of which included seeking him out. But I wanted to.

Maybe I should get my head examined, because I miss his moody ass.

The outside door to the mudroom opens and closes, followed by multiple footsteps. Then silence.

I move to the stove as Jarret strides in, wearing a t-shirt and boxer briefs. No dusty jeans or mud-caked boots.

A smile stretches my cheeks. "I set out shorts."

"I tried to tell him." Maybe walks in, clad in the cotton shorts I left for her. "By the way..." She wraps an arm around my shoulders and leans in. "You're kind of badass."

"I don't know about that." I laugh, warming at her compliment.

On my other side, Jarret reaches around me and lifts the lid on the pot.

"No, you don't." I grab the wooden spoon and swat his arm with it. "Go clean up. We're eating in ten."

"Your stomach can wait." Maybe hugs Jarret from behind and kisses his spine. "Because you're going to take a shower with me."

That gets him moving.

As they step out of the kitchen, Conor pads in, barefoot and donning a pair of Jake's gym shorts.

"I love the sign." She smiles at me with tired eyes. "It's about time someone spanked some respect into those boys."

"Spanking will be a challenge with the oldest one. He's difficult."

"And distant," she says quietly. "I'm trying to give him space and time and... I don't know what he needs."

"It's only been a week. He'll come around."

"I hope you're right." Pulling in a breath, she stands straighter. "Thank you for cooking and keeping things clean. This is..." She waves a hand at the set table. "We've never had anything like this. Never had someone taking care of us, you know. It's nice." She cocks her head. "How are *you* doing? Is Lorne...?"

Pissing me off? Driving me crazy? Twisting me up? Making me want things I shouldn't want?

Yeah. All of it.

"He's a good instructor," I say.

She sucks on her lip, scrutinizing me. "There's more you're not saying, but I'll let it go. For now. I need to go clean up."

When she leaves the kitchen, the restless flutter in my chest returns. A flutter that's reserved for Lorne and the confrontation that always awaits us.

I grin as the sound of boots enter the mudroom. A moment later, the kitchen door opens behind me.

My eyes remain fixed on the stove while the rest of my body beats and warms with the hard throb of my pulse.

The pads of his approaching footsteps indicate no shoes. He stops at my back and presses in, with his hands on my hips and his nose in my hair. "Smells delicious."

A thrill races up my spine. "Chicken and dumplings."

"That smells good, too."

I suck in a breath, bringing the addictive scent of *him* into my lungs. No man should smell that sensational, especially after a workout in the summer heat.

His chest feels like a steel press against my back as

the long length of his body edges closer, harder around mine.

In my head, I see every indention, carved ridge, and muscular curve of his physique. In reality, I've seen all of him in the buff. Except his cock, which is currently swelling against my ass.

I'm wearing one of the outfits he bought me. A green cotton slip dress that stops above my knees. The fabric is so thin the heat from his skin spreads across mine.

Is he wearing any clothes? My mouth dries as I reach back and touch his waist.

*Warm, tight skin.*

I slide my hand lower, tracing the shredded grooves of abs and hips. When my fingers meet the dense, round, *bare* curve of his butt, I spin to face him. "Why are you naked?"

The assertive glimmer in his eyes dares me to look down and investigate the extent of his nudity. I don't.

"The sign…" He hitches a thumb in the direction of the mudroom, his lips curving into a half-grin.

Have mercy, that dimple.

"Since when do you follow orders?" I prop a fist on my hip.

"When it puts that flush in your cheeks."

He brushes his thumb across my cheekbone, his mouth slightly open and bathing my face in Lorne-scented allure. Then he pivots and strolls toward the living room, giving me a jaw-dropping view of the remarkable beauty chiseled into his Adonis body.

Heat soars through my veins, cooking me from the inside out. Perspiration forms on my brow, and my breath trembles past my lips.

He can't just walk around like that. It's criminal.

"Your sister!" I shout after him.

He lifts off his hat and holds it at his side as he vanishes around the corner.

I turn to the sink and pat a wet towel across my face.

He's such a tease. What would he do if I chased him? I could walk into his room, wrap a hand around his cock, and own him in two seconds flat.

Could I do it without losing myself in the process? With anyone else, I can move through the actions while remaining totally and emotionally unavailable.

But Lorne's already in my head, consuming my thoughts and controlling the responses in my body. I can't protect my deepest self when I'm with him.

I know this, but I also know I'll go to him, because my gut whispers at me to do this. I can make him feel good. That's what I do, and it's what he needs.

"Did Lorne come in?" Jake steps into the kitchen, his gaze glued to the pot on the stove.

"He's getting cleaned up." I set out a ladle. "Food's ready. I'll be back in a bit."

Instinct carries me through the house as I concentrate my energy on locking away all emotion. If the universe wants to have its way with me, I'll let it. But Lorne can't matter to me. It would destroy me if I fell.

When I reach the closed door to his suite, a practiced persona settles over my skin. My expression transforms into that of a temptress, my body an instrument of allurement and seduction.

I become a woman who lives to fuck. She knows what men crave and how to read their cues, from the first look and initial touch to the last body-trembling orgasm. She knows when he wants sweet and demure, mysterious and quiet, or raunchy and vocal. No matter the proclivities, she always delivers, without limits or boundaries.

Lorne's never met this woman. She has no name, no

demands, no emotional baggage or insecurities. She's the epitome of desire wrapped in sensual flesh. A fantasy of forbidden urges.

He won't be able to turn her away.

14

Lorne

The walls close in around me as I step out of the shower and drag a towel over my fevered skin. My muscles clench against the absence of windows, natural light, and fresh air.

I'm not claustrophobic. I just can't stand the reminders—the feeling of being shut in, locked down, and restrained in my freedom of movement.

Every time I enter the house, I'm transported behind bars, drenched in rotten air and incessant loud noise.

Ironically, I used to sit in my cell and take a mind trip to this house, longing for the familiarity of its walls.

It's so fucked up. I know adjustment takes time, but getting there is agonizing.

Doesn't help that I'm in a constant state of throbbing, pent-up arousal.

There's only one reason why I'm standing here with a raging hard-on. I should've rubbed one out, but over the past week, shooting my load in the shower has only made me more frustrated.

I want *her*, and that craving won't go away until I give into it.

Scraping the terrycloth over my face and hair, I amble into the bedroom and freeze.

Raina stands near the door and reaches behind her to turn the lock. Her lashes sweep downward, hooding her eyes as she regards my swollen dick.

I drop the towel and let her look. Christ, I want nothing more than for her to stare, stroke, lick...

Except there's something off about her.

She looks the same. Same confident stance—shoulders back, a hand on her hip, and legs relaxed with one out at a posed angle. Same curvaceous lips—the corners resting between a frown and a smile. Same devastating eyes—molten brown and seductive. But they're lacking her usual fire.

That's it. She wants me, yet she's unnervingly detached from that want.

"Raina." I try for a warning tone, but it comes out strangled and hoarse.

All the blood in my brain descends to my cock, gnawing and tearing at my self-control.

She lifts her hands to her head and slowly, sensually slides her fingers through her hair. The motion causes the dress to inch up her thighs and pull taut across her perfect rack. Then she runs those hands down her body, straightening the fabric and taking my gaze along for the ride.

When she glances back up at me, our eyes meet, connect, and communicate. It's always been written in the space between us—the untamed chemistry, the seed of passion. But now, there's an invitation to explore it.

Whenever we're together, we stand toe to toe,

voices battling and wrestling, and hearts beating all the faster for it. We've been building to this, racing toward the moment when our bodies attack without words.

Nothing needs to be said. Millions of years of evolution carved the message into our DNA.

She and I are meant to fuck.

She walks toward me, gliding one long leg before the other. I remain rooted to the floor, ensnared by the silent symphony curling from her aura. She's a siren's song of feminine dips and bends, sensual movements, and dirty intent.

With just the right heat in her eyes, she slides up against me and tiptoes her fingertips down my chest. Her shallow breaths denote her hunger, but the pace is too steady, too deliberate.

*Sex is a job. Nothing more.*

That's true of her past. But not now. Not with me. I won't allow it.

Grabbing her hair, I yank her mouth toward mine. She dodges the kiss to bite my jaw, my neck, and holy fuck, her hand clamps around my length.

Soft, talented fingers move with diabolical precision over the most sensitive part of my head, rubbing pre-cum along the glans and gripping an inch below the tip. Her strokes are paralyzing, the friction explosive, and a swarm of electrifying tingles hits me sideways.

I stumble to remain upright, mind blown and choking for air. My fucking God, she knows how to work a cock.

All thought stops in its tracks. My vision blurs. My lungs seize, and my body swims in ecstasy as need, need, need pulses through my veins.

*Put your mouth on me. Swallow it. Suck it. Take it all.*

I grip her ass, her hair, and yank her throat to my

lips to feast, suck, and lick her skin. With her hand trapped between us, she continues to jerk me off as she tilts her head up.

She doesn't just look at me. She looks into me and acknowledges my desires.

Then she lowers to her knees.

The twist and stroke of her fist steals my breath. The pressure of her fingers tightens my balls, and the prospect of her lips wrapped around me thrusts my body toward release.

I fight it, shaking and groaning, mindlessly overcome. My knees weaken, and I clench my abs, reaching back for support. My hand finds the bed. I drop to the mattress, and she follows me down with her mouth sealed around my cock.

"Ungh, fuck!" I fall to my back and tangle my fingers in her silky hair. "So fucking good. Goddamn, Raina. Fuck!"

Her tongue is relentless, swirling and curling and doing things I can't fathom. It feels like a thousand hot, wet fingers dancing along my shaft in endless rhythm. I'm lost in the sensations, writhing, grasping, and battling the ungodly pressure to explode.

"Raina, wait." I moan, my fists flexing and releasing in her hair. "Slow down for a se— Ahhh, Christ. Don't stop. That's incredible."

The succubus peers up at me beneath the veil of her lashes, her lips swollen and throat filled with cock. It's the hottest thing I've ever seen.

With a mischievous crook of her lips, she swallows hard, clenching wet muscles around my head.

"Jesus!" My back bows off the mattress.

She slides her mouth off and drags that sinful tongue down my length. When she reaches my balls, she sucks and licks the sac until every muscle in my body strains with the effort to hold back my release.

She clasps the back of my thigh and pushes it upward, spreading my legs. Then her lips move lower, sliding beneath my scrotum, and...

"Don't." I yank her hair and clench my ass against her intrusion.

"Relax." She lowers her head and invades with her tongue, pushing and curling against my reluctant rim.

No one has ever touched me there, let alone licked and— What is she doing? Fucking hell, she's fingering my ass.

My cock goes impossibly stiff, engorged and pulsing to the point of agony. This is wrong. And so fucking good. The stimulation is unlike anything I've ever felt.

The world narrows to her tongue on my balls and her finger in my ass. The pleasure is so overwhelming I think I'm going to black out.

My head falls back on the bed, and I release a long, guttural groan.

She shifts between my legs, and her mouth closes over my cock. Sucking with abandon, she bends that filthy finger inside me, and I'm gone.

The orgasm erupts so fast and hard I can't warn her. Crashing waves of heat shoot along my shaft and hit the back of her throat in violent jets of relief. The force of it robs my voice, and my mouth hangs open in a breathless, soundless roar.

It takes me long seconds to realize I'm holding her face against me, grinding against her throat and blocking her air.

I drop my hands, panting to catch my breath. I'm utterly gobsmacked, shaken, spent, and floating in a quaking haze of wonderment.

Because of a blowjob.

I'm fucking ruined.

She lifts her head and swipes a finger along the corner of her mouth. Her hand ghosts along my pulsing, oversensitive cock, holding it steady as she tenderly kisses the tip.

Then she rises and woodenly walks into the bathroom, shutting the door behind her.

As the tingling remnants of bliss subside and my heart rate returns to normal, I'm left with cold realization.

She just made me her bitch, and she did it with total and complete indifference.

She turned me into a job.

And I let her.

I lurch off the bed and snag a pair of boxer briefs. Outrage pounds through my blood as I yank them on and storm to the bathroom.

I jerk on the handle, and it sticks. Did she lock it? In a burst of impatience, I slam a shoulder into the wood and send the door careening against the adjacent wall.

"What the hell?" She looks up from the sink, with a toothbrush dangling from her mouth.

"You locked the door."

"I did not." She spits toothpaste and rinses with water. "But if I did, a knock would've sufficed."

I step inside and mark her rigid shoulders, stiff neck, and curling fingers on the counter. The seductive act is gone, and I'm a goddamn fool.

"What?" She sets down the toothbrush and crosses her arms.

She knows *what*. Guilt lines her face, and her eyes cloud with brewing defensiveness. She's preparing for a fight, and I'll give her one. Just not the one she's expecting.

I let my arms fall at my sides and relax the tension in my back. "I didn't kiss you."

She grimaces and turns toward the shower,

reaching for the lever. "Dinner's getting cold. Go eat."

Anger surges, and I release it in two seething syllables. "Raina."

Her hand drops, and her arms pull in close to her ribs. But she doesn't give me her eyes.

"That's not how I do things." I don't step forward to close the distance. Instead, I grab a handful of fabric on her spine and haul her backwards.

Her arms fly up, and her feet shuffle with awkward grace as I shove her back against the wall.

She instantly goes for my upper lip, which I block. Her hands keep moving, striking, redirecting, and sweeping through every defense technique she knows. I anticipate each attack. I'm the one who taught her, after all. Nevertheless, she remains calm and focused, and fuck if that doesn't fill me with pride.

When she realizes she can't overpower me, she flattens her back against the wall and thrusts her stubborn chin as far away from me as she can.

"If I were anyone else, you would've escaped this position." I feather my fingers along the grinding lock of her jaw. "But I'm not *them*. I want intimacy, depth, and I'm going to kiss you."

Her expression contorts, as if the idea makes her nauseated.

I grip her chin and force her face to mine. "You just stuck your tongue in my ass, but my mouth grosses you out?"

"I don't kiss." She pushes against my chest.

I push back with my entire body. "But you've been kissed before?"

"Yes. I despise it."

"Because you've never been kissed by *me*." I drink in her dark angry eyes and shapely, fuckable lips. "As much I loved what you did back there, I'm fucking offended by your lack of interest. If I wanted a blowjob from a whore, I'd hire one."

She flinches.

"I want *you.*" I run a hand through her hair, letting the satiny texture soothe my temper. "You led me to believe you were into it. Into *me.* That's the same as lying."

"It's the way I am." Her chest trembles.

"Fuck that. Given the amount of heat you put into fighting me, I know for a goddamn fact you'd be an intensely passionate lover." I scrape a hand over my head as I consider the hypocrisy in what I'm saying. "I'm not an affectionate man, but—"

"You are." She stares at my throat, eyes wide and unblinking. "That's the problem. When you touch me, it comes from a soulful place inside you. A place of thought and compassion and connection."

She stares up at me, her expression pained. I rest a palm against her cheek, and she recoils, her complexion turning ashen.

"I'm scared," she whispers.

Now we're getting somewhere.

"The Raina I know doesn't let fear control her." Bending my knees, I touch my forehead to hers. "Give me your mouth."

The look in her eyes says she's afraid of me more than anything. She stands frozen and petrified under my command, her lips quivering as I cradle her face in my palms.

My heartbeat hammers an irregular count, quickening with each millimeter of space I erase between us.

My mouth hovers. Her breaths shiver. My lips glance off hers. We both suck in air. I lean closer, touching her with my fingers, my chest, my hips. My tongue.

The soft cushion of her lips undoes me, and her

minty taste wrenches me back for more. I surround her, pull her in tight.

Then I kiss her. A warm, wet hug of mouths and heavy breaths. I go in aggressively, not to test the water, but to shake it the hell up.

I dive and plunder, engorge and ravage, quenching an eight-year drought. My thumbs stroke her cheeks. My fingers sink into her hair, and she leans into us.

And edges back.

As she attempts detachment, I lick at her tongue, reinforcing the attraction. She gasps beneath the electricity and assesses it with a lick of her own. Then another. Hesitantly, she plunges deeper, reaching, exploring, mouth open, soft and trusting, fingertips denting skin, toes stretching her height, and slowly, wondrously, she thaws.

Her hands find my shoulders. Her groin meets mine, and she melts into me with a passion that scorches.

Cupping her face, I angle her head and draw her ardor into mine, feeding on the inescapable rightness of it. She's tiny in my arms, but her intensity is immeasurable, sparking from her skin, with a shimmery zap on every breath.

As my kiss consumes her mouth, I steal peeks at her between voracious bites. Flawlessly smooth complexion, thick black lashes over sharp cheekbones, and raven hair that tumbles around my hands—her beauty is effortless and deeply moving. Perhaps it's the sensuality within her, glowing her skin from the inside out. To hold her like this is to bathe in the warmth of sunlight.

My body leans harder, pushing her against the wall as we surrender to the flames, lips biting, tongues rubbing, and hips falling into a hungry grind.

We meld into a single desire, one wish, and we both know it's only a matter of time before I'm inside her, fucking her the way the universe intended.

Too soon, she pulls back. I chase her, stealing more greedy sips before resting my brow against hers.

Her mouth remains parted, eyes lost in emotion. She feels me, hears me, and that knowledge stirs something significant deep in my chest.

We stare at each other, breathless and searching. I tumble eagerly into the paradise of her eyes and watch in horror as they well with tears.

"Raina?"

She escapes my loose grip and moves to the far side of the bathroom with her back to me.

"Talk to me." I can't temper the demand in my voice.

"I already have a broken life, Lorne. I won't survive a broken heart. Please, just… Go."

Realization knocks the air from my lungs.

She could fall in love with me.

I've never had a girlfriend, never loved anyone outside of my family. I don't even know if I'm capable of it. Am I pushing us into something that might not work out?

Dammit, I'm willing to take that leap.

But she's not.

She turns on the shower. Then she slides the straps off her shoulders and lowers the dress down her back, wickedly and deliberately torturing me.

I want her, with every hot, hard, strumming beat in my body.

But not like this. Not until she's with me at the same burning level.

I pivot out of the bathroom and slam the door.

Raina doesn't show up for dinner that night. I tell myself I don't care and head outside to escape the crawling sensation of confinement.

For the rest of the evening, I ride Captain across the acreage, checking the fences and perimeter security around the house. Between stops, I let him stretch into a gallop. As he flies over the dark terrain, Raina's voice vibrates the air.

*The wind in my face, the freedom on his back, the feel of his strength between my legs, the sound of his loyal heartbeat.*

For the first time since the tragedy in the ravine, I give myself permission to enjoy the ride. It's not just the solace in reconnecting with my old friend. It's the memories tucked into the nature around us. The flower-picking, rabbit-hunting, stargazing memories of the trails I traversed as a child, the trees I climbed, the pond I swam in, and the fields where we camped every summer.

Happiness has been here all along, in the spirit of the land, waiting for me to wake up and be the man I'm meant to be.

*A man who's willing to dip into his soul and remember what calls to him.*

Raina knew.

She always seems to know what I need.

I don't know what time I finally sprawl on the sleeping bag. There are no watches or clocks in prison, and I've found I no longer want them.

As I lie on my back and stare at the stars, I evaluate my mental health. When inmates are released, we're warned about PTSD, anxiety, depression, and nightmares.

I've felt the tug of those things. My nerves riot in public places and social situations. I've lost the drive to take over the ranching operation. I only exercise because I refuse to be weak.

And I think about drinking. I haven't touched a bottle since that night in the stable. Haven't so much as sipped alcohol since I was eighteen. But the urge scratches through my blood.

The interests I had as a kid are gone. I didn't consider playing guitar again until Conor returned my instrument at dinner tonight. When I wrapped a hand around the frets, I relived the last night I played it, a night associated with masked men and brutality.

I have flashbacks. If it's PTSD, it only surfaces when I sleep.

Because of the nightmares.

Every night, the goddamn nightmares. Usually the same ones. I'm back in prison and don't know how I got there. I'm exhausted, and all the bunks are taken. I'm standing in the chow hall with shit on my tray, stark naked, and I can't find my clothes.

The worst is when I'm in the ravine, hands bound by

rope as Conor's rape plays out before me. Except Conor is Raina, and the man violently fucking her is John Holsten. I scream through my gag, but no one hears me. Then I wake screaming into the night. Alone.

Even with Raina's tea, I struggle to fall back asleep.

If I'm on the verge of a mental breakdown, I won't allow it to sink hooks into me. Not while I'm responsible for Raina's protection. Not while she's distracting me, grounding me, and making me whole again.

A week ago, I was numb. Now I feel this frustrating little woman in my veins. I feel every part of her in every part of me.

And she doesn't feel me back.

Except she kisses me like she does.

I know her past. She knows where I've been. We're moving forward together, whether she likes it or not.

We need *us*.

My attention drifts to the guitar at my feet. My fingers twitch to strum, and my throat clears to hum as a Jake Owen song plays in my head. It's a fucked-up song that reminds me of a fuckable woman who fucks with my head.

I sit up and drag the instrument onto my lap. I tap the wooden body. Pluck the strings. Adjust the tune. Stumble over the chords. Then I play *Alone With You*.

It's choppy the first few times I run through it, my shoulders twitching at the screeching mistakes. But eventually, I nail it, singing along with the acoustic.

Conor's a better guitarist. Jake's a helluva singer. I can do both with average skill.

The longer I play, the more I realize I missed this. I miss the jam sessions, the connection through music, the emotions it evokes. I miss the people who mean everything to me.

As the last note echoes across the field, my hands

fall from the strings.

That's when I hear her.

Every molecule in my body tunes into Raina's location behind me before she stirs.

Her breath releases. Her feet pad through the grass, and she kneels before me with a thermos in her hands.

"That was…" She searches my face for the answer. "Beautifully lonely."

My chest tightens, and I set the guitar aside. "I haven't played in—"

"Don't stop."

"I just did."

"I mean, don't make this the only time. Your family would love for you to play with them again."

At my nod, she hands me the thermos of tea. I inch over, making room for her beside me on the sleeping bag, and together, we lie back and drink in the starlight.

"Did you eat?" I ask.

"After everyone went to bed. What are you teaching me tomorrow?"

I walk through the shooting practice and defense techniques I have planned and update her on the security around the property.

"How are we going to find John?" she asks.

"He'll turn up." I'm surprised he hasn't already. "The sheriff will call when he does."

"What happens if John shows up here?"

"There are six people who wouldn't hesitate to kill him, and we would be in our lawful right to do so. This is our property. Trespassers enter at their own risk."

"He knows that?"

"Fuck yes, he knows."

"If I went into town and did things, like grocery shopping, I could lure him out."

"No. That's non-negotiable."

# Booted

Jarret and Maybe bring in the food. That won't change until Raina's safe.

"You haven't left the ranch in five days," she mutters.

I lean up on an elbow and bow over her. "Why are you out here?"

"Why do you ask me that every night?"

"Because you always give me that shit about the universe, and for once, I want a real answer."

She squints. "We're being truthful?"

"Yes, goddammit. Always."

Her gaze dances across the moonlit sky and takes its time returning. "This is my favorite part of every day."

I relax with a lightness in my chest. "Mine, too."

She rests calmly on her back beneath me, wearing one of my t-shirts and nothing else. I could roll on top of her right now and lose myself in her tight body.

And it wouldn't matter to her. Not the way it matters to me.

She's been fucking since she was fourteen, in every position and with more men than I care to imagine. I haven't had sex since I was eighteen, and while I was wildly experimental, my experience is no match for hers.

But that doesn't mean she's in control. She caught me off guard today and owned me with admirable skill.

It won't happen again.

In an unhurried glide of motion, I rise to my feet. My shirt, hat, and boots came off a while ago, but I'm still wearing jeans.

"Flip over." I hook a thumb under my belt and assume a loose, confident stance. "On your knees with your head on the ground."

Her eyes flash. Her mouth parts, and she slowly pushes to a sitting position. "Lorne?"

"Now." The boom in my voice makes her jump.

She touches her throat, her chest rising and falling. A moment later, her fear melts away, replaced by the Jezebel who milked my cock before dinner.

I'll let her wear the mask. It won't stay on for long.

In a mesmerizing, serpentine twist of her body, she rolls onto her chest, tucks her knees beneath her, and arches her ass in the air.

I crouch behind her and flip up the hem of the shirt, revealing lacy black panties that cut high across her gorgeous cheeks. I selected those in Cora's shop while imagining the stunning view before me now.

My erection jerks against my zipper, and my breathing loses rhythm. I'm enslaved by the sight of her, and I haven't even seen her naked.

She peers over her shoulder, her eyes lidded and inviting, almost pleading, as if that's the look I want her to wear. She assumes this is for me, that I'm going to fuck her just like every other dick that's seen her in this pose, and she's prepared to let me.

But tonight is about her. I'm going to strip her down to the center of her heart, starting with that mask.

I rear back an arm and slam my palm against her backside, spreading a sting through my fingers.

She yelps, and her body lurches forward with the impact.

Adrenaline floods my blood. I'm starved for this— the domination, the power and purpose—but I rein in my exhilaration and focus on her.

"Wipe that counterfeit look off your face." I spank her again.

Her head whips around, and she shoots me a murderous glare.

"Better." I caress a soothing hand across her heated skin. "I want honest answers." I continue to tenderly rub her sore flesh. "Have you ever had an orgasm with a man?"

# Booted

She lowers her eyes to the ground, then her head, leaving her ass perched skyward. After a moment of silence, I let my hand fly, delivering a fiery smack.

"No." She gulps air, trembling and tense. "I haven't."

"Has anyone gone down on you?"

Her fingers curl against the sleeping bag. "Yes."

And she didn't come. Because they didn't have a fucking clue what they were doing.

I stroke the hot, prickling skin on her butt and drag my touch along the cleavage, dipping low and deep while imagining the clinch of that forbidden entrance. "How did you know I'd allow your finger in my ass? That I'd like it?"

She lifts on her elbows and twists her neck to look at me. "After what happened to you in prison, you've been forced to imagine what it would feel like to be penetrated there. It terrifies you, but it also stirs a dark curiosity. It's one of those hate-to-love-it things. Most people have kinks like that." She chews on her lip. "But a finger is your limit. If I tried to peg you with a strap-on, you'd stop me. Even though it can be immensely pleasurable for a man, you're way too alpha for that. The only way you'd enjoy anal sex is if you're the one doing the fucking."

I sit back on my heels, awestruck and painfully turned-on by how accurately she knows me. "Lie on your back."

She obeys, without the sexual swagger from before. "Have you ever fucked a girl in the ass?"

"No."

High school girls were way too squeamish for that.

I stretch out beside her, with one hand propping up my head and the other resting on her flat stomach. "What's your hate-to-love-it kink?"

She tenses and angles her face away.

I grab her chin and yank her back to me. "Your

kink."

Her nostrils widen and relax. "I didn't have one until today."

I tighten my grip.

"You," she whispers.

"Be specific."

She makes a pained sound in her throat. "This is hard."

Her fingers wander along my forearm and around my hand. She doesn't pull to break my hold. Instead, she clings.

I let go of her chin and weave our hands together, shifting them to rest between her breasts. "Tell me."

"I liked putting my mouth on you, on *all* of you. I'm sorry, but you have an outrageously sexy body."

There's nothing wrong with physical attraction. Hell, I'm consumed by it every time I look at her. But...

"You're deeper than that, Raina."

"That's exactly it. I've never been deep with anyone. Then you went and kissed me and..."

I press my body along the side of hers and lower my mouth to her neck. With my lips tasting her throat, I adjust our laced hands to cup the soft mound of her breast.

She's built like a porn star—exaggerated curves, delicate bone structure, and lean muscle. Only she's all natural.

Molding my fingers around hers, I plump the flesh beneath our hands, guiding our touch into a kneading, titillating caress.

"I kissed you and...?" I kiss her now. Her neck, her jaw, and the sensitive spot beneath her ear.

"You pulled me under and drown me, Lorne. It's just how you are. Your assertiveness, the command in your voice, the overbearing way you push me... I hate to love it."

# Booted

That's her turn-on. Deep down, she yearns to be sexually dominated by a man she has feelings for while fighting him all the way.

Subconsciously, I already knew this. We've been playing with the power exchange since the day we met. Hearing her vocalize it, however, heats and hardens everything inside me. It's as if her words have given my body permission to proceed.

With our hands on her breast, I press my thigh against the apex of hers, trapping her leg beneath my weight.

As much as I want to grind against her, I hold my hips still and measure my breathing. "When was the last time you gave yourself a release?"

"In the shower a few hours ago."

A groan escapes my throat. She thought about me while touching herself. I'm certain of it. That means I affect her, and fuck me, I ache to affect her some more.

"Before that?" I lick the hollow of her throat.

She swallows against my lips. "It had been two years."

Because she was with John.

I shove that thought away and turn my attention to our hands. Veering them downward, I use her fingers to trace the winding contours of her body.

She knows how to touch herself. This isn't about self-pleasure. It's about keeping her with me while *I* pleasure her.

It would be more effective with the shirt off, but her nudity would rage a war inside me I wouldn't win. The impulse to sink into her soft, squeezing heat roars at me, shaking me to my core.

I breathe through it, bathing her neck in hungry gasps as I steer our exploration south.

Lying half on her with our bodies aligned, I edge my

thigh away from her panties and slide our entwined fingers beneath the lace. My breath stammers at the feel of her short, coarse hair.

My gaze falls into hers as I imagine the black curls beneath my touch, the way they glisten and shine with her arousal. She's so wet. Soaked through the lace. And I've only just begun.

I drive our journey lower, deeper between her thighs and slowly dip into her swollen slit.

Her legs twitch with restlessness, one trapped beneath mine, the other dragging her foot along the sleeping bag.

"Lorne..." Her plea is breathy, strangled. "Stop."

"This is unstoppable."

We're unstoppable.

I attach my lips to hers, stalling her protests. As I plunge my tongue, I sink our fingers into the hot, tight clasp of her body.

With the kiss comes the flex of her thigh against my hand, the clamp and release of her inner muscles, and the loll of her tongue against mine. Just the right blend of acceptance and resistance, without a fight or a care.

She's trying to be indifferent. Probably telling herself not to let a man know how much power he wields over her in this position. She wants to let go and feel me, but she's terrified of falling.

So she doesn't lean up, doesn't try to lead my finger inside her or heighten the intensity in any way. Because that would confess her desire, her hunger to be a part of this.

I brush my lips across her jaw and move in so close she can feel *my* hunger stabbing against her. She can feel my strength, my breaths, and my aggressive grip on her cunt, and her mind is probably already joining us together, playing out the slap of flesh and stabbing strokes as we fuck.

I mimic the fantasy with my fingers, thrusting in and out, stretching her open, building her toward orgasm while making her wait for the peak. I can hardly bear it. My lungs slam together, my erection a steel bar of pressure. Fucking Christ, my bones and guts burn with so much need for this woman, I'm going to go up in flames.

I need to taste her, lap her up, and eat the fuck out of her.

With my mouth on her skin, I kiss every swerve and bend as I inch down her body. Our hands separate. Hers, falling to my hair. Mine, sliding aside the lace between her legs.

The sight of her wet, pink pussy reduces me to a ravenous, shaking, predatory creature of need. Hunger and elation thickens my cock. A full, hot feeling invades my prostate. My skin aches to be touched, and all thought narrows into the mindless drive to grab, thrust, fuck, and claim.

With a strangled groan, I rub a hand down my brow, my mouth, and around my neck as I fight to get a grip on my control.

I haven't done this in so long I don't even know if I'm good at it.

Gripping the backs of her thighs, I spread her open and lower my head. The warm, thrilling scent of her arousal waters my mouth. I run my nose through it, then my lips, reveling in the sweet, wet promise of sex. Then I devour the aroma straight from the source.

Without restraint or hesitancy, I bury my face and ravage her cunt with tongue and teeth. I kiss her deeply, ferociously, endlessly sucking and tugging at the silky tunnel of her heat.

Her hands pull my hair as she bucks and twists her hips, moaning, panting, and gripping around my tongue.

I have her now. She wants my cock. Fucking hell, she's so hot and wet she's trembling for my hard, ruthless thrusts.

Yanking hard on my hair, she bares her teeth. "Just fuck me already."

If I do, she'll convince herself it's only sex. That I'm taking, chasing my own needs, and leaving her when it's over. Just like all the others.

I crawl up her body and straddle her leg. Putting my face in hers, I drive three fingers deep inside her and fuck her with my hand.

"You're going to come when I say." I lick the sultry rim of her gaping mouth. "With your eyes on mine and your emotions spilling all over your pretty face."

"Lorne, I can't." She grips my forearm.

I circle my thumb around her clit, flicking it until her back bows off the ground. Then I kiss her. Delicate bites of warm lips, at odds with the brutal drive of my fingers. I keep the aggression in my hand and the affection on my mouth, and within seconds, the combination crumbles her shields.

She liquefies beneath me. Her legs fall open. Her breaths burst in short, wheezing gasps. Her hips lift, seeking, and her eyes stare up at me, dark with desire and round with fear.

She's letting me see her, hear her, in the sweetest, most profound surrender. She's never been stronger or braver with me than in this moment.

As I torment her pussy, I glide my free hand along the side of her face and hold my lips to hers, breathing in her sighing moans and tasting her submission. I'm addicted to her scent, her sounds, the feel of her soft flesh around my fingers. And her eyes.

Edging back, I watch her watch me with a shared awe that drives the rhythm of my fingers inside her. She's on the brink of climax, and she doesn't know whether to fight it or give in.

"Come for me." I rub her clit, the outer edge of her cunt, the walls deep inside, stirring soaked flesh and shoving her off the edge.

Her hands fly to my neck. Her eyes open wide, and she comes with an exquisite scream. "Lorne, oh my fuck, fuck, fuck—"

I kiss her through it, sucking and groaning as I memorize the liquid, pulsing sensations around my fingers. I don't think I've ever felt a woman come like this. If I have, it wasn't memorable. It wasn't her.

Slowing the motion of my hand, I bring her down gently, relishing the twitches in her body and the kicks in her breathing.

When her lungs catch up, I lift my soaked fingers to my lips and draw them into my mouth, one by one. She regards me from beneath dark fringes of lashes as I savor her taste, torturing myself with her essence.

Settling on my side, I pull her close and kiss her hair. She doesn't curl up against me or push me away. She goes still and quiet, her forehead lowered to my chest and hands slack between us.

The hypnotic tempo of her breaths lulls me into the zone between alertness and sleep. With her skin against mine and my demons at bay, contentment finds me. For minutes. Hours. I don't know how long I drift before she slips from my arms.

I lift my head as she sits out of reach and pulls her knees to her chest. Distancing herself.

"Raina," I growl.

"I don't want to fight." She stares out into the darkness, her face taut, shoulders hiked, and voice achy. "Please, Lorne. Not tonight."

She's peeled open, defenses down, raw and

enticingly vulnerable. If I wanted to hurt her, now would be the time to do it.

This is exactly where I want her. I only need to reach in, and my fingers would brush her soul.

I'm not a romantic. My boots stick to the ground, and my heart beats with the rhythm of the land. But a long time ago, I knew how to treat a woman.

I grab my phone and pull up a song. As I set it aside and stand, *Come A Little Closer* by Dierks Bentley strums through the speakers.

Her brows gather as she meets my eyes.

"Dance with me." I hold out a hand.

"I don't know how." Her broken whisper cleaves between my ribs like a knife.

"I'll show you."

She unfolds from the ground and steps forward, wearing a look of tortured uncertainty.

I remain where I'm at and let her come to me. When her toes reach mine, I hold up a palm. She touches it, and a jolt of awareness crackles across my skin.

The music guides my body into a slow, swinging cadence that compels hers to do the same. Our hips sway together, hovering around the sliver of space between.

Her palm rests against mine, joining us by that single point of contact. There's no urgency. No expectations. No demands. It's just her and me and the connection of our eyes.

I lift my other hand to her elbow and whisper my fingertips along her upper arm. She breaks out in goosebumps as I lightly follow the delicate curve of her shoulder.

My barely-there touches set the footing. My hands move, and she follows my lead. Fingers kiss skin, brushing, roaming, and indulging as we rock gently together in tune with the melody.

# Booted

I'm certain she's never permitted herself to touch a man this way, to caress and explore for her own curiosity and pleasure.

She peruses me with her eyes, learns me with her hands, and matches my steps with a slow, seductive roll of her hips.

Each verse brings us closer, and closer, until our foreheads meet, and our breaths mingle. I stroke my nose along hers, my hands gliding down her arms and pulling her in with just the friction of our skin.

Our caresses tease, light and airy, as if a heavier touch would break the natural rhythm between us. We become one. One dance, one body, caught up in the electricity of closeness.

She reaches for the back of my neck and idly traces my shaved hairline. I shudder and press in, seeking the pounding reverberation of her heart and taking comfort in the beauty she emits. A beauty that floods my senses with life.

Her hand slips through my hair, cupping the base of my skull. Her lips float to my cheek and graze the scratchy stubble. Then her head tilts back, offering her gorgeous face, and I touch it, with my hands, my breath, my gaze.

As the song leads us, we move in exquisite synchronicity, staring at each other, lost in the sensations while cradling the solidarity of our souls.

This is the most intimate we've ever been, yet no part of us below the waist makes physical contact. We embrace without arms, kiss without lips, and fall with the ground firmly beneath our feet.

"I hear you." She gazes up at me, her eyes bright and mouth against mine in an almost-kiss.

"I hear you, too." I rest my head against hers, swaying to the music, tranquilized by her nearness.

When the song ends, I walk her back to the house,

my fingers woven around hers and my thoughts on the bed that awaits.

She pauses at the door and finds my eyes. I lean in, run my hands around the graceful column of her neck, and sink into the long strands of her hair.

Then I kiss her. Slow and gentle, our tongues touch and slide together. Breaths stroking, lips curving, it's a kiss that marks a moment, not the end of one, but the beginning.

We come up for air, and she steps inside the house. Then she glances back at me.

If she asks me to come in, I will. I'll take her to bed and spend the rest of the night inside her.

But she doesn't ask. She closes the door and rests a hand against the glass, regarding me from the other side.

The currents shift between us. Creases fan out from the corners of her eyes, and her expression twists with turmoil.

She seems to be trying, and failing, to grasp something that will pull her free of this thing between us. I won't help her with that.

Her desperation beats against me, and I welcome it. I'll accept every emotion she offers. Because I want all of her. Every fear and desire, weakness and strength, nightmare and dream.

But she's not ready for that. Not yet.

"Lock the door," I mouth.

She turns the lock.

## 16

### Raina

"No! Absolutely not!" Lorne plants his boots in a wide stance on the front porch, his eyes wildly scanning me before swinging back to Conor. "It's too risky."

Going out for a family dinner wasn't my idea. After last night, I prefer some time alone to sort the bleeding, ugly mess he made of my insides.

"Fine. We'll take a vote." Conor crosses her colorfully inked arms, glaring at her brother. "All those in favor of eating at a quiet, safe restaurant say *Aye*."

The whole family is here for the intervention, and a chorus of unanimous *Aye's* echoes around me.

I'm the only one holding my tongue.

He needs to leave the ranch and interact with society, just for a couple of hours. At the very least, he needs to spend time with the people who mean the most to him. His family waited eight years for his return. Their reunion is as important to him as it is to them.

I can only imagine how hard it is to build those

relationships back to what they once were. He's not that eighteen-year-old kid anymore. But fighting them on something as simple as going to dinner only increases his emotional distance.

At the same time, I understand his concerns about leaving the ranch. No place is safe right now. He won't let me stay here alone, and he doesn't want me in public where threats can't be controlled.

Conor doesn't take her eyes off him. "Those opposed say *No.*"

"No." He towers over her. "My vote is the only one that counts, because she's *my* responsibility." He stabs a finger in my direction. "*My* decision."

"Possessive much?" She arches an auburn brow, and a knowing smirk steals across her lips.

Yeah, he's possessive. But he's also been training me for the day he lets me go. I was never meant to stay here.

My purpose is to kill John Holsten.

"I didn't vote." I shove back my shoulders and meet his heated gaze. "*Aye.*"

Green flames ignite in his eyes beneath the brim of his hat. His anger is so effervescent it thrashes and spits sparks in a deadly dance of intimidation.

Fury hardens every inch of him, from his square jaw and aquiline nose to the thick muscles stretching the denim on his thighs.

He stands several feet away, yet his strength and authority press against me from all sides. Chills invade my arms, and I rub my hands over the prickles.

"Get in the house." His command is a roar with teeth, meant to make me blanch.

I can't stop my body's reactions to him. He terrifies me, but in a different way than he did when we first met.

Something changed between us last night. Or

maybe my perspective of him changed. But as he stands before me, looking for all the world like he's going to break my face, I know he won't.

He would never lay a hand on me out of anger. He isn't John Holsten. He isn't like any man I've ever encountered.

He's worse.

He broke me apart beneath the stars with his kissing and touching and dancing. I'm still trying to pick up the pieces. Needy, shameful pieces that cry out for him and make me crave things. I want to kneel for him, bend to his will, and put my trust in his capable hands.

But I won't.

I don't need him to take care of me. I need him to stand at my side when I'm kicking ass and say, *I'm with her.*

We haven't spoken about what happened. In fact, I haven't seen him all day, because some of the cattle escaped through the fence. He's been in the pasture for the past ten hours helping the guys gather the herd.

We should both go inside and talk, but I'm not ready for that. Certainly not in his current mood.

"You're outvoted." I gesture at Conor and the others. "We're going to dinner, with or without you."

"Is that why you're dressed like that?" He sneers at my legs in the jeans I cut into super short shorts. "Are you hard up for male attention? Maybe the waiter will give you something to swallow for dessert."

My heart folds in on itself.

How can the same mouth be so clitorally pleasurable and emotionally painful?

Jarret steps forward, hands clenched, as Conor shouts, "Take that back!"

"I don't know what's going on between you two." Jake gives Lorne a baleful glare. "But Raina's been good to you. Good *for* you. As small as she is, it takes grit to put you in your place. A woman like that deserves admiration, not disrespect."

Lorne's hateful lips bow into a deep scowl.

Beneath the ache in my throat simmers a comforting sense of embracement. I feel like I'm part of something, a member of a six-person unit. It's so staggering and precious I don't want to let go of it.

As I zip up my hemorrhaging emotions behind a blank expression, Lorne zeroes in on the ragged hitching in my chest.

"Raina..." Regret tempers his tone, but he won't retract the accusation.

He's too desperate, too willing to do whatever is needed to keep me here, including hurting my feelings.

I close the distance with unhurried steps, lift my hand, and slap his viciously handsome face.

He glares at me, nostrils pulsing.

The urge to run burns my legs, but I lock my knees and confront his temper head on.

A wordless argument follows. His eyes snarl and demand. I remain icy and resolute. We're at an impasse, and I'm not backing down.

"Who I am riding with?" I walk toward the parking lot.

"You can ride with us." Conor falls into step with me, glancing behind her.

"Maybe will ride with you." Lorne stalks past her. "Raina and I are with Jarret."

Damn him and his hot-and-cold, back-and-forth bullshit.

He'd rather eat barbed wire than go with us, but he would never stay behind while I go. He's putting his need to protect me over his anxiety of public places.

No one has ever made me feel as safe as he does, yet

so incredibly vulnerable and reckless at the same time. He's a paradox of extremes. Temptation and aversion. Protection and danger. A slow burn and a quick fuse. There's no middle path with this guy. He's either all in or all asshole.

He follows me into the cab of Jarret's truck, wedging me in the center. After checking the glove box for Jarret's pistol, he settles into brooding silence.

It's a miserable ride.

An hour later, the six of us sit in a fine-dining steakhouse several towns over.

For a restaurant that's only been open for a month, I expected it to be busier. Only half the tables are occupied, each one draped in linens, silver, and soft-glowing candlelight.

Conor chose it for its lakeside view and raving reviews.

The servers don black suits and pour water into stemmed glasses, and the scent of seared meat permeates the air. It reminds me of the places John used to take me. He liked to wear me on his arm and mingle with the upper-class like he was one of them.

Lorne sits beside me, hands on his lap, stiff and motionless. His eyes move frequently, watching everything and everyone around him. That is, when he's not watching me.

I feel that green gaze like a kiss. *His* kiss. It caresses my skin, seeking and finding erogenous zones I didn't know I had until last night.

He watches me through courses of soup, salad, and fancy little appetizers. When the guys order beers, he drinks water and continues his vigilance, speaking only when prodded and smiling only at his sister.

But he doesn't offer dimpled smiles. He's too on edge.

I'm still mad at him and refuse to give him my eyes or any compassion for his discomfort.

Until he leans across the two-foot distance between us.

"Move closer." He grips the seat of my chair. "Please."

It's the *Please* that reaches through my resentment and shakes me.

I lift my weight and let him slide me to his side. The position doesn't look odd, seeing how the other four are already paired off in the same way.

Lorne stretches an arm along the back of my chair, and his fingers sink into my hair. As he idly strokes the strands from roots to tips, his entire demeanor relaxes. He sits back, muscles loosening and breaths slipping into silence. The slow, rhythmic slide of his hand through my hair is so palliative and trance-inducing I could curl up on his lap and fall asleep.

The serenity of nightfall blankets the lake beyond the wall of windows and spills into the dining room. Muted whispers, soft clinking china, and dark wood furnishings add to the ambiance.

The servers bring out the main course, and everyone digs into their steaks, chops, and roasts. The tender meat melts in my mouth, the vegetables buttery and crisp. The food is as comforting as the atmosphere.

As Conor and Lorne talk about her veterinary practice, it becomes apparent that he finally stopped by to see it today. At least he's doing something right.

My stomach pinches. I shouldn't judge him too harshly. He has a strong constitution and a courageous heart. He survived prison, hasn't turned to alcohol, and here he is, sitting among strangers without losing his shit. I'm proud of him.

When he isn't being a jerk.

# Booted

Jarret orders another beer, and Jake teases Maybe about the critters that died under the farming machines that harvested her salad. By the time the plates are scraped clean and desserts are ordered, the mood has lifted into easy conversation and content smiles.

Lorne's hand returns to my hair, his attention on his family. "When are you getting married?"

"We're waiting for things to settle down." Jake pointedly looks at me.

My shoulders tense. What does he mean? Are they waiting for John Holsten's death? Or is he implying something else?

"We're kicking around the idea of one wedding." He brushes away an auburn lock from Conor's cheek.

"You would share your wedding days together?" I glance between Conor and Maybe.

"Sure." Conor turns into Jake's palm, touching her lips to his scar. "We could go small. Just our family in the backyard."

"Or we can do it in Sandbank," Maybe says with a grin, "and invite the whole town."

A shadow caresses Lorne's face before a flicker of candlelight chases it away.

"Which would you prefer?" he asks.

My breath stutters when I realize he directed that question at me. "Why would it matter what I—?"

"It's hypothetical." His fingers clench in my hair. "Breathe."

I draw air through my nose as everyone at the table stares at me.

"Now tell me." His hand trails down my back. "Do you want a big wedding or a small one?"

His hypothetical inquiry is making me hypersensitive to the invasive, unwavering way he's observing me.

187

"I don't know." I go still beneath his eyes. "I've never thought about it."

A week ago, I didn't even like men. Not enough to willingly attach myself to one.

The server appears with our desserts, saving me from further scrutiny. Lorne ordered the Grand Marnier soufflé for me and a coffee for himself.

I scoop out a spoonful of jiggly orange pastry and offer him the first bite.

He shakes his head and stares at the table.

Is he thinking about the jab he made about me swallowing waiter's *dessert*? Or the question about the wedding?

Maybe he's just appreciating the coffee cupped between his huge hands.

Sometimes I catch him drifting off in thought while holding something so seemingly inconsequential, such as an ink pen, a television remote, a cup of coffee, or the necklace he's never removed from his wrist. The little things people take for granted are the things he values most. The things he didn't have access to in prison.

I take a few bites, savoring the creamy goodness while watching him in my periphery.

"You okay?" I lower the spoon.

He doesn't respond.

"Lorne?"

He blinks, and his head jerks up. His body goes rigid, and his eyes dart around the dining room, searching every exit and window. Then he looks at me, and an odd grunt sounds in his throat.

His shoulders relax, and he returns his attention to the cup in his hands. "I used to make my dad's coffee before I went to school."

Across the table, Conor stiffens.

"The smell..." His eyebrows knit over pensive green

eyes. "It's nostalgic, in a good way."

"I have good memories of him, too." She smiles sadly. "It's okay to miss him, Lorne. I miss the man who lived at the ranch. When he moved to Chicago…" Her expression shutters. "That wasn't Dad."

Out of compulsion, I slide a hand over his thigh. He grips it, trapping my palm against denim and muscle.

After a moment of wretched silence, Conor closes her eyes. "Will someone change the subject?"

Jake jumps in, redirecting the conversation into happier territory by announcing that the cattle operation will have its most profitable quarter in two decades.

As he talks, I finish off the dessert and squirm against the pressure in my bladder.

A hallway leads into the back, near the kitchen. The restrooms must be there.

"I need to use the lady's room." I move to stand.

Lorne tightens his grip on my hand, stopping me. "Wait until we're home."

"It's a forty-five-minute drive."

His jaw clenches, and he glares at the other patrons in the restaurant, as if they're all concealing guns.

They probably are. I mean, we're still in cattle country.

Blowing out a sharp breath, he adjusts his fingers around mine and rises from the table.

With my hand imprisoned in his, I follow him through the dining room and down the hallway. The tendons in his shoulders and neck are so taut they look like they're going to snap.

He doesn't stop at the door to the women's bathroom. He shoves it open and hauls me inside.

A middle-aged woman stands at the sink, her eyes bulging at his reflection in the mirror.

"Get out," he barks.

"I'm sorry." I yank my hand from his and give her a grimace. "He didn't take his meds today."

She grabs her purse, walks a wide berth around him and darts out the door.

He swerves toward the stalls, checks each one, and wriggles the handle on the locked closet door. No windows. No bogeymen hiding in the toilets.

He prowls back to me, his gaze hard and threatening. He closes in and doesn't just step into my personal space. He devours it.

His chest touches my nose, and the width of his shoulders blocks my view of everything behind him. Strong hands rest on the front of his jeans, thumbs hooked under the belt, fingers framing the metal buckle.

With his chin angled down, the black Stetson sits low on his brow, making his dark expression all the more darker.

I shiver. He's brutally arresting and overwhelmingly intense. His meanness runs deep, but when he directs that malice at me, it's always followed by remorse.

"You lash out at me when you're upset." I tilt my head back, searching his eyes.

"I lash out when I *care*." He cups a hand beneath my chin, and his thumb feathers across my cheek. "I'm sorry for what I said at the house." He sets his brow against mine. "You're stunning, and I don't want to share the pleasure of looking at you with anyone else."

My breath catches. The next one comes out ragged, clawing at the air between us. "I won't fall for your sweet talk."

"You fell apart for it last night when I sweet talked your pussy."

My nipples tighten, and a quiver races along my inner thighs. He wrecked me so thoroughly with that insatiable tongue I still feel him inside me.

# Booted

"I'll be right outside that door." His thumb kisses my lips and slips away. "Then I'm taking you home."

He steps out of the bathroom, leaving me standing in the lingering tingles of his touch.

I try to shake it off, but it sticks. He sticks. His words, his gaze, his captivating presence—he's holding me under water without a breath of air.

My mind runs a marathon as I wander to the middle stall and empty my bladder.

Is it his confidence? His masculine beauty? His strength? John Holsten possesses all those traits, and it did nothing for me when we met.

I don't understand what's happening between Lorne and me, but I feel protective of it. The thought of never seeing him again fills my gut with ravenous protests.

Maybe it's all the talk about weddings.

Maybe it's the comfort of being included in such a tight family.

Maybe it's just... *Him.*

The automatic flusher erupts as I finish. I swing open the door of the stall, head down, my fingers zipping and buttoning my shorts.

Something moves in my periphery. A sound near the last stall and...

The closet door is opening. Only it's not a closet. A dimly lit, linoleum-lined corridor stretches out from the man bursting in.

White Stetson, dark scowl, and brown eyes I know horrifyingly well—all of it slams into me so fast I don't have time to react.

John's palm covers my mouth. His body pins me against the wall, and his other hand holds up a phone with something paused on the screen.

My pulse explodes as I rear back a fist to drive it into his upper lip.

"Your sister's alive." He presses his mouth against my ear. "Make a sound, and that will change."

My heart stops. My insides ice over, and everything shuts down as an excruciating cry reaches for my throat. The gag of his hand presses harder, as if to trap my pain, but I'm already swallowing it down, hanging on his words, and pleading with my eyes.

She's alive? Is it true? What about the death records? Were they fake?

He holds the screen of the phone to my face and starts a video of Tiana's tiny body curled up in a hospital bed. A doctor walks into the camera view, and Tiana lifts her head, blinking huge brown eyes. Tubes snake around her. Sickness pales her skin, and long black hair clings to her three-year-old shoulders.

*Four.*

She would be four now.

He stops the video and pockets the phone. "When your mother drugged herself to the eyeballs, I moved Tiana to a safe place in Texas. She needs you."

Another sob tries to burst free, and I gulp, and gulp again, fighting to keep silent.

His arm slithers around my back, tugging me against him as he holds my mouth.

"Not a sound," he whispers. "We're going to walk out of here without drawing attention. Through the kitchen. Right out the back door. I told Tiana you're coming. Don't disappoint her."

My heart howls for her. My precious, innocent baby sister. It's been so long since I've held her, kissed her, and smelled her sweet scent.

"If you fight me," he breathes in my ear, "I'll kill her for good this time."

Defense techniques play on a reel in my head. Any one of the maneuvers would knock his hand from my mouth. My scream would alert Lorne and...

*Tiana will die.*

I blink up at John, at the handsome features that look so much like his sons. Very few lines crease his face, his eyes chillingly cold and lips curled back to bare the clench of his teeth.

The door he came through is shut. Twenty feet away, Lorne stands behind the other door. If I delay much longer, he'll storm in to check on me.

Has John been watching me this whole time? Did he follow us from Sandbank and hang out in the service hall, waiting on a chance that I would enter the bathroom alone?

If Tiana's alive, why did he tell me she was dead? Why remove the only leverage he held over me?

Because he didn't need that leverage. Not when he could hold me in chains and torture me with lies.

My stomach turns with horror and hope. I can't risk her life.

But what about Lorne? If I slip away quietly, he won't believe I ran. He'll know it was John, and he'll blame himself for not protecting me.

"Ready to be a good girl and see your sister?" Fingers dig into my cheek as the other hand grips my breast and squeezes. "Fuck, Raina. You have no idea how much I missed you."

Nausea threatens, watering my eyes. I shut out the memories and give him my gaze, shaking and breathless, heart in my mouth, begging for kindness. I need him to tell me Tiana's okay, even if it's just words. I need him to promise.

Except his promises are filth. He vowed to take care of her, swore she would receive a transplant and the best medical treatment.

I surrendered our lives for lies, cruel intentions, and

manipulations.

As much as my entire being clings to the hope that she's alive, I can't be blinded by it. I can't let him win.

Tears burn in the back of my throat as I nod.

"You'll be quiet." The hand against my mouth clenches and shoves, slamming my head against the tile wall. "Or she's dead."

Pain ricochets through my skull, and I nod again.

He uncurls his grip from my lips and quietly opens the door.

I wait until he steps into the hall. I wait until he leads me out with a possessive hand on my ass.

I wait until he convinces himself I'm going to cooperate.

Each step away from Lorne ratchets my blood pressure. My skin loses warmth. My stomach turns to lead, and a primal scream builds in my throat.

Ten steps from the bathroom, my nerves take over. My hand flies, and the heel of my palm crashes against his upper lip.

"Lorne!" I scream at the top of my lungs as my strike forces John's head back. "Lorne! Lorrrrrrrne!"

John doesn't stumble the way I expected. He's too strong, too fucking relentless as he bows back into me. The look on his face is a death threat, signed in Tiana's blood.

I throw myself at him with fists and teeth, heedless in my attempt to stop him from escaping.

A crash sounds in the bathroom. The door?

*Please, please, please let it be Lorne.*

John's eyes dart toward the noise, and he pushes away with evil fuming in his black eyes.

I grip his shirt, and he whirls on me, ramming a fist into my gut so violently it feels like the slow rip of lining tearing away from my stomach.

# Booted

I can't breathe, can't think past the pain.

"Raina!" Lorne bellows from the bathroom.

*Don't let John escape. Don't let him get to Tiana.*

The agony in my belly crashes me to my knees. I crawl, dragging my legs, reaching. But the monster's already gone.

17

Lorne

I've never felt so much rage. It bundles in my chest as I race toward the open closet. It flares through my fists at the sight of Raina crawling down a corridor I didn't know existed. It incinerates my breaths as she grips her stomach and tries to stand.

I lurch to her side, but I can't touch her. I'm shaking too badly, seething with the need to reduce the world to rubble.

"Was it John?" I stare down the empty hallway.

It veers off in multiple directions with no signs of danger and no clear shot of an exit.

"Yes." She staggers to her feet and bends over in pain, hugging her waist.

He put his hands on her.

He fucking hurt her.

I roar with all the fury of a wildfire. Flames engulf my vision. Gasoline replaces my blood. I punch a hole in the wall and burst down the hall, burning to ignite everything I come in contact with.

"Which way?" I swing in all directions, scouring for a throat to carve open.

Raina stumbles forward and grips the wall, her face contorting in an expression she's never worn. "Tiana..."

Tiana? What the fuck did he say about her sister?

"Which way?" My voice explodes like shrapnel in my ears.

She winces, and a sob tumbles out. Then more sobbing as she tries to speak. I can't make out her distressed words, but I catch *kitchen* and *back door*.

I take off down the corridor, leaving her hurt and alone. Her cries chase me as she calls out her sister's name. But I can't comfort her, not right now, for what I'm feeling isn't human.

As I stalk into the kitchen, someone steps into my path.

"Sir?" A server in a suit holds up his hands. "You can't be in here."

I knock him out of the way without a backward glance.

My insides twist and distort around the instinct to destroy. The knife from my boot warms my hand, and I don't know how it got there. The boom of my heartbeat doesn't sound like my own.

My wrath is a soulless executioner, stretching beneath my skin, tightening, scorching, and ordering me toward the slaughter.

I weave around employees and steel tables, searching, hunting, eyes fully open, and posture bowing into the flames of violence.

Then I see it. On the far side of the kitchen, the mocking white glow of a Stetson slips out the back door. Anger unleashes without thought of consequence, and I run, shove, and swerve, locked in tunnel vision and intent on blood.

He booted me off my own land, hired the men who raped my sister, and dared to come after my girl.

I killed before. For Raina, I'll kill again.

When I reach a long row of gas stoves, I wildly grope for a way around. The surface sizzles with fire and seared meat. The length of it extends from one wall to another, and the back door waits on the other side.

Panic rises. I'm caught in a goddamn maze, and he's getting away!

Doubling back costs me precious seconds. I dart around a food prep table and sprint toward the exit, pulse hammering and fingers flexing against the knife handle.

My shoulder collides with the door, crashing it open. Outside, the parking lot glints with cars under the streetlights and fades into the surrounding darkness.

Nothing moves. No one stirs. Where the fuck is he?

I prowl around vehicles, senses sharp and blade held out at my side. If he's hiding, I'll find him. Gut him. And strangle him with his goddamn intestines.

The squeal of tires turns my head. On the far side of the restaurant, an expensive pickup peels out of the lot. Gravel flies. Rubber burns, and I explode into a sprint.

My arms pump hard as I stretch my stride and run faster than I've ever run in my life. My boots pound pavement. My chest screams for air. I push faster, harder, chasing him down the lakeside road, unwilling to lose him.

But I lose ground.

He hits the gas, and his taillights vanish in the distance.

"Fuuuuck!" My rage thunders across the lake.

I can't contain the vibrating, thrashing madness inside me. I throw the knife, rip off my hat, and slam it against the ground.

Then I pace, heaving and panting, shaking and

pulling at my hair.

He hurt her, and he can hurt her again. Because I fucking failed.

I lace my fingers on my head and tilt my face to the sky, eyes closed, lungs burning, unable to catch my breath.

I left her by herself. Unprotected. What am I doing?

I need to calm my ass down.

Bending at the waist, I grip my knees and breathe. In. Out.

She's alive.

In. Out.

He didn't take her.

In. Out.

She needs me.

I collect my knife and hat and jog back. From my pocket, I remove my phone and dial Jarret.

"Where are you?" he asks after the first ring.

"Your dad showed up. He got away. I'm in the back lot." I disconnect and pick up my pace.

When I hit the parking lot, my gaze falls on the slender silhouette near the back door of the building.

She runs to me, one hand falling to her stomach.

Did he kick her? Punch her? In my mindless fury, I didn't even check to see if she was bleeding.

When she reaches me, she reads my eyes, and her voice cracks. "He got away."

My stomach hardens, and I pull her against me, pressing my lips to her hair. "I'm so sorry."

"Tiana's alive." She pushes back, voice rising. "He said if I didn't go with him, he'd kill her."

"What?"

As she angrily rushes through what happened, I crouch before her and lift her shirt. No stabs or cuts. No blood. I prod the skin on her abs, and her words break into a cry of pain.

My molars slam together. "I'm going to kill him."

"*I'm* going to kill him." She shoves down the shirt, her eyes brimming with tears. "First, I have to find my sister."

Christ, this woman. She's so fierce and beautifully hopeful I can't bring myself to deny her anything.

Maybe Tiana's alive in a hospital somewhere in Texas, but I'm not counting on it.

"She's our number one priority." I lift her into my arms and scan the lot for Jarret. "I need you to trust me."

"I've never trusted anyone." Her arms wrap tightly around my neck, confessing otherwise.

The sound of an approaching engine turns me toward the street. Jarret veers the truck in beside me and swings open the passenger door.

I meet his ice-cold eyes and in that flickering moment, I see every bullet he's fired. Every blade he's bloodied. Every life he's taken. Killing his father was a burden he never wanted, but that conflict no longer resides in his expression.

"Jake is taking the girls home." His gaze darts around the perimeter.

I slide in with Raina and shut the door. "We're going to see Fletcher."

"Thought you might say that." He steps on the gas.

While I update him on the last twenty minutes, I hold Raina on my lap, close to my chest. Fuck the seat belt. I'm not putting her down.

During the drive, she falls unnervingly still, almost lethargic, much like the way she was the night I met her, right after she was pulled from John's house.

I run my hand over the back of her hand, attempting to soothe her. Until my fingers slide through wetness.

"The fuck?" I hold my hand up to the moonlight,

and my nails glisten with blood. "What happened to your head?"

"He slammed me against the wall. It's just a cut." She pulls my arm down and wraps it around her. "Please, just... Keep holding me."

My nostrils widen with the flux of my anger. But I manage to rein it in for forty-five agonizing minutes.

Jarret pulls into Sheriff Fletcher's driveway, holsters the gun from his glove box, and strides to the front porch. I follow him with Raina in my arms and set her on her feet at the door.

When Fletcher answers the knock in his plaid pajamas, Jarret shoves his way inside.

"John paid us a visit tonight in Lindville." He makes a beeline for the office off the foyer.

"That's out of my jurisdiction." Fletcher storms after him. "Get out of my house."

"I want police records." I grip Raina's hand and pull her inside. "Death records. Autopsy reports. Anything you can pull up on Tiana Benally."

His eyes flit to Raina and harden. "I don't have access to that, and even if I did—"

"Fletcher?" His wife, Mary, pads into the foyer, wrapping a robe around herself. "Everything okay?"

She looks us over, and the soft wrinkles around her eyes deepen. She's known us our whole lives. She also knows what the papers printed about me, but I doubt she knows the corruption her husband's involved in.

"It's just business, sweetheart." He steps toward her and kisses her on the forehead. "Go on back to bed."

"Okay. It's good to see you boys." She gives Raina a concerned look and leaves.

Fletcher turns back to us. "Why are you digging up information on a dead girl?"

I explain what happened at the restaurant and the

threats John made. His brows knit together, his expression otherwise unreadable.

"Have you heard from John?" I lead Raina to a chair in the office and help her sit.

"No, I told you I'd call if—"

"Pull up the damn police records." I don't believe a word out of his mouth. I need to see records loaded from secure databases.

More than that, Raina needs to see them.

He could fight me on this. It's a risk to his job. But I'm a scarier risk, and he knows it.

With a grunt, he charges toward his desk and powers on the computer. I don't even know if he has access to this kind of information, but his dirty fingers seem to always find a way.

It doesn't take long before he shoves back from the desk and points at the screen. "Here it is."

Raina stands and approaches the computer, her eyes stark with dread.

"Move." I motion at him to surrender the chair.

He rises, his scowl bending beneath his gray mustache.

As she lowers into the seat, I push her forward and lean over her, eyes on the screen.

Documents line up side by side—a death certificate, a police report about unclaimed remains, and even a testimony by the doctor who was treating Tiana in the hospital. It's all there.

Tiana died with her doctor as a witness.

"The video he showed me..." Raina touches the screen, her voice brittle.

I crouch beside her and hold her quivering jawline in my palm. "It must've been old footage."

She covers her mouth with a hand, her soundless cry dominated by profound grief. Her eyes shine with deceived pain and the reflection of the screen that inflicts it.

I hear her deeply. I feel every hurt and broken dream as my own.

She wanted so badly to believe John's lie. He couldn't have dealt a more agonizing blow. But he underestimates her. She'll come back from this, because she's a force unlike anything I've ever encountered.

Sliding my arms beneath her, I scoop her out of the chair and carry her to the door.

"If you see John Holsten..." Jarret leans into Fletcher. "If you hear him, smell him, or so much as get a sense that he's in town, you'll call us immediately."

Fletcher sets his jaw and gives a stiff nod.

It's only a matter of time before he's slithering behind my back to suck John Holsten's dick. The day he does will be the worst day of his life.

"Whatever he threatens you with," I say, "just remember my threat is bigger." I lower my voice to a harsh whisper. "He doesn't have what it takes to break your wife into pieces."

"Don't you dare threaten me, boy."

I just did.

# 18

## Raina

Sadness is a river of splintered glass that cuts between the soul and body. Being alone in this pain is the same as being no one at all. That's the true sadness.

Whenever I hurt, I've always been alone.

Until now.

Lorne leads me through the estate and into his suite. The austerity of the space is a stark reminder that I've never moved in.

Neither has he.

With his hand clamped around mine, he escorts me into the master bathroom and flicks on the light. Only then does he release me for the first time since we left the sheriff's house.

I miss his touch instantly.

Digging under the sink, he gathers gauze, mild solution, and antibiotic cream—the things leftover from my first two days here. Before I stole his truck and ran.

That feels like ages ago.

After he treats the cut on the back of my head, he checks my abdomen. The soreness lingers, but it doesn't compare to the initial shock of the punch.

"Do you want a shower?" He stands close enough to infuse my breaths with his clean masculine scent.

A shower... Is that what a person needs on the night her dead sister resurrects and dies again?

"No." I want to stay right here with him.

His hand slides beneath my hair, gently combing and lifting. As he slowly releases the strands, he watches them fall, his eyes a velvety green shade of contentment.

I know how much he loves the softness, the sedation in the strokes. It calms us both in a way I never expected.

His touch moves across my cheekbone to my lips, his demeanor a world away from the man who chased after John. That Lorne was chillingly cold and deadly. Had he caught John, Lorne would've been hauled away from a murder scene in handcuffs.

He would be sitting in a jail cell right now, awaiting sentencing.

I could've lost him.

"There's so much we need to talk about." I drop my hands to the counter, my body sagging beneath the weight of it all.

He brushes the hair from my face, waiting for me to elaborate.

"The past." I swallow.

"Tiana's death."

I nod. "The future."

"Our relationship." He steps into me and in one gentle pull, he intertwines our bodies in a tight embrace.

I can't pretend there's no relationship. It's wrapped around me, holding me as I fall.

"The present." I rest my head against his strong chest.

# Booted

"John Holsten."

There aren't enough hours left in the evening to discuss how we're going to proceed with that.

As he continues to touch my face and hair, I lose the will to talk at all.

Angling my head back, I dive into his eyes. "I want to go to the water."

His dark brows form a *V*. "Water?"

"The pond on the east side of the property. The one enclosed by a cliff and—"

"I know the one. I used to swim there." He doesn't move to take me.

"John won't come here tonight."

"Or ever. But if he did..." His eyes darken with bloodshed.

Then he blinks, straightens. His hand laces mine, and he tugs me into the bedroom. From the closet, he removes the shotgun, confirms it's loaded, and straps it onto my back.

He moves toward the door, but his gaze stays with me, fastened like the fingers around my heart. If he wants it, he only needs to pull. I won't fight. I won't shut him out.

Because I ache for another dance under the stars.

Maybe he'll hurt me in the end. It's possible he'll never love me. But he's worth the pain, the heartbreak.

He's worth the fall.

"I hear you thinking." A long-legged step brings him back to me, and he releases my hand to cup my face.

I've made so many mistakes in my life. Every time I ignored my gut and the messages of universal energy, I suffered greatly.

The silence urged me not to sell my body. The wind begged me not to climb into John's truck. I dismissed it all for my sister, and I lost her.

Then I went out tonight, against the protests of the

man trying to protect me, and I lost her all over again.

Tiana's death is a wound I will carry forever, and John Holsten just ripped it open. But sometimes, what seems to be the hardest thing to bear is the universe's attempt to wake me up.

Tonight forced me to accept two things. One, Tiana isn't coming back. Two, Lorne feels deeply and fiercely for me.

The moment he realized I was attacked, he turned into an indomitable predator, both beautiful and terrifying, mercurial and logical. He's a courageous man in his essence, who loves as passionately as he fights.

Leaning into me, he touches my neck and zings a frenzy of static across my skin. His mouth moves closer, holding me in transitory paralysis.

Is he going to kiss me? My pulse thunders for it, but his lips veer off to my ear.

He doesn't whisper, just breathes, and my insides shiver in an intoxicated dance of energy.

"The universe is speaking." I marvel out loud.

"Are you listening?"

I nod my head against his.

With a chuckle, he lifts me off my feet, shotgun and all, and carries me over his shoulder and out of the house. In the stable, he puts me in the saddle. Then he rides me out to the water.

The swimming hole stretches about fifty feet in diameter. A steep rocky cliff forms a horseshoe around it and slants into the starry sky. The reflection of the moon on black water floats like a milky spotlight. I'm drawn to it.

Sliding off the boots and socks, I walk barefoot to the shoreline. My toes dig into earth and wet grass, my senses attuned to the buzzing of nocturnal life.

Behind me, Lorne ties Captain to a tree. "Why are we here?"

# Booted

"My ancestors believed that water is sacred."

"You want to swim?"

"I want to cleanse."

There are no pastures here. Livestock doesn't use this pond. So I set the shotgun on the ground and remove my shirt, shorts, and undergarments. Muggy air kisses my nude skin, and I lift my face, soaking in the moonlight.

It's refreshing, liberating, to be so exposed and close to nature.

Focusing all thought and energy on the water, I enter east, into a pond that is silk and shadow.

My feet slip over the muddy bottom, and gentle ripples lap at my toes, my ankles, then my calves. The water is neither cold nor flowing as it should be. I was never a very good student in the sacred ceremonies, but I remember the basics of this tradition from my grandmother.

I walk forward until the surface rises to my chest. Then I dip seven times, once in each direction—east, north, west, south, above, below, and here in the center— while being mindful of the spirits in all directions.

Each plunge beneath the water purifies, renews, and nourishes. I release my guilt and failures, my resentments and griefs, while concentrating on my blessings.

Tiana's very short life left a huge impact on me. She gave me the experience of sisterhood and showed me the purity in unconditional love.

She instilled in me the desire to be a mother someday. The kind of mother she deserved.

By the time I finish, I feel lighter, brighter, and at peace.

I'm not a committed believer in the old ways, but I'm not a non-believer, either. I'm open to what feels right deep in my center.

Tonight, this felt right.

I turn and wade my way back to the shore. Halfway there, I pause, stirring the knee-deep water.

Lorne hasn't moved from where I left him. He stands twenty feet away, hands at his sides and posture stiff. The Stetson angles down, concealing his expression, but I don't need to see his face to sense his tension.

He's looking at me. At the glow of my bare skin in the moonlight.

When he put his mouth between my legs last night, he didn't remove my shirt or panties. He's never seen me naked.

He takes his time staring. I assume he's been staring this whole time.

I hold still and wait. The passing seconds bring a trickle of tremors. The lingering of his gaze hardens my nipples. My pulse quickens. My skin heats. My entire body anticipates.

Slowly, he removes his hat. His hands reach behind him to pull his shirt over his head, back to front, in that strange way that men strip. Then those confident fingers unbuckle the belt.

His boots go off next. Followed by his jeans and briefs.

The sight of his hard, long cock sends me backward, seeking the cover of the water. It's not fear. Though part of me will always fear the strength of his hands around my heart.

What I feel is inevitability, and it's coming for me in the form of a proud, naked, very hungry cowboy.

He prowls into the water, eating up the distance with powerful strides, sinews twitching with intent, and eyes hunting.

I've never had sex for pleasure. I've never chosen a man simply because I want him. I revel in the freedom of this choice, though it isn't a choice at all. It's an imperative. I need him beside me. With me. Around me. *In* me.

Submerged to his waist, he dives, spearing his body like an arrow and sluicing beneath the surface.

He's coming.

# 19

## Raina

My heart pounds as I kick against the muddy floor of the pond, splashing and spinning at a depth that reaches my chest. Lorne's under there somewhere, but the water's too dark.

I tremble in a ring of ripples. Where is he?

A current of movement swirls around my legs, and he comes up for air with his face inches from mine.

Sweet mercy, he's arresting. Wet black hair sticks to his forehead and spikes in chaotic perfection on his head. Beads of water cling to thick lashes, and a faint row of freckles dots across his nose.

No single feature defines his beauty, but his eyes come close. It's not the color. Though the vibrant hue of green deserves its own enchanting name. Amid those irises glows a raw intensity, an unapologetic bluntness, that rivals the inflexible angles of his square jaw.

He looks at me like I'm the only star in his sky, and that's a pretty high expectation to bestow on someone. He hasn't been with a woman in years. How does he know there isn't a brighter, better one out there?

I'll offer him all that I am and everything I hope to be, but after... What if the starlight dims and he decides I'm not what he's searching for?

In the end, it would hurt both of us.

"You have options." I float backwards and let the water wash over my shoulders.

He stays with me. "I only see one."

"Cora likes you. She has the prettiest gray eyes, and her smile—"

"I don't want Cora." He swims forward with determined strokes.

I kick away, splashing water while drowning in hope. "There are a lot of single women in Sandbank. Docile, well-behaved women."

"I don't want that shit." He captures my ankle, then my thigh, and drags me against him. "I know who I want." His lips lower to the corner of mine. "But I need to matter to her the way she matters to me."

"You want her without barriers." I grip his shoulders and wrap my legs around his waist. "You need her without shields." With a press of hips, I grind against his swollen length. "You already have me without demanding."

He leans back and hears me with his eyes. In that suspended moment between stillness and movement, our souls lace together. The air and water churn, hugging us in sultry warmth as our skin fuses in a glide of heated wet satin.

It's hard to hold back, to draw it out and make it last. My body craves him without fear. My mind trusts him without questioning.

My heart loves him, freely, openly, and he hears that, too.

"You're my whiskey." He takes my mouth, groaning

into the kiss. "My addiction." His tongue traces mine. "My freedom."

Molding together, tasting each other, we sink into a rolling swim of entwined arms and legs, mouths and tongues, moans and thrashing breaths.

Our lips fit impeccably, every curve and dip made to connect and sizzle, meant to fall into incinerating harmony. I whimper beneath the intensity and match his hunger, breathing fast, heart rate faster. Then he's moving, slicing us through the water and scattering moonlight across the surface.

Near the cliff, he hoists me up and sets my butt on the ledge of a massive rock. The smooth surface floats just above the pond, and water laps beneath my thighs as he moves to stand between my knees.

Since it's not deep here, he's able to position me on the edge and hook my legs around his hips. His balls hang heavily in the water, and his erection juts between us, a trajectory of masculine need and strength.

My nerve endings thrill, and my pussy aches. Breathless and empty between my legs, I reach for his thick, full, beautiful cock.

He catches my arm. "If you wrap those succubus fingers around me, I won't last two seconds."

Our eyes lock, and I see the urgency in his, the tenuous restraint.

"I bet you recover with impressive speed." I cup the back of his neck.

He grips mine, mirroring me. "Even without your magic tea."

My mouth curves, stretching my cheeks.

He kisses my grin. Then he kisses me with his whole body. Arms and lips, heart and breath, we explore at a pace that's soft, hard, slow, urgent, and everything in between.

Our hands roam, lightly and assertively. Mine slide over his wide shoulders and into his hair. His fall around my ribs and wander to my back.

Every fingertip leaves an imprint on my skin as they coast upward to trace the shape of my shoulder blades. His touch splays on either side of my spine, engulfing my back with tingling heat, and his gaze ambles a sinful caress along my bare breasts, paying homage to every detail.

Considering how long he's gone without sex, I expect him to hold me down, shove himself inside me, and deliver an unholy pounding.

But that's not his method of torture.

He's calculating and wicked, holding me on the edge with only his eyes and the tease of his touch. There's no sanctuary from the need he kindles inside me, no reprieve from the force of his eyes. This is meaner than the hardest, cruelest fuck.

"Lorne." I tremble and squirm beneath the torment of his fingers as they rove down my back and linger on my tailbone. "Stop delaying."

"Quiet."

"Just put it in me."

I'm perched on the rock at just the right height to line us up and pull him inside. I wriggle closer, until the hand on my hip stops my movements.

"I say when and how." He grabs my neck and gives a warning squeeze. "And you will shut the fuck up."

There's the ruthless cowboy beneath the soft caresses.

Panic ripples up my spine, followed by a surge of desire so big it swallows everything in its path.

Those cruel lips call to my heart. The grip on my throat moves my spirit. His hard voice makes my life dance. He's my battle song in the war of love.

He stares at me. I stare at him, and when we know

we're safe with each other, he releases my throat and kisses me.

"I've been so fucking hard for you." His kiss turns into a winding lick that travels down my chest, my stomach, and delves between my legs.

The electric jolt of his hot, filthy mouth goes all the way to my toes. I fall back on elbows, spine bowed, and release a long, deep-throated moan.

He eats me ravenously, greedily, lapping and sucking and groaning against my pussy. His hand slips up my body to stroke my breasts, and his other enters from below to join his mouth in the delicious attack.

His fingers sink deep and thrust hard as his tongue circles my clit in an assault that sabotages my breathing and wrings my core into a tight coil of need. I'm so close. Right there. Right there...

He brings the pleasure to a halt and nibbles a path to my breasts, his hands trailing, light and taunting.

"Don't stop." I'm stretched to the point of snapping. My body pulses and contracts for more. I need. I want. I have to come.

"I want you so bad." His head returns to my thighs.

He licks me again, using fingers and tongue where I need him most, while studying my reactions, feeling how my legs move, and watching my body buck and writhe.

"Beg." He stops and touches his lips to my inner thigh.

My breaths come so hard and heavy all I manage is a moan.

In a blink, he's on me again, fucking me with his mouth, his fingers, just long enough to short circuit my brain before pulling back.

"I'm waiting, Raina."

"Fuck you and your evil mouth." I grip his hair and pull.

"Not until you beg."

I release a scream of frustration that ripples into a breathy cry. "Please, Lorne. Please fuck me with your tongue and your fingers and your hard, fat cock. Give it to me. Make me burn. Please, let me come."

His huge grin pops that dimple, and I'm owned, completely and utterly.

"Come on my face, you dirty girl." He crashes his lips against my pussy.

The orgasm slams into me a glorious wet rush, my legs sawing around his head, and my brain shimmering with sparks.

He licks me through it, coaxing my inner walls to clench and clench and clench until the tingles ebb into sweet, swishing bliss.

"You're fucking gorgeous." He leans up with his lips stretched back in a wolfish smile, panting past clenched teeth.

"So are you." My heart sighs with post-orgasmic affection.

Gripping my waist, he yanks me off the ledge and into the water. Desire coats his mouth, and serrated breaths expose the edge of his control.

"Hold onto me." His voice is crushed rock and carnality.

I loop my arms around his neck and angle my body over his hungry cock.

With a hand on the ledge behind me, his other grips the base of his length. His eyes flick to mine. His jaw clamps, and he slowly enters my body, sinking, stretching, possessing, inch by consuming inch.

Pleasure swarms my blood, and every cell in my body sings for more, more, more.

He stops breathing, his chest hard as steel as he presses deeper, mouth open and shoulders tight.

# Booted

I grab hold of his face and watch his flawless features twist and contract through the pleasure, the relief, and the glory.

When he's fully seated, his breathing bursts into a surge of gasping groans. His arms come around me, and he searches my eyes.

Our exhales rise in invisible clouds, and his cock jerks inside me.

"I'm not going to last." His fingers dig into my back, shaking.

"Don't last. Just let go."

He pulls out and slams into me with a demand of hips and strength. I cry out, grappling for any part of him I can cling to.

"Your body feels so damn good." He plunges again and again, commanding me to take him, to accept every thick, ruthless inch of him. "Look at you. So fucking beautiful when I'm inside you."

The rocky ledge behind me grinds against my spine, and the water slaps at our legs. We battle to squeeze closer, deeper, bending into each other with a passion that turns into teeth and nails.

He's a hair-pulling, nipple-biting, skin-heating fury of aggression. No thrust is hard enough, no kiss punishing enough.

He watches me through it all, holding my weight, bouncing my breasts, and ramming into me with a burn that strokes my insides with flames while pushing me further, hotter, harder...

My release implodes in a sucking grip of spasms that devours all the air and shoots along my limbs in iridescent bubbles of rapture.

"Lorne!" I scream, choking, staring into his eyes as my whole body quivers and jerks.

"Fuck, Raina. I'm gonna come." He grunts, his hips

erratic, his gaze dialed into mine. "Let me come in you. I need to—"

"Yes." My toes curl, and my back arches in anticipation. "Please."

"Raina, oh, God. Oh, fuck." His forehead crashes against mine. His lips hunt and claim as he groans and rages and pumps my body full of come.

The flexing strength in his torso, the taut cords in his neck, the blown pupils in his feral eyes... I've never seen anything more beautiful than this man in the throes of orgasm.

When he collapses against me with shallow breaths, I brush away the black strands from his brow.

"Are you concerned about catching a disease from me?" I mumble.

A twisted smile adorns his face. "I don't fucking care."

He pulls me closer, his cock softening inside me, as he hauls me toward the shore.

Lifting me out of the water, he carries me to a bed of damp grass and lowers me to the ground. He follows me down, still buried inside me, and slowly rocks his hips.

"What about pregnancy?" I hug him to me and kiss his reckless mouth.

"If it happens, it happens." He thrusts gently, feeding his need and growing harder. "I want you. Without barriers. Damn the consequences."

He deepens the kiss, and I push him back.

"I'm clean." My breaths soften.

His quicken.

"John?" His jaw sets. "He made sure, didn't he? He had you checked?"

"Yes. He also gave me regular injections of the birth control shot." I run a hand across his cheek, trying to smooth the tension. "I'm glad, Lorne. If I'd gotten pregnant..." I shake off the thought. "I have a month before I need another shot."

With the door wide open on every nuance in our lives, there's nothing separating us. Nothing but the fire he stokes with his thrusts.

He holds my head in his hands, rests his eyes on mine, and makes love to me on the soft, wet patch of grass.

Our bodies slide in a leisurely grind that allows us to savor every second. Hands caress. Lips worship. He's gentler than I've ever felt him, though he isn't gentle at all. His bearing is too intense for that, his body too rugged and muscular. But he's relaxed, unhurried, as if he simply enjoys the pleasure of moving inside me.

I make wanton noises, and we laugh carelessly together. The silence doesn't recoil in judgment, and the surrounding trees don't hover around, wondering what to do. The universe sways with us, glittering and vibrating with approval.

When we come, it's a soft, sensuous wave of pleasure, pulsing with the lulling rhythm of the night.

We watch each other as we dress. He rides Captain to the stable and holds my gaze during the task of putting away the gear.

At the house, he fucks me in the shower, rough and fast, then again in the bed, as if it's been days since he last had me.

Afterward, we lie in a heap of slick limbs, sated breaths, and incoherent thoughts. With a leg thrown over my hips and an arm stretched beneath my head, he trails knuckles around the curve of my breast, his eyes hooded and sleepy.

My core cramps from bowing and crunching through orgasms, and the tissues between my legs tingle from hours of penetration. I struggle to focus my eyes, my head heavy and entire body twitching from his endless attention and stamina. But my chest has never been fuller.

He smashed my heart against my ribs to make room for his. Now we beat side by side, stretching and growing together in the shared space.

His lips brush against mine, his breath so familiar and comforting. How did I live so long without it? How could I ever return to that lonely, hollow woman.

I can't.

The past two years simmer from the creases of my mind, gathering and building a swell of overloaded emotions behind my eyes.

"We're never leaving this bed." His mouth settles against my neck, his voice a rumbling embrace of promise. "I'm never letting you go."

My breath skips. "You want me to live here?"

"You're officially moving in." He glances around the empty, unfurnished room. "We both are."

My skull pounds with a flood of sadness and joy, fear and relief. It's been there all this time—the horrors of my past, the hope for something better. His declaration scrapes it all out and sets it free.

The bottomless torrent bombards me with achy, breathless sobs, and I'm too spent to stop the purging.

I cry, silently and cathartically. He holds me through it, supporting me with his arms and encouraging me with a gravelly hum in his throat, while silently promising I'll never be alone in the hurt again.

Lorne

As Raina drifts to sleep against my chest, I let myself absorb the colorless, empty room for the first time. I don't like ceilings, floors, or walls. I hate closed doors and spaces with recycled air. But I like this.

It's a blank canvas for something new, something extraordinary, with Raina.

In my throat and on my tongue dwell feelings that can't be shaped into words. But the molecules in my body understand. They multiply and spread out, consuming my veins with purpose and acceptance.

I need this love. I want it. I want to need it. From her.

I want the fiery frustration she ignites in my stomach. I want the strangle around my lungs whenever she's near.

I want the agony in my heart at the thought of losing her. It keeps me sharp, vigilant, aware.

Tightening my embrace around her naked body, I

run my nose through her hair, savoring the silky texture and breathing in her botanical scent.

For the first time in eight years, I'm home. Not home in a prison cell. Not home in my childhood room. It's the home of my future, and I can turn it into anything I want.

Jarret did this for me. He built me a place to call my own.

I reach for my phone on the night table and launch the internet browser. I'm still trying to adjust to all the changes in technology, but I'm learning how to shop online.

I have a credit card and a small inheritance from my father. I also have an untouched savings account from my labor on the ranch all those years ago.

As I type into the browser's search bar, I notice a number of bookmarked websites I didn't put there.

My gaze lowers to the sleeping woman on my chest.

She claims she doesn't want a phone, but she borrows mine often to look up recipes and herbs and whatever else she does with it.

I click through her bookmarked links and open pages for furniture, bedding, wall art, and Native American decor.

She's been thinking about this. Dreaming about furnishing this room. For me? Or for us?

A grin pulls at my lips. Perhaps this is a subtle attempt to nudge me, but honestly, the woman doesn't have a subtle bone in her body.

Either way, she made the task a million times easier.

For the next twenty minutes, I purchase everything she bookmarked and other things she didn't.

That done, I turn off the light and wrap my body around hers.

Then I sleep.

# Booted

As always, the nightmares come, rousing us both with my choked gasps.

When I wake for the third time, it's after a hauntingly sick dream of her and John in the ravine.

"Are you okay?" She peppers kisses along my jaw.

"Yeah."

It wasn't real. She's right here with me.

"You want some tea?" She runs a hand through my sweat-damp hair.

"I want *you*."

I crawl over her warm body, fit my hips against her, and sink into her heat in one long, exquisitely slow stroke.

By morning, I've lost count of how many times I've been inside her in the last twelve hours.

Maybe a man shouldn't slack his needs in a woman every hour of every day, but I don't give a fuck. I'll never stop getting hard for her. Never stop finding solace in her body.

After breakfast, I lean against the fence railing that corrals a bullpen for horse training. Only the trainees today are Raina and Maybe.

With Raina on Captain and Maybe astride Jarret's gelding, they listen to my animated sister explain the basics of horse riding.

This was my idea, a way to keep the girls occupied and in our sights while we discuss John Holsten.

Conor canceled her vet appointments for the day, but only after a heated argument with Jake and me at breakfast. We can't keep her from her job, but we will until we have better security in place.

The horses trot at a controlled gait with Conor walking alongside them, gesturing as she talks. Maybe's British White Park heifer scampers after them like a thousand-pound, ankle-biting dog and nudges Conor's hand for a pet.

"Chicken..." Maybe leans down in the saddle and points a finger at the critter, smiling. "Stop distracting us with your cuteness."

Raina shakes her head and laughs, her bronze complexion glowing in the sunlight. Her entire aura glows with happiness, and I like to think I had something to do with that.

As always, she wears my old jeans, this pair unaltered and bunching around her boots. Raven hair drapes over the graceful lines of her shoulders and swings against the small of her back.

Her fists slide over the reins, and the memory of what those hands can do sets my brain on fire.

She's a vixen.

My vixen with fingers of sin.

"I know that look." Jake rests his forearms next to mine on the fence.

Beside him, Jarret's lips twitch, his gaze never straying from Maybe.

"You slept in your room last night." Jake studies me from a foot away. "With Raina."

"I also ordered furniture and other shit. I'm moving in."

"'Bout fucking time." He narrows his eyes. "But that's not what's putting that look on your face."

"I'm watching a beautiful woman ride my horse, thinking I'd just like to ride *her*."

"It goes deeper than that."

He's right. She's a fathomless desire with bewitching brown eyes and pouty lips sucking on my soul.

"I love her." Three words are painfully inadequate for what I feel.

"I saw that coming a mile away." He watches the girls for a moment, and his lips form a flat line. "We need to talk about branding week."

# Booted

Our date of brand falls on the third week of every June. That's next week.

We'll be immersed in the longest days of the year as we gather as many hired hands as we can to administer shots, castrations, and branding. I used to oversee the annual operation. Hell, at eighteen, I supervised the entire ranch. I'm the oldest of the four of us, the big brother, and the one they once looked up to for guidance.

It's time I step back into those boots.

"John knows when we brand." I turn to Jake and Jarret and inch up my hat. "He knows we'll be distracted and dog-tired the entire week. Raina and Maybe will be with us, but we won't be able to watch them every second of the day. And Conor..."

"She won't close the clinic for six days." Jake shoots a concerned look at my sister.

Branding isn't something we can cancel or delay. This is our livelihood. If our cattle aren't vaccinated and tagged, we can't sell them.

"I have some money," I say. "Not a lot, but I'll cover the cost of a security guard for the week. What I really want is to hire a man to track down John."

Where is he staying? What is he planning? Should I try to set a trap to catch him? Or wait him out?

I don't know what to do. I'm a damn cattle rancher, not a detective.

"Private investigators aren't cheap." Jake blows out a breath. "I emptied my savings account keeping an eye on Conor all those years."

"It's not just that." Jarret tips his head toward us. "I have concerns about hiring someone to track the man we plan to murder. Some of those detectives are retired cops. And anyone we hire could be called in to testify in court regarding the surveillance. I don't know how this will all turn out, but if we're suspected of killing John, I don't want the added risk of an outside party saying, *Oh, yeah. Those guys hired me to find him.*"

None of us want that risk. Especially not with all the bodies in the ravine.

"I agree." I prop a boot against the rung of the fence. "But I want a security guard, a body guard, someone to patrol while we're distracted. Just during branding week."

"I'll get recommendations from the PI I used for Conor," Jake says.

"In the meantime, we can't leave them unattended." I direct my eyes at the girls. "Not for a second. When my sister's at work, one of us will be watching her on the cameras."

"I'll do it. I have a lot of paperwork to catch up on anyway." Jake's mouth wobbles, hiding a smile, as if we don't already know how much the dirty fucker enjoys watching her.

I turn toward the fence, eyes on Raina, and explain to the guys all the qualifications I want in a security guard, my expectations from the role, and how he'll man the cameras and patrol the property while we're in the field for fifteen-plus hours every day. Then I outline the logistics of the branding operation, the things I want to improve and my ideas on how to make it run smoother.

When I finish, Jarret and Jake stare at me like there's no grain in the silo.

They can fuck off if they don't like what I'm saying.

"Spit it out." I straighten, ready to ram heads. Or fists, if we're doing this the usual way.

"You're back." Jake's frown crooks into a shit-eating grin.

"Thank fuck." Jarret leans against the fence, wearing the same smile. "The foreman position is still open, waiting for you. If you want—"

# Booted

"I want it." I rest my hands on my hips and let the responsibility settle through me. It feels good. "But I'm making changes, starting with how we castrate. We're switching to elastic bands. It's more efficient. More humane."

As I detail a few other revisions I'll make after branding week, my pulse increases, and my chest expands. I read a lot of books in prison, studying as much as I could about anything and everything, including how to run a successful ranch.

Jarret regards me with a look he doesn't wear often. Eyes bright and glossy, face slack, open body posture—he gives himself away before he moves in and suffocates me in a constrictive, hard-bodied hug.

My hands lift, giving him an amicable pat that does nothing to express the soul-deep affection I feel for him.

Then I do what's expected and shove his chest. "Get your ugly ass off me."

He shoves back, grinning. "How ugly?"

Jesus, how old are we? I haven't played this game with them since we were stupid little shits. But as he waits expectantly, I shake my head and give in.

"So ugly we had to hang a pork chop around your neck to get the dog to play with you."

Jake laughs. "He's ugly enough to scare a buzzard off a gut pile.

"Uglier than a pocketful of assholes."

We go back and forth a few times before falling into quiet grins, heads down, appreciating happy memories.

"We missed you." Jake's gaze shifts to the bullpen, tracking the smiling redhead. "Conor's been... Worried. Impatient. She doesn't know what to do, except to give you more time."

A pang of guilt hits my stomach. "The adjustment took me by surprise. I was so fucking ready to get out and return home. Then I got here, and nothing felt the same. I'm not the same, but I'm starting to accept that, day by day."

"If you need anything..." Jarret says.

"I need to end this thing with John and put it behind us."

We spend the next hour, leaning against the fence and watching our girls while kicking around plots of murder.

Jake and Jarret single-handedly took out John's creditors and hitmen over the years, but they had intel from Sheriff Fletcher and John's computer—addresses, dates and times of meetings—and the element of surprise.

John knows we're coming for him, and he's a crafty motherfucker.

The weaponry and self-defense training will continue with Raina, because I want her to have those skills. But there's no way in hell I'm putting her in John's sights.

*I* will end this, one way or another.

## 21
### Lorne

That night, Raina and I join the others on the back porch, and the first thing I notice is there isn't enough seating.

The arrangement of two chairs and a loveseat is all we ever needed.

For the four of us.

Now our family of four is six.

We all feel the significance of that as we gather around, piling in laps and squeezing in. Raina sits beside me on the couch, and the others pair off in the chairs.

Extra seats could be brought out, but no one bothers. It's as if there's an unspoken consensus to fill in all the pockets of space with the voices, bodies, and smiles of the Holsten-Cassidy tribe.

Conor's smile is the biggest. Perched on Jake's lap, she leans toward the coffee table at the center and holds out a hand, palm up.

The sight of her scar stills the breath in my chest.

Jake extends his arm in the same manner, placing

his welted palm beneath her hand. Jarret follows suit, cradling theirs.

I'm the last to move, sliding in at the bottom with my scar holding up the others.

Blood, revenge, unity, victory—it's all there in four hands, twenty fingers, and eight years.

Maybe clasps Jarret's leg, and Raina's slender arm slides around my back.

Her dark eyes find mine, her expression soft with understanding. We talked about the scars during our nights on the sleeping bag. In the short time I've known her, we've shared every secret, every failure and triumph.

"We did it." Conor's smile teeters. "It's been a brutal ride, but you know what? Fuck them. Fuck everyone who tried to break us apart. We're stronger for it. We're still together and still kicking ass."

"Can I get an amen?" Jarret shouts dramatically, teasing her.

She jerks her hand from the pile and tries to knock off his hat, laughing as she tackles him.

As I lower my arm and sit back, I realize how proud I am of how far we've come.

We could've turned our moment of reflection into a harrowing mood leaden with tragedy and bitterness. But we're beyond that. We don't need to relive the memories or rehash our feelings about it. God knows, we've done enough of that for a lifetime.

Instead, the atmosphere vibrates with love and celebration. Because Conor's right. We did it. We survived.

"You know what this calls for?" I reach behind the couch and grab my guitar.

"Some bluesy redneck shit?" Jarret pulls out his harmonica.

"Yup. I'm thinking... Wheeler Walker Jr."

"I know exactly what song is in your filthy head." Conor points at me as she stretches for the acoustic Jake recently bought her.

When she settles on his knee with the guitar on her lap, I give her a chin lift, signaling her to start.

She bends over the frets, plucks a few notes, then strums the snappy chords of *Eatin' Pussy/Kickin' Ass.* Jarret jumps in on harmonica, followed by me on backup guitar.

When Jake starts singing, Maybe and Raina sit up, captivated, smiling widely, and a few verses later, laughing their asses off.

Raina curls a hand around my neck and puts her mouth at my ear. "If this were our song, it would be *Kicking Pussy and Eating Ass.*"

Laughter bursts from deep in my chest. Her gaze zooms in on my dimple, and my grin widens.

I introduced the twins to this song when we were kids, before any of us were eating or pounding pussy, and look at us now. We're belting the lewd lyrics, tapping our boots, and turning up the heat with our girls.

I forgot how well these jam sessions nourish the bond between us. The chorus of closeness waves away stress, triggers the release of happiness, and takes the mind off our problems.

When we play together, we communicate on a whole other level—with notes, our eyes, and our laughter.

Raina curls up beside me, her cheeks stretched in a permanent smile. She may not be able to relate to the connection I share with them, but she will. A year from now, ten years from now, she'll have her own bond with this rowdy group.

We jam for the rest of the night, drunk on the music and the comfort of camaraderie. As it grows late, the song selections tumble into mellow, slow-dance territory.

Jarret rises, leaving his harmonica and his girl in the chair, and steps toward Raina.

"I want a dance," he says, "before the Neanderthal hauls you into his cave."

She stares up at his ridiculously charming grin, and her pink lips part on a breath. "Okay."

As he leads her to an open area on the porch, I set my guitar aside and approach his blonde fireball with a hand extended.

"Are you shitting me?" A smile explodes in Maybe's blue eyes, and she leaps up, grabbing my fingers. "I knew I'd grow on you."

"Like a rash." I hold back a smirk and pull her across the porch, positioning us near Raina and Jarret.

"You know what you need?" Her hand folds around mine, the other resting on my shoulder. "A baby calf. That would soften you right up."

"I'm down with that." I slide her into a two-step. "I can already taste the tender veal melting in my mouth."

"Ugh. Have you met Chicken?"

"You mean the spoiled, cow-shaped dog living in the stable?"

"You think she's adorable. Admit it."

"The rash is starting to itch." I swing her into a fast turn, which shuts her up.

For two seconds.

"Do you want to talk about Rogan?" She peers up at me.

I never met my half-brother. Never knew I had one until Maybe came along. I don't care. Blood-related or not, it's hard to feel any sense of loss for a con-artist who plotted against the people I love.

But that's not what she's asking. She wants to know that she and I are okay, that there are no ill feelings. It matters to her, because she has a big heart, and she's invested every inch of it in this family.

"We're good, Maybe." I guide her around Jarret as he speaks quietly at Raina's ear.

When my attention returns to the blonde in my arms, I find her studying me, as if probing my expression for the truth.

She came to the ranch as a reporter, but in reality, she was a fashion journalist. Though she doesn't wear a speck of makeup, she seems to prefer dresses, like the frilly one on her now.

I squint at her. "Do we need to bond over hair braiding and toe painting?"

"Is that on the table?"

"No."

"Then I'll be content with more dances."

Across the porch, Conor transitions into *Ride* by Chase Rice, and Jake leans into her, breathing the lyrics in a rumbling voice that causes her fingers to miss a chord.

Maybe makes a noise in her throat and lowers her arms. "This is baby-making music."

Behind her, Conor winks at me and turns back to Jake and her guitar.

With a hand on Maybe's back, I escort her to Jarret and reach for Raina's arm.

"I need my girl." I pull the black-haired beauty against me and spin us toward the stairs.

"Under the stars?" she asks.

"Under me."

Her lips curl into a sexy smile.

I lead her off the porch, where the overhang doesn't obstruct our view of the sky.

With my fingertips grazing the silky skin above her waistband, I bring her in tight and sway against her hips, flowing with the rhythm of the acoustic.

I know her hands, and I know where they go. On

me. Anywhere. I just want to feel her touch, her pulse, her love.

She gives it to me. A palm resting on the back of my neck. Fingers sifting through my hair. Breaths heating my throat. Heartbeat knocking against mine.

"I hear you," she whispers.

"I love you, too."

Her eyes widen slightly as she inhales my declaration and sighs it back against my lips.

On the porch, Jarret and Maybe move in their own whispering dance as Jake and Conor serenade us through one of the most sensual country songs I've ever heard.

"You love me." Raina slides against my body.

"Deeply." I lick the words from her mouth and trace them to her neck before taking them on a journey across the plump rise of her breasts.

Her eyes stay on me, and her hands join the connection, caressing, gripping, and igniting my blood.

She's impossible to resist. Her gaze, her skin, her mouth... I devour it all, rolling our hips together, laving my tongue, dragging my fingers, and turning the stars into flames.

Jake continues to sing, his voice growing deep and husky as he drawls out words like *hotter*, *loving*, and *fucking*.

Raina chuckles against my throat. "When did country music start dropping *F* bombs?"

"This is the dirty version."

"I bet you think this song's gonna get you laid."

"I think..." I kiss her mouth, her jaw, and swirl my tongue around her earlobe. "I'm going to spend so much time inside you in the infinite future that your panties will get wet at the sound of my zipper."

Her breath catches. "I should probably steal some more panties."

# Booted

"A lot of desperate days coming your way."

"It'll be hard." Her hand lowers to my belt, and her fingers splay over my swelling cock. "Feels like it already is, but we'll work through it."

We'll work through it right now. And not while I'm watching my sister get worked up with Jake.

I grab her hand, yank her into the house, and toward our room. It's a zigzagging trip as I back her against every wall to indulge our hungry lips.

By the time we reach the suite, we're stumbling in a tangle of arms and tongues and frenzied breaths.

When I close the door, she pushes away from me and walks backward with a wicked twinkle in her eyes.

Her shirt hits the floor. Then her boots. As she reaches back to unclasp the bra, I hiss between my teeth.

I want to slow it down, just for a minute.

"Stop." I wait for her to obey and remove the phone from my pocket.

Flipping through the playlist, I select *Like a Wrecking Ball* by Eric Church.

"Proceed." I set the phone aside and clasp my hands behind me. "Do it to the music."

Just the very first note of this song inspires friction and tangled sheets. But it has nothing on the salacious striptease that fills my view.

It's an unhurried torment of discarded clothes and wandering hands. As each dip and curve is revealed, all I can think about is sinking into my home.

I prowl toward her, follow her down to the bed, and surrender to the gasping heat of her mouth and body.

She pleasures me with passion.

I love her with fire.

Together, we reduce the night to ashes.

## Lorne

Nine days later, I collapse onto our new king-sized bed in a pile of sore muscles and overworked joints. We're only halfway through branding week, and I'm dead.

"Think of it like this," Raina says from the bathroom. "At least it's not your ass getting branded or your penis being whacked off with a dull knife."

"We remove the testicles, not the..." I lift my head, and my throat dries.

She stands in the doorway, backlit by the bathroom light. The rounded outline of her hourglass figure beneath the thin nightgown is even more erotic than her nudity.

But it's her riveting eyes that hold me, luring me like a drug. There's something so mystical in the way she looks at me. It's a look that listens and finishes sentences without an uttered word.

"Don't even think about getting hard." She walks through the furnished room, picking up clothes and setting things away. "You need sleep."

I'm already hard, but she's right about the sleep.

At least our room is finished. When the online purchases arrived last week, we decorated the space, fought and seethed while assembling the furniture, and reconciled in a sweaty heap of stripped clothes and panting breaths.

We officially moved in, marking the start of our future together.

If I could only wrap up the damn loose end in our past, I might actually sleep through the night in our new bed.

During the few days we had left before the branding began, we worked on practicing her aim with the shotgun. She's improving and gaining confidence with it. She understands every part of a firearm, how to assemble them, and the proper procedures when they jam.

I would never send her out to take down John Holsten, but she has the skill to do it.

"I have something for you." I roll my tired ass to the nightstand and remove a small envelope.

She approaches in a swirl of warmth and flowers that intoxicate my brain.

"What is it?" She accepts the package and sits beside me on the bed.

"Open it."

Her fingers feather over the paper, and she slides out a bracelet of woven wire that matches the color of her bronze skin.

"Lorne..." She traces the brass ball ends that gather like charms where the bracelet fastens together. "Are these your guitar strings?"

"Yeah. They needed to be replaced, so I ordered new ones. But I couldn't throw the old ones away."

They're the same steel strings I played the night at the ravine. They lived on my guitar all these years and survived just like the rest of us.

I don't have to explain the meaning of that to her. It's there, in the glistening sheen of her eyes.

"I used the entire set of six strings. Since the steel is wrapped in copper and silk, it shouldn't irritate you. And I didn't weld them. They're just braided together and held by this." I tap the tight coil of wire near the grouping of ball ends. "If you loosen the coil, the strings will unravel and return to their original shape."

She slides it on her wrist with trembling fingers. "I'll cherish it, Lorne. It's..." Her chin quivers, and she turns to me, hands on my face and lips against my mouth. "It's beautiful and perfect and... Thank you."

"Thank *you*." I hold up my arm, indicating the dream catcher necklace I'll never take off.

As she touches it, the appreciation in her eyes imparts an echo on my soul.

This is just the beginning. Someday, she'll wear my mother's ring, and if I'm lucky, she'll carry my child.

She leans her forehead against mine and whispers over my lips, "I love you."

"I hear you, too."

Our noses fit together, sliding side by side as our breaths mingle without expectation. There's desire there. It keeps a constant vigil between us. Her tongue peeks out, tasting our chemistry, eager to feed it despite the late hour. But I hear her protest before it migrates to her vocal cords.

"We're going to sleep," I say.

She's putting in as many hours as I am at the ranch, in addition to preparing our meals and keeping the house clean.

A sigh pushes off her lips, making them pout. "I need to check the laundry and—"

"Come here."

I pull, and her body falls against mine in a delicious blanket of velvety hair and warm skin. We already showered, and I'm stripped down to my briefs.

Gripping her nightgown, I lift it up and off. Then I position her in the center of the bed and extinguish the light.

"How are you getting along with the security guard?" I curl into her and trail my fingers along her hipbone, eliciting a shiver along her skin.

"Erin is...different."

Erin is ex-military. And a very stern woman. I should've known Jake wouldn't hire a man to watch Conor on the cameras. But that's not all Erin does.

She has an extensive technical background and improved the functionality of our surveillance equipment. She's able to shadow Raina's every move while monitoring Conor on a mobile device.

I still worry every time Raina leaves my sight, but Erin has enabled me to focus on the cattle and the tasks that must be finished.

"Only a few more days." I run my fingers through her hair.

She releases the sweetest sound, a whispering moan of comfort, and snuggles deeper into my chest.

She makes me ache. An ache that twinges as much as it soothes.

Sometimes, when I wake at night and feel her motionless against me, I can't breathe until I check her pulse. Or when I come home for dinner and she's at the back door waiting for me, I'm paralyzed by an unguarded pang of longing.

I can't compartmentalize the depth of these feelings. I've never experienced anything so exquisitely intense or as terrifyingly vulnerable as the love I feel for her.

# Booted

More than anything, I want to shackle her to our bed while I hunt down and fight John Holsten to the death.

Because if I lost her...

I can't. I won't let it happen.

I fill my lungs with that conviction, but the dread doesn't recede. It multiplies.

## Raina

The next afternoon, I climb the rails of the steel fence around a temporary corral and scan the sea of twitching ears and mooing mouths. Sweat trickles between my breasts. My limbs shake with exhaustion, and to think, we only have eight excruciating hours of work left today.

I've been manning the chutes with Maybe since before dawn, operating the gates and herding cattle from one location to another. The heat from the sun and the endless walking and lifting is taking its toll on my body. I can't wait to crawl into bed tonight with my cowboy and sleep away the aches.

But right now, I need to get some food in these ranchers before they pass out.

I spot Lorne's black Stetson near the standing stocks, where the cattle await examinations, branding, and vaccinations.

He crouches beside a calf, his handsome face shadowed with fatigue and tension.

When I climb another rung and rise above the herd, he goes still, as if sensing me all the way across the corral.

His head lifts, followed by those green eyes, and my stomach buzzes like a bee hive. There's such a powerful, self-confident aura around him I can feel him all the way from here.

"Lunch," I mouth.

He rubs his nape and scowls in the direction of the estate, at the security guard standing off to my side, and back to me.

Yes, I have to run to the house to grab food. Yes, Erin will be with me at all times. And yes, I'll hurry right back.

He hears me. He doesn't like it, but he gives me a nod of assent.

Since Erin doesn't ride horses, she drives me back in her SUV.

At the house, I hurry through the kitchen, chopping fruit and slapping together barbecue sandwiches.

Erin sits at the table, staring at the device in her hand with a pinched expression. She never initiates conversations and usually only responds with single-syllable answers.

Her brown hair smooths into a ponytail that sits high on her head. Minimal makeup highlights her sharp cheekbones, and cargo pants bunch around her slim frame. She's pretty in a stern, militant way.

If I had to guess, she's in her late-thirties and single.

"So…" I stuff the food into a large cooler. "Are you married? Any kids?"

"No," she says absently, her eyes fixated on the screen. Then her teeth clench. "Dammit."

A cold jolt flashes in my skull. "What's wrong?"

"Nothing. *Yet.*"

My feet carry me to the table, and my skin chills as I

lean over her shoulder.

The screen in her hand is divided into multiple camera views of the vet clinic. Inside, outside, the footage doesn't show Conor anywhere.

"An older woman brought in a Basset Hound." Erin flips between camera angles, enlarging portions of each one. "She and Conor exited through the back door with the dog on a leash."

"Oh." A relieved breath slips out. "They're just getting a stool sample."

"Yes, I know. But the damn dog led the woman out of view. A minute later, Conor followed." Frustration leaks into her voice. "I specifically told her not to leave the camera's field of view. I even showed her where the boundaries are."

"Call her." My pulse quickens, and I clench my fingers on the back of her chair.

"Her phone's on the counter." She changes the screen to show the back room of the clinic, zooming in on the cell phone.

She returns to the view of the lawn behind the clinic. Trees encircle the area. The same woodland that once formed a canopy over the ravine.

The live feed of grass and dirt is so still it could be a photo. Nothing moves. Seconds tick by and Conor doesn't return.

It could take minutes or longer for the dog to do its business. Even as I tell myself this, my stomach twists into a knot.

"I need to go check." Erin stands, grabs her keys, and pauses to consider me. "I can't leave you here."

I'm already moving. I chase her out of the house and skid to a stop halfway to her SUV. "I'm going to run back and grab a gun."

"No." She glances at the screen in her hand, without

slowing her swift gait. "She's still not back, and I'm not waiting. Get in the car."

Her usual blank expression creases, her complexion a terrible shade of pale. She's worried.

My throat stings as I hurry into the SUV.

The only information Jake gave her about this assignment is that his abusive father has been threating Conor and me. Erin has John's physical description, and she knows he could be armed and not working alone. But she doesn't know how truly dangerous and cunning he is.

The clinic is only a couple of miles away, near the south pasture. Conor usually walks it or takes her motorcycle. But Jake's been dropping her off and picking her up all week.

Erin pulls onto the road in front of the estate and takes the quickest route there, her sharp gaze darting between the screen on her lap and the windshield.

"I need you to call Jake." She calmly lifts her phone, glances at it, and returns it to her pocket. "Never mind. There's no signal."

I hug an arm around my waist as painful trembling rips through me. "Do you think something happened to her?"

"I'm paid to be hyper-aware and open to every possibility."

That's not an answer.

She turns onto a gravel path that cuts through dense trees. Knee-high weeds grow between the tire tracks, and every bump rattles my rioting nerves.

She veers around the next corner and slams on the brakes. A few feet ahead, something lies in the road. Something human.

My muscles lock up, and my breath freezes in my chest.

Conor sprawls face down in the gravel, red hair

shrouding her face, her body motionless and twisted, as if she collapsed in the middle of a sprint.

"Oh no oh no oh no." Panic grips my spine, and my lungs slam together.

Was she running from someone? Is she hurt? Dead?

No. No, that's not possible.

I fumble for the door handle with numb fingers.

"Stay in the car." Erin removes a handgun from her shoulder holster and turns her flinty gaze to me. "Lock the doors and do not get out. No matter what happens. Understood?"

With a nod, I release the door handle and clap a hand over the sob crawling from my mouth.

I'm unarmed and nearing hysterics. Lorne's paying this woman to protect me, and her cool composure is testament to the fact she knows what she's doing.

She leaves the car running as she exits, closes the door, and trains the gun in a ready stance. I hit the locks. Then she moves.

Light footsteps, weapon sweeping with the shift of her body, she creeps toward Conor without taking her attention off the surrounding trees.

As she approaches, Conor doesn't stir. Not a twitch.

*She can't be dead. She can't be dead.*

My mind floods with horror. Nausea grips my gut, and my ears ring with godawful pounding.

*Please, Conor. Please, wake up.*

Erin stops beside her but doesn't look down. Her eyes probe and scrutinize the perimeter, the gun steady in her outstretched hands.

The span of stillness turns me inside out.

Finally, she crouches and places two fingers against Conor's throat.

I hold my breath.

Her jaw angles toward me, and I watch her mouth

form the word, *Alive*.

My lungs release in a great rush of relief, bringing forth a well of tears.

She stands, and her gun jerks toward the trees a millisecond before the boom of gunfire shudders the air.

The reverberation punches through me as Erin drops in a slow-falling crumple of knees, hips, shoulders. When her head hits the ground, the hole between her eyes spurts blood across the gravel.

My hand flies to my throat. My jaw locks to the point of pain, and my breaths explode in hyperventilating gasps.

A woman emerges from the tree line, gray hair pulled into a loose bun and a pistol trained on Conor's catatonic body.

Her unfamiliar eyes lift to mine, and her thin pale lips shape the command, *Get out*.

Lorne is miles away on the other side of the property. No amount of gunfire would alert him. Have I been gone long enough for him to come looking for me?

Erin took her phone with her, so I can't make an emergency call. The SUV is still running, but if I try to drive away, she'll shoot Conor.

If I step out of this car, they'll take me.

The thought hits me with a wave of dizziness, shooting black dots across my vision. I feel like I'm going to puke.

Without moving my upper body, I slide my hands around, searching the glove box and the spaces between the seats and console. Locked. Empty. No weapons. Nothing I can use to defend myself.

How badly is Conor injured? There's no visible blood or injuries. Did they knock her out? What if she wakes in the middle of this?

She's a fighter. She'll get herself killed.

An engine sounds in the distance. Up ahead? Heart

racing, I lean forward as a sedan tears around the corner in reverse, coming straight at us.

The woman doesn't acknowledge it. Doesn't move the gun away from Conor. Doesn't take her finger off the trigger.

The car stops a few feet away from her. A man climbs out of the driver's seat, and the trunk pops open. Silver hair and dusty jeans, he looks around the same age as the woman.

They don't glance at each other as he ambles to Erin's body, lifts her, and tosses her into the trunk.

Pain stabs through my chest and simmers bile in my throat.

John's behind this. He sent these people for me, and if I don't cooperate, Conor won't live.

I would choose death over going back to him, but I would never choose Conor's death.

He knows that.

They brought Conor here to ensure I go quietly.

"Get out of the car!" The woman bellows, shaking me into full-body tremors.

Instinct screams at me to run, to jump behind the wheel and slam the SUV in reverse.

But Conor... I can't leave her.

The woman leans down, touches the gun to Conor's head, and meets my eyes through the windshield.

My body refuses to move, my limbs frozen and unresponsive.

Until she applies pressure to the trigger.

I launch toward the door, smacking at the lock and handle, and tumbling out. "Don't shoot. Please, don't shoot."

"Listen up, little girl." The woman eases back on the trigger, but the gun remains against Conor's head. "John doesn't want the redhead to die. He said he'd hate to do that to his son. But if you don't do as you're told, I'm pulling this trigger."

She already killed Erin without remorse, and she looks dead set on adding Conor to the trunk of that car.

I hold up my hands as my heart jangles in a block of ice. "Whatever he's paying you, we'll pay more. Name the price."

Lorne and Jake would sell the ranch in exchange for our lives.

"Not everything has a price." She sneers.

So John offered them something invaluable. It's either blackmail or he's dangling the life of a loved one over their heads.

"Is he threatening one of your children?" I glance between them. "A son? A daughter?"

The man tenses, and his eyes lose focus.

"Is this woman your wife?" I ask him.

His hand forms a fist at his side, fingers curling around a wedding band.

"John told me he'd save my baby sister." I take a cautious step toward Conor. "Three years old. Huge brown eyes. She had this smile…" I draw in a breath, and my mouth quivers into my own smile. "You just felt it, you know? Every time she looked at me, I felt that precious smile way down deep. But I'll never experience it again. She died eight months ago."

The couple shares a look of pain and resolve before the woman turns back to me.

"My husband's going to give you a shot to make you sleep. If you fight him…" She lowers to a squat, straddling Conor's legs, and digs the gun into the tangle of red hair. "This one joins your sister."

My entire body becomes one throbbing heartbeat, increasing my sensitivity to the rumble of the motor beside me, the crunch of gravel beneath the man's shoes, and the sprinkle of sunlight filtering through the canopy.

The man removes a syringe from his breast pocket and advances. Is that what they used to knock out Conor?

"She'll wake up from this?" My knees wobble. "You won't kill her."

"She'll wake soon. We'll even drag her off the road so she doesn't get hit."

What am I supposed to do? Self-defense training and shooting practice didn't prepare me for this. If I attack, Conor's dead. If I scream and run, Conor's dead.

There's only one way to save her.

Shaking uncontrollably, I grip the bracelet on my wrist, slide it above my elbow, and wedge it high on my arm. I don't want to lose it. Whatever happens, I need a piece of him with me.

*I'm so sorry, Lorne.*

I step forward, holding my gaze on Conor and my arms up.

The man reaches my side and stabs the syringe into my neck while pressing the plunger.

The sting brings my hand up to slap at it. I'm certain he hit a major blood vessel, because all movement and thought instantly slows down.

I take a step, and fuck, that's hard. Everything seems like too big of a task.

I wave a hand out in front of me, reaching for something to grip as I float, spin, and tumble into blackness.

## Lorne

With clenched teeth, I wrestle a calf into position and sweep my gaze over the corrals for the hundredth time. Raina's been gone a while.

How long? Thirty minutes? Longer?

My chest tightens. She should've been back by now.

I drop the branding tools and jog toward the chutes, dialing Erin's phone along the way.

It goes to voicemail.

My scalp chills. If Erin stayed between here and the house, she wouldn't be out of service range.

I try again.

Voicemail.

"Jake!" I search for his wide shoulders amid the chaos of herding and sorting cattle and spot him near the trailers. "Jake!"

He wraps up his conversation with a ranch hand and strides toward me.

"Raina's been gone too long." My heart hammers as

I approach him. "Erin isn't answering my calls."

His gaze drifts across the field, and his eyebrows knit beneath the hat.

"Fuck." He removes his phone and makes a call.

An eternity comes and goes before his dark eyes flick to mine. "Conor isn't picking up."

We alert Jarret and race to the house on horseback.

It's the longest ride I've ever taken. Longer than the ride to hunt down Conor's rapist. Longer than the ride in the police car after I killed Wyatt Longley. Longer than the eight years I spent behind bars.

My mind plunges into a howling abyss of nightmares that ends with Raina and Conor lying bloody and lifeless on the kitchen floor.

Jake and I reach the back porch, dismount, and charge into the house.

Music blasts into us as we open the door. Deafening and eerie, the raspy voice croons an alternate version of *Ain't No Sunshine* through the speakers.

I know the song well, but this isn't a cover I've ever heard.

"Raina!" I bellow over the din.

Jake takes off toward the office, and the chilling melody follows me into the empty kitchen.

A partially packed cooler of food sits on the floor. Unfinished meal preparations scatter the counters.

My stomach bottoms out.

I check the mudroom, common areas, bedrooms, and both porches. No one's here. No sign of struggle.

And Erin's SUV is gone.

Did they run an errand? Raina's not supposed to leave the property.

I try Erin's phone again and get voicemail.

*Don't panic.*

In the background of my roaring pulse, *Ain't No*

# Booted

*Sunshine* comes to an end and starts again.

The humming instrumentals have an undertone of Native American influence. The original song is haunting, but this version laces my bones with ice-cold dread.

I storm toward the stereo to put my fist through it, but I pull back as Jake runs out of the office.

"Conor's not at the clinic." He rips his hat off and shoves his fingers through his hair. "I went through the video recordings. She stepped outside with a customer—a woman and her dog—and didn't return."

My hands clench so hard the joints pop beneath the pressure. "And Raina?"

"She left with Erin." He paces toward me, his face a sheet of white and his eyes on the camera mounted in the kitchen. "Erin was at the table, monitoring the video feeds on her device. She would've seen Conor move out of view. I assume she left to check it out. Raina went with her willingly, but they never showed up at the clinic."

We stare at each other through a fog of disbelief, denial, and looming dread. The heaviness of the music penetrates our crippling shock, every note resounding like a slow-firing cannon.

"This is Wovenhand." Jake cuts his eyes to the stereo. "A twisted rendition of John's favorite song."

"I fucking know it's John's song, but how the fuck is it playing?"

"The cameras and sound system can be accessed by any device that has the password."

"Like Erin's." My pulse beats beneath my skin.

"She's either involved in this or he confiscated her electronics."

"Change the password."

"I already did."

My muscles tighten as a surge of manic energy quakes through nerves and limbs.

257

The song is a message from John, his sick way of telling us he infiltrated our security, our guard, and our girls.

We don't know where he is or how to find him, but we can't just stand here. We have to go, search, hunt, and get them back.

Jake's chest heaves as he comes to the same conclusion.

We move simultaneously.

Out the front door and through the lot, I head toward my truck. "I'll drive."

We jump in, and I punch the gas, palms slick and throat on fire.

Jake attempts to call Erin and Conor again as I speed toward the vet clinic, spitting gravel. I take the back way through the woods, and that's when I see her.

Tires screech in my attempt to stop.

"Oh, my God." Jake opens the door while the truck's still moving. "Conor!"

She stands in the middle of the path with a hand cupped to her neck. My relief crashes in waves with an undertow of horrifying realization.

Raina isn't here.

Jake runs out of the truck as Conor raises her arms, reaching for him.

"What happened?" I'm right behind him, scanning the trees and road, my ears straining for sounds of movement. "Where's Raina?"

Jake lifts Conor into his arms and buries his face in her hair.

"I don't know. I..." Her breath hitches, and her hand returns to her neck. "I was injected with a tranquilizer. A woman... She brought her Basset Hound in for parasites. I went outside with her and stayed in camera range until she started screaming. She collapsed over the dog, claiming it was having a seizure. I didn't think. I just reacted and ran to her." She sucks in a sharp breath, and her gaze flies to me. "Did you just ask where Raina is? Is she missing?"

Jake meets my eyes and carries her to the truck. Setting her on the seat, he paws and probes her body for injuries. "What kind of tranquilizer? Should we go to the hospital?"

"No, I just..." She touches her throat. "My neck's sore. As fast as it immobilized me, it was probably Etorphine or something similar. The main risk is overdose, which causes instant fatality. I'm still here, so..." She shrugs.

"Goddammit, fuck!" Jake launches at her, kissing her face and tangling a hand in her hair.

"Raina's missing." Impatience burns up my spine. "I need to know everything you remember. Every detail about that woman and everything she said."

"Oh, no. Oh God, Lorne." Her expression fractures through her shock and terror as she quickly outlines physical descriptions of the woman and the thirty-second conversation they had about parasites. "When I bent down beside her outside the clinic, she must've had the syringe ready. I didn't even see her move. I was focused on the dog, trying to figure out why the woman was screaming. Then I felt a pinch in my neck. I knew what it was, but I had no time to react. It hit like a ton of bricks. Then I woke here. Alone." She gestures at the road. "Maybe three or four minutes before you showed up."

Jake glances at his watch.

"How long?" I ask.

"She was comatose for an hour."

I pace away from the truck, shaking and flexing my hands. "An hour for the bitch to bring Conor here, where there are no cameras, and make the trade."

"A trade for Raina?" Conor gasps.

I nod stiffly. "It would've been easy to watch the estate from the main road and determine our patterns over the past four days. Raina goes to the house to grab lunch, always around the same time, always with Erin, and she's never left alone. John expected Erin to notice you missing and head this way, and he knew Raina would have to come."

This was a trap for Raina, using Conor as a hostage. An exchange of one life for another.

John took her.

He has her in his possession, and I can't begin to imagine the vitriolic state of his mind.

I own the land he wants, run the cattle operation he lost, and claimed the heart of the woman he's infatuated with.

He'll punish her for transgressions he believes she and I committed against him.

I stare at the end of the road where it winds out of view. The choices I make and the actions I take from this point forward will determine the rest of my life, as well as Raina's.

My heart rate thunders, waging a battle inside me.

On one side is an inferno of hailing gunfire, madness, and mindless anger. On the other is a sharp sword of logic, focus, and frigid steel.

A snarling, impulsive, impassioned firestorm versus a methodical, emotionless, unforgiving blade.

The one that wins is the one I feed.

When John attacked Raina at the restaurant, I fed the fire, and he got away.

I need control. Diligence. Calculation. Heartlessness.

Something switches inside me, and in that terrible, defining moment, I lose my humanity.

In its place rises one purpose. One thought. One

emotion.

Ice-cold cruelty.

I return to the truck, focused, sharpened, and planning ten steps ahead.

"Where did they get the tranquilizer?" I climb in behind the wheel.

"It would be used for really large animals." Conor shifts to the center of the seat, allowing room for Jake.

When he slides in, I shove the truck into drive.

"I don't have anything that potent at the clinic." She rubs her neck. "But I've seen it used to bring down raging bulls that escape in town. The sheriff would have something like that."

*Sheriff Fletcher.*

John is penniless and desperate, and he turned to the only friend he has left.

Of course, Fletcher's involved. I counted it.

He won't offer up John's location easily, but I'll give him no choice.

Ice hardens my muscles. I don't feel it. I don't feel anything but lust.

Lust for blood.

I'm intoxicated by the need to slowly, callously eliminate every person who earned my wrath. The potency of it crystallizes my blood and solidifies my veins.

"We'll get her back." Conor touches my thigh and yanks her hand back when she feels the inhuman rigidness in it.

When I reach the ranch, I park, enter the house, and stride to the bedroom. Single-minded and reined in, I don't slow down or take detours.

"What happened?" Jarret runs toward me.

My jaw is a steel frame of lethal teeth, trapping the gnawing, relentless need to crush bone and sinew.

In the bedroom, I gather guns, ammo, blades, and

other gear while mentally mapping how each weapon will be used.

Raina embeds the very air in this space, but I don't look around. I can't. It would run a knife through my heart and debilitate me.

When I have everything I need, I take steady, efficient steps to the truck, my mind anchored on the next stop.

The sheriff's house.

On my way out, I breeze past the conversation in the foyer. Jake must be updating Jarret and Maybe on what happened.

As I tread onto the front porch, Jake shouts, "I'm going with you."

Good. I need him.

"I'm going, too." Conor says.

"No, you're not," Jake and Jarret growl at the same time.

I'd lock my sister in the tack room before I'd let her come with me. Wouldn't be the first time.

I leave them to work it out and climb into my truck.

Jake doesn't make me wait.

"Jarret's staying with Conor and Maybe." He slides in beside me and stows his pistol.

As I pull out and drive toward Fletcher's, I center my mind and prepare to risk everything.

Halfway there, I break the silence.

"I'm going for zero." I meet Jake's gaze. "Zero warning. Zero mercy. Zero survivors."

Except my family. The six of us *will* survive.

For the rest of the drive, I lay out the plan and what I expect from Jake.

He listens with his eyes closed and pulls in a long, shuddering breath. When I finish, he refocuses on me, resolution forging his jaw.

# Booted

I enter Fletcher's neighborhood from the back side and park a few streets away from his house. We walk to his front porch, and his SUV isn't in the driveway.

As planned, we beat him home from work.

Jake knocks, and I let him navigate the manners and niceties. He tells Fletcher's wife, Mary, we want to catch up with her husband. They go back and forth. She wants to call Fletcher. Jake says not to rush him.

No calls. No warnings. We need the element of surprise.

When Jake flashes the smile that always works on my sister, that's all it takes.

Mary invites us in and seals her fate.

We gather around the kitchen table, where she feeds us buttery biscuits and coffee. Jake does most of the talking, keeping the conversation light and nonthreatening. She tells us stories about going to school with our mothers. I maintain a civilized exterior and feel nothing for this woman. I can't feel. My humanity is dormant. It has to be if I want my family to survive this.

Jake steers the discussion back to topics on weather, vacations, and town gossip.

And we wait.

After an hour of teeth-grinding chitchat, panic creeps in. Plaguing images. Gruesome thoughts. My mind pulls into a vortex of despair for the woman I miss with my entire being.

The things John is doing to her... I don't have to imagine it. I've seen the kind of dark brutality that lurks within a rapist. I was forced to watch it in the ravine.

That experience prepared me for the agony that festers in me now. I freeze out the burning impulses with cold reasoning. Emotions must be kept under strict control. The only way I'm getting Raina back is with icy precision and a clear head.

Eventually, Fletcher's SUV sounds in the driveway. Jake remains at the table. I stand with Mary as she moves to the counter to pour her husband a cup of coffee.

I hold out my mug for a refill so she's not suspicious of my hovering.

As she fills it, Fletcher strolls into the kitchen and stops.

His knees lock in the brown uniform pants. Tendons stand out behind the buttoned collar. His lips pale beneath the gray mustache, and his hand hovers over the gun at his hip.

His fear shows itself in that split second and disappears just as quickly.

"Good evening, boys." He removes the brown triple brim hat, with the obnoxious gold acorn cords and badge, and sets it on the table. His gaze slides to Mary, looking her over for signs of distress, then returns to me. "To what do I owe the pleasure?"

"Where's John?" I calmly set the coffee aside as bloodlust shivers beneath my skin.

"Mary," he says without looking at her. "Why don't you go—?"

"Mary stays." I grip her frail arm. "Give me John's location."

She tugs against me, more in alarm than in an attempt to flee. "Fletcher?"

Fletcher scowls, his hand twitching for his gun. "I don't know where—"

I yank her arm straight, holding the wrist and elbow, and crack the ulna bone over my knee. I feel the break, hear the screams, and swallow down the regret that inflames in my throat.

The sheriff goes for the gun on his hip, but Jake already drew his own and trains it at Fletcher's head from a few feet away.

# Booted

Mary sags to the floor, sobbing and cradling her arm. I grab the gray bun on her nape and drag her to her feet.

"I'll break every bone, Fletcher." I swat away her efforts to fight and position her good arm in front of me. "Then I'll start cutting off pieces."

"Tell him where John took the Indian!" She trembles and wails. "Tell him, Fletcher!"

Mary knows? She obviously doesn't know the location. She would've leaked it after the first break.

"Hand over your gun." Jake inches closer, pistol aimed and steady.

He and Jarret murdered a lot of men, and his skill with a firearm is impeccable.

I give Mary a shake, drawing her attention. "Tell me what you know."

Fletcher's face reddens. "Mary, don't—"

"He helped John get the Indian girl today. I don't know where he took her, but I..." Her voice grinds into sobs. "I just want all this to go away. All this business with your family... It's an infection. I want it out of our lives."

Goddammit, I ache to crush her for smiling and serving us coffee and talking about our mothers. She knew the whole time that my girl had been taken from me. Fucking bitch.

She tucks her broken limb against her side and shrieks as I wrench her other arm out and over my knee.

"Stop." Fletcher holds up his hands, his eyes wild with pain and desperation. "I'll tell you. Please, just don't hurt her."

"The gun," Jake says. "Slowly."

He slides it from the hip holster and hands it to Jake. "I have a cabin at Loblolly Lake. On the south side. That's where he's holding Raina."

"Did you provide the tranquilizers?" I tighten my

265

grip on Mary.

"Yes."

He didn't just help John capture Raina. He gave John a secure place to rape her.

I know they're lifelong friends, but I didn't understand the depth of that relationship until now. John has nothing to offer Fletcher. They're in this together because that's what friends do, and they've been doing it since my mother died and probably long before that.

They're a cancerous lesion on the flesh of the soul that can only be removed with gunpowder and sharp steel.

I release Mary and lift my handgun from its wedged position between my belt and tailbone. As she runs into Fletcher's arms, I toss Jake the keys to my truck.

He waits until my weapon is trained on Fletcher before leaving the house without a word.

He'll pull the truck around and follow the rest of the plan.

Meanwhile, Mary cries against Fletcher's chest as he gingerly exams her broken arm.

"I need to take her to the hospital." He looks up at me, eyes pleading. "I'll give you directions to the cabin. Anything you need. Just let us go."

"Don't need directions. You and Mary are taking me there."

25

Raina

I wake on my back on a concrete floor, vision blurry, muscles weak, mind groggy. So tired. So many questions. Is Conor okay? Does Lorne know what happened? Where's John?

Where am I?

I lift my head and stop breathing.

Empty storage room, concrete walls, steel door, duct-taped wrists, scattered clothes—it's all in my periphery, but my attention is locked on my body.

I'm completely nude, and I don't have to touch between my legs to know he's been inside me. I feel the wetness. The abuse. The violation.

My stomach heaves, and I roll to my side, fighting for air and trying not to puke while remaining as quiet as possible.

He raped me while I was catatonic.

He forced me when I couldn't fight.

Tears smear my eyes, and I drag my bound hands

across my cheeks, wiping, whimpering, and trembling all over.

I don't remember it. I wasn't forced to feel him, smell him, or hear him. I know it happened, but I've been spared the memory.

I won't be so lucky next time.

My breathing grows faster, louder. Sweat drenches my skin, and fear overwhelms my body as I take an inventory of the cramped room.

The bolt on the door requires a key. There's nothing in here but the clothes he stripped from my body.

How am I going to escape this?

My shoulders curl in, and I press the duct tape to my forehead, rocking and shaking violently. Coldness seeps into my skin, my blood, my bones. I can't hear over the thundering drum in my ears.

This is happening.

I'm caught. Caged. Naked. I can't make this stop. I can't take it away. The beatings, his temper, the hands on my skin, the sickening sensation of him moving inside me... I can't face this.

I won't do this again.

When he raped me before, I was different. I was detached, hardened, jaded, and fighting for Tiana's life.

But I still have a life to fight for.

My own.

For Lorne.

If I don't find my way back to him, it'll destroy him as much as it will me.

I have to fight through this crippling fear. I need to think, prepare, and be strong.

Bringing the duct tape handcuffs to my mouth, I start chewing while focusing all my senses on the silence outside the door. The steel barrier is so thick, would I even hear anyone? There are no gaps around it, nowhere for sound to slip through.

Is this some kind of safe room? It's the size of a small closet with no windows and cinder block construction.

My teeth snag on the duct tape, stinging an ache through my gums.

Why am I chewing? Lorne showed me how to escape this.

Pulling my feet beneath me, I stagger to stand and catch myself against the wall. The room spins, and my legs tremble to give out.

How many times have I been drugged?

Prodding a finger along my throat, I feel bruising around two injection sites. Another one flares on the inside of my elbow.

I grit my teeth and raise my bound arms over my head. Out of the corner of my eye, the guitar string bracelet glimmers on my bicep. I still have it. Lorne's with me. The thought makes it easier to breath.

Steadying my stance, I tighten my abs and ram my arms downward as fast and hard as possible against my stomach while pulling my elbows apart.

The duct tape rips off. No pain. Small victory.

I scan my clothes and consider my options. The square toe of the boot is hard leather. Could I hit him over the head with it? Would it knock him out? The panties would rip if I tried to choke him with the strings. Not sure what I can do with the cutoff shorts and t-shirt, but the under-wire bra is the right length and shape for strangulation.

Once I'm booted and dressed in everything but the bra, I turn my attention to the single light bulb in the ceiling. There's no pull switch or lever on the wall.

I'm an inch too short to twist the bulb, so it takes a few jumps to knock it loose in the socket.

Blackness floods the room, and I release a breath. When he opens the door, he'll let light in, but the shadows will give me an extra second to take him by surprise.

Wrapping my fingers around the straps of the bra, I stand near the hinges of the door and wait.

After ten minutes, maybe longer, a key slides into the lock. My muscles tense.

The tumbler slides open, and the door scrapes along the floor. My heart rate explodes.

Light spills in, casting a white stripe through the room. John's tall silhouette moves past the door, and I launch.

Hooking the bra around his neck, I fall against him and grapple with the straps, trying to twist them tighter, harder around the column of his neck.

Terror engulfs me, shaking me to my bones as he swings an arm and nails me in the face. I lose my grip and adjust my hands, grunting, panting, and climbing his towering frame. But I'm at the wrong angle. Hanging on his side, fighting his arms, I can't get a good handhold.

Spinning around, he tries to shake me off. Every movement causes my fingers to lose purchase.

"Enough." He reaches back and jams the cold, hard, undeniable barrel of a gun against my head. "Let go."

My heart thunders. My breaths wheeze, and my fingers curl tighter around the bra wires.

"I missed you, Raina." He digs the gun against my scalp. "But I won't hesitate to blow your brains across the wall."

Panic, adrenaline, terror—all of it floods my system. I can't defend myself against a gun.

If I run, he'll shoot.

If I fight, he'll shoot.

I release my grip and scream, "Help! Somebody help me!"

# Booted

He whirls around, clamps a hand over my mouth, and shoves the gun under my chin. "Save your screaming for when I'm inside you. There's no one around for miles."

Tears sear my throat and ache in my eyes.

Where are we? Another isolated property in the middle of nowhere? A place where Lorne will never find me?

He yanks me out of the closet and into a bedroom furnished with log cabin decor. Beyond the window lies a blue lake that stretches toward the setting sun. Woodland creeps in from all directions. No other houses. No cars or boats. No people.

I scan the room for clues and hone in on a row of picture frames on the dresser behind me.

My stomach clenches. I know those faces. It's the same couple in every picture.

Mary and Sheriff Fletcher.

"Fletcher helped you." I glare at John.

"Of course." He gestures toward the door with the gun. "Walk."

I shuffle out of the room, flexing my hands to stifle the trembling. "Where's Conor?"

"Living in my house. Fucking my son. Or... if Jake's anything like me, *he* is fucking *her*."

"He's nothing like you."

The instant I say it, I know it's not true.

It's hard to look at John without seeing Jake and Jarret in his face. The brown eyes, full lips, square jawline, symmetrical features—he's sickeningly, disturbingly handsome.

Without the hat, he appears older, thanks to the silver peppered in his dark hair. He carries extra weight in his midsection, but his arms and legs are muscled and toned. Every time I've fought him, he's overpowered me.

I step out of the bedroom and enter a large living

area with a stone hearth. A couch and chairs face a wall of windows that overlook the lake. The back door leads to a deck, and the lock requires a key.

Straight ahead is the kitchen, and beyond that, an interior door that likely opens to the garage. Opposite the picturesque windows is the front entry with another lock that requires another key to exit.

Even if those doors stood wide open, I wouldn't reach them before John filled my skull with lead.

He trails me as I pass the chairs, the couch, and...

I yelp and shuffle back, bumping into him.

Those are dead bodies.

On the kitchen floor.

Holy fuck, that's the old couple that kidnapped me today.

With bullet holes in their heads.

Dead.

A chill grips my spine.

"Why?" I blink rapidly, my shoulders hunched and tingling.

"I promised them I'd get their son back. Problem is their son is buried, wherever my boys bury bodies."

If Jake and Jarret killed their son, he would've been a hitman or a dirty creditor. I don't feel anything for him or the parents who abducted me.

Erin died because of them.

I'm here because they sold their souls to the devil.

John has caused so much death and torment, and it won't end. Not while he's alive.

Hatred simmers like acid in my veins. I jerk away from him and back up, shaking and clenching my fists.

I want to run. I want to fight.

My gaze shifts to the pistol in his hand.

I want to live.

"I really don't care if you hate me right now." He

advances. "You're here because that's what I want."

"Fuck you, you sick fuck."

"Damn, you're beautiful." He licks his lips. "Your feisty spirit, sexy eyes, tight body…" His slow perusal crawls over my skin. Then he softens his voice. "You remind me of Julep. She was such a firecracker. Huge brown eyes like yours, and a heart of gold. Being with her made me a better man. Then I lost her and…" His forehead furrows, and he rubs a hand over it, smoothing away the creases. "When I'm with you, I feel young again."

"You're a psychopath."

His nostrils pulse, and he stabs a finger at the couch. "On your back. Arms over your head. Legs spread."

Staring down the barrel of his gun, I know without hesitation that I'd rather die. I can't bear the thought of him touching me, putting his despicable mouth on me, and unzipping his pants.

If I turn and run, he'll shoot me in the back, and this will all be over.

It's the only way.

My muscles tense on the verge of springing, but a soundless command holds me in place.

*Live,* my heart whispers.

A heart that's tethered to a man who would feel my death like his own.

Lorne is out there looking for me, and his ruthlessness is an unstoppable weapon. He'll find me. I just need to survive until he does.

Surviving means enduring the thrusting, panting pestilence of John Holsten's lust.

"See that?" He points at a control panel on the wall near the front door. "Fletcher's high-tech security system will sound if anyone approaches the property. If, by some miracle, Lorne learns your location, I'll know he's coming." He wriggles the gun. "I saved a bullet just for him. Now get on the couch and open those legs."

I sway beneath the weight of hopelessness, but my resolve holds steady. I'll brave this with the determination to escape.

I'll sustain by transforming into the woman I once was with him. The numb, robotic creature who detached and endured.

My pulse pounds in my stomach. My mouth floods with excess saliva, and my skin feels heavy and hypersensitive as it prickles and tightens against my bones.

I try to distance myself, but the feelings inside me are too deep, too human. I don't know how to separate from a heart that's so swollen and raw with love.

Lorne lives in my soul, always with me, and he'll be with me through this.

I swallow, choking against the burning revulsion in my throat.

Dread leaks from my eyes.

Agony stabs through my chest.

My insides shatter into panic-stricken tremors as I sit on the couch and spread my legs.

26
Lorne

Sheriff Fletcher drives his SUV with Mary in the backseat. I sit beside him, my pulse beating a cold, steady rhythm and my pistol trained on his sobbing wife.

As we approach the lake cabin, my jaw locks.

Raina's in there. She's so fucking close I can feel her in my skin. As much as I want to storm in with guns blazing, I can't.

Fletcher warned me about the security system, so this won't be a smash and grab situation. Right about now, John's being alerted of intruders. He'll use Raina as a hostage, and there will be a standoff. Since Fletcher's a wild card, Jake is my only backup. My biggest concern is Raina getting caught in the crossfire.

My plan accounts for all of this. It's complicated, risky, and fucking perfect as long as there isn't a single misstep.

Up ahead, Jake parks my truck on the vacant road. He'll do a perimeter check and catch up.

Fletcher motors past him and pulls into the driveway.

"If you don't give me your full cooperation," I say, "Mary dies."

She whimpers from the back seat.

"I said I would." He stops the SUV and kills the engine, his face gaunt and pale.

Before we left Sandbank, he gave me the keys to the cabin and a layout of the floor plan. Then Jake returned his gun to him.

Fletcher rolled over on John, and John will feel that betrayal the instant Fletcher enters the cabin with me.

Arming the sheriff with a gun makes him more pliable. Whether he turns that weapon on Jake or me is uncertain. Doing so would risk Mary's life, which is why he didn't try to shoot me on the way here.

But the night is still young.

"Get her." I motion at Mary.

He carries her to the door, and I follow, scanning the empty windows of the one-story cabin. He steps aside so I can push the key into the lock. Then we're in.

The door opens to a vast sitting room, wall of glass, and open kitchen. I'm aware of everything. Every shadow. Every creak. I'm so reined in and calm I don't react to the two dead bodies on the floor near the back.

One is a woman, probably the kidnapper from the vet clinic. If so, John cleaned up loose ends I won't have to deal with.

I keep Fletcher and Mary in front of me, my pistol sweeping between them and the surrounding rooms.

A few more steps into the cabin brings John into my line of sight.

He lies face down on the couch with Raina struggling beneath him. Hips thrusting between her kicking legs, he pins her arms above her head and holds a gun to her cheek.

A sucking, roaring maelstrom of madness and violence implodes beneath my skin, and I brace against it with everything I have, desperately trying not to let it pull me in.

He slows his vile humping and slides his soulless gaze to mine.

My self-control is a jagged crag on which cold fury teeters. I dangle an impulse away from filling this room with hailing blood and carnage.

His finger curls around the trigger, the gun aimed at Raina. He only needs to squeeze.

He may not have it in him to murder his sons, but the rest of us mean nothing. If I shoot, he'll pull that trigger. If I so much as move, he'll kill her.

I take calming breaths, center all thought on the plan, and leash the ravenous storm inside me.

With a clearer mind, I'm able to acknowledge the details, like the fact that she's wearing clothes. Her shorts are fastened. Her cries have fallen quiet, and her liquid brown eyes find mine from across the room.

She's scared. Terrified. But not broken.

John isn't inside her. Doesn't mean he hasn't already violated her, but he's in this position because he wanted me to walk in and find him bucking on top of her with a gun to her head.

He intended for me to see it, imagine the worst, and come unglued.

I lost my shit when I was eighteen, and I paid gravely for it.

Lesson fucking learned.

"Don't move." He pushes off her, pointing the gun at her chest.

Her eyes stay with me, questioning.

John and Dalton taught me how to shoot. John is the

best marksman I know. He can probably hit her *and* me before I fire a single round. One false move and we'll both be blown to bits.

I give her a slight shake of my head and fight the pull of fear.

Fear is the rope around wrists in a ravine. It's a knife in the heart, slowly twisting.

It hammers in my head and throbs behind my eyes, but I shake it off.

I need to be the one tying the rope and twisting the knife. I must keep my shit together.

John looks at Fletcher for the first time, his sneer laced with malice. "How could you?"

"John, listen to me. I didn't have a choice." Haggard and edgy, Fletcher inches to the closest chair and lowers Mary onto it. "He broke Mary's arm and would've hurt her more if I didn't cooperate. If it was Julep, you would've made the same decision."

John grits his teeth and yanks Raina off the couch, with the barrel wedged against her ribs. "So what happens now? Are we all going to shoot each other?"

No one will shoot Raina.

I touch her with my gaze, wishing it was my arms.

The door opens behind me, and I swing my pistol from Fletcher to John, confident the tread of Jake's approaching boots means his weapon is pointed at the sheriff.

"How's Conor?" John looks at his son without a hint of surprise or concern.

Jake doesn't answer, following the plan. We're here to lead the questioning and control the end result.

I loosen my rigid fingers on the pistol and seek the comfort of Raina's proximity.

Held at gunpoint, she stands strong and noble. There's no withering. No waterworks. It's not that she's fearless. Given the shaking of her fists at her sides, she's fighting an avalanche of emotions and holding herself together through sheer willpower. It's fucking awe-inspiring.

Christ, I love her. I love her magnificence, her fortitude, and her spirituality. Her presence weaves through the bloodlust in my veins, pacifying me and keeping me focused.

"You booted me off the ranch for eight years." I meet John's dark eyes, burning to stab the life from them. "But you couldn't boot me out of the family. In the end, you're the one who lost it all—your job, your sons, your wife, and your fucking soul."

"It's not over, boy." John stiffens, his finger twitching against the trigger.

I mark the aim of every gun in the room, the trajectory of every possible bullet, and draw a map in my head of where Raina should and shouldn't be when everything goes south.

"You killed my mother." Jake stands at my side, gun aimed at Fletcher, eyes on his father. "And Ava O'Conor."

The air coils, the tension locked and loaded.

I feel it inside me, like icy, liquid metal sliding through my veins. My legs twitch, fighting the impulse to run for Raina, my throat thick with the need to roar.

I reach for her through eye contact, and she reaches back with a soft unblinking gaze.

We're going to get through this.

"Julep wasn't supposed to be in that car." John brings Raina tighter against him, an arm around her back and his thumb intimately stroking her upper arm.

*Get your hands off her.*

My nerves rampage, my heightened senses prickling and stretching me beyond my physical limits. I can't watch Fletcher, John's trigger finger, and his wandering hand all at once.

I focus on Raina, on the strength in her eyes, and check my rage before shifting back to John. "You killed my mother for the land."

"Of course, it was for the fucking land. Ava was dead set against drilling on her precious inheritance. It was irrational fucking bullshit. That oil would've made us rich."

"So you killed her and lost your wife in the process. Then you discovered Conor and I own the land, not my mother."

He could've murdered us when we were small, but he wasn't *as* evil then. He's always been greedy. Always wanting more, more, more. But he wasn't desperate enough to kill innocent children for it. That didn't become an option until he ran the cattle operation into the ground and found himself owing bad people a lot of money.

"Julep's death will always be my biggest regret." John says remorsefully, as if he isn't holding a gun to Raina's heart. "I hope someday my sons will forgive me."

How different things would've been if Julep hadn't climbed into the car with my mother. From what I know about her, she would've kept John and Dalton on the right path. The four of us kids would've been raised by a mother.

I doubt John's words move Jake in any way, but he reacts as if they do.

"Go to hell, you selfish prick. You took our *mothers* from us, because you wanted more money, more power, more possessions and bullshit. You will never be forgiven. Not for the heinous crimes you committed over the past twenty years. And not for the atrocities you've done and are *currently doing* to Raina."

A furious tide of anger rises up John's neck. "She's mine, and I'll do whatever—"

# Booted

"Shut the fuck up." I concentrate on his trigger finger, holding mine steady with the pistol's sights lined up on his chest so very close to Raina's head.

My teeth saw against the inside of my cheek, and the copper taste of blood fills my mouth.

Any second, someone's going to shoot. It could be me. From this distance, maybe I can land a kill shot. Or maybe I'd miss and hit Raina. Either way, John will react and pull his trigger. I can't take that risk.

"And you." Jake swings his stony gaze to Fletcher. "You were there when our moms died." The tendons in his forearms strain beneath the skin. "You covered the whole thing up. Always wiping John's ass and cleaning up his shit."

"Calm down." Fletcher moves closer to Mary's chair and grips her shoulder. "Lower the gun, Jake. I'm not the enemy here."

No, he's worse. People trust him. The town loves him. There's no indication of evil intent, no hint of corruption. He wears his badge and deals death by way of a knife in the back.

There's a special place in hell for Sheriff Fletcher.

"I want to hear you say it." Jake inches away from me, putting Fletcher and Mary in his line of sight. "Admit you covered up their deaths."

The sheriff blinks rapidly and rubs a hand down his pants near the hip holster, his gaze darting between Mary and the exits.

Nervous energy pulses and tugs at the air. Quickening breaths, dilated pupils, erratic eye contact, facial tics—it strangles every expression in the room.

We're reaching the breaking point.

## Raina

The tension in the room is strung so tightly it wraps my chest in rubber bands and restricts my breathing.

The only thing holding me together is the ever-present caress of Lorne's gaze. It touches me continuously, always watchful, always protecting.

He has an innate way of loving me with his eyes. As he stares at me, the guns and chaos fuzz into the backdrop until all I feel is his intense, dominating presence.

He came for me.

He saved me from a fate worse than death.

He risked his life and his freedom. For me.

I don't know how he knew to go to Fletcher for my location. It's clear Fletcher isn't here by choice. He seems only intent on keeping himself and Mary alive.

Jake continues to roar at him, poking the already edgy and unpredictable man, who also happens to be professionally trained in apprehending violent threats.

But I understand Jake's need for closure. He

deserves answers about his mother.

Lorne, on the other hand, hasn't spoken or moved. I'm not sure he's breathing behind that pointed gun.

I've experienced the full spectrum of his moods, but this is the coldest I've ever seen him. He's chillingly quiet and detached, as if he shut down all parts of himself except the imperative to get me out of here.

Is he waiting for a clear shot to take down John? I don't know how he can do that without John pulling the trigger.

Paralyzing fear shivers through my body. My feet tremble, and I clench my fists, fighting back the burning wetness in my eyes.

John wants me alive, but he'd kill me to save himself. He would shoot Lorne in a heartbeat. His loyalty to Fletcher is questionable. If he's capable of love at all, Jake is the only one in this room safe from his gun.

If only I could disarm John without starting a gunfight.

His thumb slithers along my arm, making my flesh crawl. I jerk my shoulder and knock away his hand. The movement loosens the bracelet from my bicep and sends it sliding to my wrist.

"Don't move." His thumb returns to my arm.

I curl my fingers around the guitar strings and meet Lorne's eyes.

His gaze lowers to the bracelet and comes back, his face smooth and unreadable.

*If you loosen the coil, the strings will unravel and return to their original shape.*

I heard that Hitler used piano strings to hang people. Would guitar strings work the same way?

Across the room, Fletcher gives Jake vague answers about the car accident, his tone biting and nervous.

I hold my hand against my stomach and discreetly

unravel the bracelet. It only takes a little bending of the fastening and the strings instantly spill out of their circular shape. As they straighten, I switch them to one hand and lower them out of view at my side.

Lorne watches it all. His gun doesn't waver, his eyes giving nothing away.

"Put down your weapons." John digs the gun against my ribs, his arm clenching around my back. "We can discuss this without killing one another."

There are too many guns with too many flaring emotions. My heart thumps wildly. I'm trying to remain calm, but every second lasts an eternity as I stand perfectly still, terrified I'll set off the first bullet.

"You killed two innocent women!" Jake's temper spirals out of control, seemingly fueled by years of harbored resentment.

"Jake." John's voice booms through the room. "Put down the goddamn gun and let's talk."

"I've already decided your fate, *John,*" Jake snarls. "I'm just trying to determine whether the sheriff will go with you."

I hold my breath, heart hammering.

Mary snaps out of the chair, her broken arm forgotten as she whirls on Jake.

"This hasn't been easy for my husband." Her chest rises and falls with vehemence.

I tighten my fingers around the guitar strings, my heart in my throat as I wait for the right moment.

"It's okay, sweetheart." Fletcher reaches for her. "You need to sit—"

She swats him away with her good arm while scowling at Jake. "Have you even tried to put yourself in Fletcher's shoes? He risked everything for your family. His job. His freedom. Our lives. When he fixed things with the car accident, we were supposed to get a piece of the land.

Do you know how much we've been compensated? Nothing. We haven't seen a God *dern* inch of that property because you sniveling brats keep interfering."

She knew the whole time. She fucking knew what John put his family through and expected to profit from it?

Lorne doesn't blink, but his shock glows in the whites of his eyes.

Jake goes unnaturally still, his gun aimed at Fletcher as the force of his scowl targets Mary.

"Jake." John's fingers bite into my arm.

"You know what I think about that, Mary?" Jake swings the gun, trains it on her chest, and shoots.

The blast ricochets through my skull, and I jump. John flinches with me, but his gun doesn't move from my ribs.

Mary slumps to the floor, her shirt blotched red with the blood pooling around the hole in her chest.

The room falls silent.

A breathless, stunned, half-second of silence.

Then Fletcher roars.

While the high-pitched sound of agony is still echoing off the walls, he grabs the gun on his hip and fires at Jake.

My heart stops as Jake stumbles backward, mouth hanging open and a hand over his chest. He aims his gun at Fletcher, but the sheriff is already firing again. One round after another, the bullets keep coming.

Jake jerks with each shot and crashes to the floor behind the couch.

I choke, and my entire body turns to ice.

*Oh fuck, oh fuck, no! This isn't real.*

A scream tears from my throat. Paralysis locks my joints, and everything around me moves in a jarring fog.

Fletcher continues to fire in the direction of Jake's fall, filling the room with deafening reverberation.

# Booted

"Noooo!" John buckles over, taking me with him and grinding the gun against my ribs. "Please, God, no! Not my son!"

Lorne seems to be in shock, with his pistol frozen on John and head turned toward Jake's body.

When Fletcher's clip empties, I feel the shift in the air, the creeping arrival of anguish, and the scratch of lines being drawn through the room.

Fletcher killed Jake. The agony of that lands in my stomach with a weight I can't carry.

*He must die.*

John straightens, and his arm falls from my back.

The gun digs into me, and my pulse tears through my veins, beating so viciously I feel like I've been thrust from my body. I'm overcome with shock and inconsolable loss, but there's something else.

Something's off.

Lorne's too calm, too unaffected, his posture rigid and sharp like a blade.

He's twenty feet away, separated by the couch and chairs. He doesn't look down at Jake's body. His eyes and pistol are fixed on John when they should be pointed at Fletcher.

"You son of a bitch." John turns the gun away from me and levels it on Fletcher. "You killed my son."

Fletcher pivots toward Mary's lifeless body as John opens fire. The kill shot takes him down with a bullet through the heart.

"You fucking killed him." John bellows and squeezes off another shot with his back to me.

I wrap the ends of the guitar strings around my shaking hands and wait for him to empty the magazine.

But he doesn't.

He turns the gun on Lorne.

My heart explodes as I spring. The guitar strings

loop over his head like a noose, and I yank the ends with all my strength, twisting, cinching, twisting, cinching. The wires are wrapped in copper and silk, but they still dig into my hands. It hurts, but not nearly as bad as it's hurting the tender skin on John's neck.

"Raina!" Lorne edges around the couch. "Hold on. Just hold tight."

John's hand goes to his throat, and he fires off a shot at Lorne. My breath stalls and restarts as the bullet veers off wildly, missing him.

My sweaty hands slip along the strings, but I've twisted and knotted the garrote enough to keep it in place. The wire noose is so tight it cuts into John's skin and draws blood.

He crashes to his knees, shooting at Lorne to keep him back. Every time the gun fires, I die inside. Any of those bullets could hit their target, and Lorne can't shoot back because John's thrashing keeps knocking me in the way.

I don't know how much longer I can hang on. I can't see John's face, but there's no gasping, no voice. This has to be working.

How long does it take to strangle a man? How many bullets does John have left? How is he still moving and shooting and dragging me around when he can't breathe?

An eternity of bucking and choking and gunfire passes before the gun clicks.

*Empty.*

John falls to his side, dropping the gun and wrapping both hands around his throat. Crimson tinges his face. His legs kick beneath me, and his mouth gulps for air.

"Raina." Lorne drops to his knees beside me, tense and panting. "We'll do this together, okay?"

My voice hides beneath an overload of adrenaline,

fear, and hours of nerve-wringing stress, but I manage a nod.

He places a hand over mine, where I white-knuckle the knot of guitar strings. His other hand angles his hunting knife over John's heart.

"This is the knife that cut Jarret and me out of the rope in the ravine." He stares into John's bulging, dying eyes, his voice a blade of ice. "It's the knife that scarred our hands and sealed our blood oath to end Levi Tibbs. And it's the knife that will end you."

He looks at me, and my skin tingles with horror and urgency. I wrap my fingers around his on the handle, and together, we drive it between John's ribs.

The blade sinks hard and fast, and John's body falls still, his eyes open and unseeing.

I drop back on my butt, and my gaze darts across the room.

"Jake." The sob that's been waiting in my throat bursts free, followed by a torrent of tears.

I crawl on hands and knees toward the couch, defeated by exhaustion and driven by grief. I just need to see him, to make sure.

"Raina. Shhh." Lorne tackles me and hauls my body onto his lap.

His arms come around me as movement sounds near the kitchen.

My breath freezes, and my fingers curl into Lorne's shoulders.

A hand emerges from behind the couch, followed by the man who was shot multiple times in the chest.

"What?" My heart races, and a wave of dizziness washes over me. "How?"

Jake strides around the furniture, his expression taut as he glances at his dead father.

"I took Fletcher's gun before we came here." He

kneels beside us and rests a warm hand on my arm. "He assumed I returned it with live ammunition."

"Assumption is the mother of all fuck-ups." Lorne brushes the hair away from my face.

It takes a moment for reality to sink in, even though it's right in front of me, larger than life. "They were blanks."

Jake nods. "If Fletcher hadn't been under duress, he might've noticed the difference in the sound."

Jake's alive. Lorne's unharmed. John's gone, and he's never coming back.

It's finished.

In the seconds that follow, I feel Lorne's arms squeezing around me and mine reciprocating. No longer will we be hiding behind security alarms or looking over our shoulders.

We can finally put everything behind us and *live*.

Jake stares blankly at his father's body, his voice flat. "John died under the belief that I'm dead."

"That was the plan." Lorne removes his hat and scrapes a hand over his head, his eyes tired and bloodshot.

"I'm glad." Jake stands, removes his phone, and makes a call. "It's over." He ambles toward the kitchen. "Yeah, we're all fine..."

Lorne lowers his face to mine, sharing his breaths as easily as he shares his heart. "Are you okay?"

That's a loaded question, one I'm not emotionally stable enough to answer, but... "I'm alive, thanks to you."

"*You* saved *my* life, Raina." He cups my face. "If you hadn't used the guitar strings the way you did, I would've lost that gunfight. I counted on John shooting Fletcher, but I thought he would continue firing until he ran out of ammo. I should've known he'd save bullets for me."

"That whole thing was planned? Jake turning on Mary, Fletcher shooting Jake, then John killing Fletcher?"

"Yeah. We improvised a little along the way, but it was all planned, starting with Jake picking a fight with Fletcher and Mary about our mothers."

"You didn't know about Mary's involvement."

"No." A muscle tics in his jaw.

"You were going to kill her anyway?"

"No mercy. No survivors."

*Ruthless.*

I don't care. He was ruthless when I met him, and I fell in love. His hard edges and vicious heart lures me in and lulls me to peace. His complexities captivate me, and his proximity owns me.

I drift toward him, slowly, needfully, until my mouth absorbs the raw, rich, masculine flavor of his power.

Loving Lorne is like loving a sharply-honed, meticulously-crafted blade. He's so pretty to look at he should be put on display. But a true sword lover would never do that. I'll always keep him at my side, like an extension of myself. His lethal danger will obliterate anyone who threatens me, and I'll sharpen those edges and take care of him.

Jake goes into the garage, and a few seconds later, he steps back into the house. "Erin's body is in the trunk of the car."

My chest constricts. "How are we going to get away with this?"

Lorne grazes his lips over mine. "We'll explain it away as self-defense."

"No." I jump to my feet and scan the room. "There are six dead bodies, and one of them is a sheriff. You won't get away with this. Not with your criminal history."

"Lorne won't be involved." Jake walks through the room, collecting bullet casings from the floor. He holds up one and studies it. "A forensic analyst can tell a blank from a live round just by the residue left behind." He pockets it and continues his task.

"Was that the plan?" I turn back to Lorne. "You're going to leave before we call the cops?"

"I never agreed to that." He unravels the guitar strings from John's throat and tucks them in his boot with his bloody knife.

Neither he nor Jake need to be involved in this. I have a reason for being here. I was abducted. I can play into that, put all blame on John, and make it appear like John and Fletcher killed each other in a gunfight.

The evidence doesn't support that, but I can take care of that, too.

"Are there security cameras here?" I ask.

"No." Jake wipes down a handgun. "Fletcher doesn't have recording equipment. Nothing that could be used as evidence against him."

I scrutinize the room, and my attention lands on the half-burned candles sitting on pedestals on the side tables. Stepping toward them, I rifle through the drawers until I find a lighter.

"What are you doing?" Lorne stands over me, exuding an intensity that churns the air.

"I was kidnapped and brought here." I light the candles. "A rape kit will validate my story."

His fists squeeze at his sides, and his breathing surges into a seething whirlwind.

I grip his hands, then his face. Leaning up, I touch my brow to his. "We'll work through it. I promise."

He wraps his arms around me in a hug that constricts my ribs. "I'm so fucking sorry."

"Lorne, don't." I push against him. "You came for me. I love you. Now I need you to go."

I sweep an arm out and knock the candles over, sending them rolling across the couch and armchairs. A couple of them burn out. The others catch on fabric upholstery and flicker to life.

"There was a fight." I stride toward the front door. "I escaped."

"Goddammit, Raina." Lorne chases after me, followed by the tread of Jake's boots. "What if they pin this on you?"

"They won't." I step into the blackness of night, cross the front lawn, and turn to face two scowling cowboys. "There won't be any evidence if the house burns down before someone arrives. How far is the closest neighbor?"

"Miles." Jake rests his hands on his hips and surveys the surrounding fields of nothingness.

"You'll both be called in for questioning," I say, "because I live with you and because of your relationships with John."

They stare at me, as if they're not going to go along with this.

"You've risked everything to protect those you love." I move into Lorne's space and slide my hands around the back of his neck. "My risk here is minimal, and my love is huge. Let me do this."

"You're killing me." He attaches his lips to mine and kisses me angrily yet achingly slow.

Then he pulls back and spends the next thirty minutes telling me exactly what to say to the detectives.

He and Jake refuse to leave until the fire roars out the windows. When they finally drive away in Lorne's truck, I sit on the front lawn and wait.

But the real wait is over.

I have amends.

Family.

Love.

Lorne.

I have the better that comes after the worse.

**28**

*Raina*

**TWO MONTHS LATER...**

Emotional growth is a lot like learning to shoot a gun. Some days, I kick ass. Other days, I suck it. But the more I practice, the stronger and more confident I become.

My mistakes are many, and I'm learning from them, learning how to be a better half of the whole I share with Lorne.

When I met him, I was emotionally fractured and guarded. I didn't know how to trust or open up, and looking back, I can see how unhealthy my perspective was on sex and intimacy.

Lorne's helping me through the things I don't like to talk about—my sister's death, John's abuse, my history of neglect and prostitution—and I'm learning how to ask for help when I need it.

It's a *no pain, no gain* effort, because it forces me to look inside myself and make the changes I need to make.

This doesn't mean everything is love and peace. Lorne and I challenge and argue and say things we don't mean. But in the end, we always find a solution together.

We always listen.

It's important to pause sometimes, in the midst of a great, big, scary, wonderful life, to take a look around, feel the wind, and heed the silence.

"I hear you." Lorne sits beside me at a picnic table, bending over a plate of Indian tacos and licking his fingers.

"I hear you, too."

I'm not the only one working on self-improvements.

He hates crowds and public places, yet all around us are the mesmerizing colors, scents, and soulful music of Native American festivities.

He surprised me with this weekend trip. At the crack of dawn, he put me in his truck and drove three hours to attend the annual festival hosted by the six north-central tribes of Oklahoma.

We've spent the day watching inter-tribal dancing, browsing eye-catching paintings, pottery, jewelry, and clothing, and sampling traditional food.

I knew events like this existed, but I'd never been to one. The only exposure I had to my heritage was through my grandmother.

Being here among the culture and people, I feel a sense of belonging. It's peaceful and eye-opening. But more than that, it's nice to just let go and have fun. And boy have I had fun teasing my cowboy about his rugged, booted presence in a sea of tomahawks and feathered headdresses.

It's been the best day of my life, and I owe it all to him.

He planned this trip for me.

*And maybe for the tacos.*

He bites into the fried bread and chili with a groan.

# Booted

His strong jaw flexes as he chews, his tongue darting out to catch a drip of salsa.

That sexy mouth is a potent, erotic power tool. Whether he's eating, barking orders, or kissing me senseless, I'm captivated and shivering in ways I've never felt before.

There are a lot of things I never experienced until Lorne, like dancing under the stars, holding hands in the grocery store, romance and feelings, tender and slow, whispering, cuddling, and other giddy nonsense.

I used to grimace at the notion of *making love*. But that was before I understood the profound bond and commitment it requires.

Anyone can fake sex.

No one can fake making love.

"You're smiling, shivering, and stroking your throat." He watches me from inches away, his green eyes dancing in the sunlight. "You better be thinking about me and not the half-naked men on the stage."

I drop my hand and glance at the traditional dancers as they stomp and twirl to the intoxicating beat of drums.

"Always you." I cherish every second I share with him. "Are you enjoying yourself?"

He wipes his mouth on a napkin and sets his empty plate aside. Then he leans in and runs his nose along my neck. The masculine essence of him saturates my senses, and the intensity of his love fires my pulse.

"I love watching you smile," he breathes at my ear. "The way your eyes glow as they take everything in. The way your entire body comes alive amid the colors and music. All of this..." He motions at the sights around us. "It helps me understand the magic that lives inside you."

"You're part of that magic." I trace a finger along the sharp line of his jaw. "Thank you for this."

"You're welcome." He laces his hand with mine and

sits back to watch the dancers.

He still wears my necklace on his wrist, and I treasure the guitar strings on mine.

Maybe it's morbid to wear a murder weapon on my body. But after he scrubbed the strings and wove them back into a bracelet, he slid it onto my wrist and said, "This symbolizes the strength in our survival."

I love that.

We survived so much just in the past two months. There were doctor exams, police interrogations, and plenty of gossip surrounding the death of Sandbank's sheriff. But the skeletons John and Fletcher kept in their closets burned to ash along with their bodies.

The night they died, I was detained for hours of questioning, along with the rest of the family. By morning, we walked away with our freedom.

"You want to stroll through that section?" Lorne points at a row of tents on the far side of the festival.

"I'll go anywhere with you."

We spend the rest of the day perusing Native American crafts. When nightfall casts the streets in shadows, he drives me to a one-room cabin he rented for the weekend.

Isolated in the woods, it overlooks a pond that twinkles in the starlight. He builds a fire in the outdoor pit, plays mellow country music on his phone, and sprawls in an oversized wicker armchair like a lazy lion.

I sit beside him, close enough to touch, and wait for him to make his move.

What will it be tonight? A little spanking? Some growly dirty talk? Bondage with rope? Wild and urgent? Slow and torturous? Anything is possible as long as he's the one commanding and restraining.

For a moody, complicated man, his sexual proclivities are straightforward. He simply wants to be inside me, in any hole, any time, any place, and any way he can get me.

As I watch the flames dance in the fire pit, my skin heats. It's less from the warmth of the fire and more from the predatory gaze caressing the side of my face.

His silent assertiveness thrums my nerve endings and melts my blood into lava.

"You're staring." I draw my bottom lip between my teeth, eyes on the crackling flames.

"Take it off."

"Take what off?"

"The clothes you don't need anymore."

My heart sprouts wings as I rise from the chair and stand before him, just out of reach.

He loves to watch me undress, especially when I tease.

I start slow, inching fabric, tracing buttons and clasps, sliding fingers along skin, and subtly swaying to the gentle music.

His moonlit eyes glint in the shadow beneath his hat, his jaw a rigid slope of self-restraint. He sits in a reclined position, arms and legs spread out in a relaxed and confident way, taking up space and owning the air.

His chin angles down, and a hand rests beneath his mouth with fingers loosely curled. It's a pose of casual indifference, but there's nothing casual or indifferent about the way he stares at me.

I remove the last of my clothes and stand before him, a little lust-drunk and totally nude.

He makes me wait through a long, lingering perusal before his gaze meets and holds mine.

"Touch me." He removes the hat and sets it aside, his hooded eyes soldering our connection.

My nipples pucker in the night air, and a sublime quiver ripples through me.

Three unhurried steps bring me into the *V* of his legs. I place my hands on the armrests and bend in to gently graze my lips across his forehead. Then I slowly veer over to his temple and down to his mouth, trailing the kiss as lightly as possible while stirring the barely visible hairs that cover his face.

The sweet, subtle brush of lips makes his breath hitch and his dimple pop. I nip at the sexy rivet and glide away to his ear, hovering there while releasing a languorous sigh meant to tantalize.

"You drive me crazy." He groans, sinking deeper into the chair and stretching his legs out around me.

"You love it."

"Fuck yeah, I do."

His head falls back, exposing the sensitive tendon that runs from his ear to his shoulder. I go after it with my mouth, starting at his earlobe and working my way down the ridge, randomly alternating between languid licks, nibbles, and flicks with the silky underside of my tongue. The constant back and forth keeps his senses on maximum alert.

By the time I reach his shoulder, his breathing is shallow and fast. He yanks off his shirt and returns to his sprawl, his gaze demanding and possessive.

With a smile, I trace my mouth along the alluring lines of his muscled torso. He doesn't move to grab me or rush this. He loves to prolong the agony as much as I do.

"You're stupid sexy." I nip and tongue every hard, sweet spot from his throat to his eight-pack. "I lose brain cells every time I look at you."

"Less talking, more licking." His growly bedroom voice curls pulsing heat between my legs.

His eyes haven't strayed from mine once, his body tight and hot beneath me. Each of my featherlight kisses makes his pecs twitch and bounce, and he clenches his hands around the armrests.

I edge toward the hand with the scar and touch the tip of my tongue against the webbed area between his strong fingers.

His grip relaxes, and I lick along the sides of each digit, stimulating sensitive nerves.

His eyes briefly close, lips separating, and the denim between his legs tightens around the hard, swollen length of his arousal.

I use only my mouth, my hands never leaving the chair, as I roam to his buckle. There, I lightly blow on the treasure trail of sparse hair that leads to where we're both aching for me to go. It's a prize-worthy trail, and I show him by licking the spot below his belly button, drawing some of those soft hairs between my lips, and pulling, just hard enough that he feels it.

Right about now, pinpricks of edgy pain are sending jolts of electricity through his abs and low below his belt.

His hips shift beneath me, and the cords in his neck strain beneath his five o'clock shadow.

From under his tousled black hair glows eyes the color of the forest in the moonlight, like the greenest leaves absorbing bits of the stars from the night sky.

I know what he's thinking. He wants me to yank down his zipper and suck him to the back of my throat. I want that, too, but I also want his mouth.

Sliding up his body, I straddle a rock-hard thigh and angle toward him. With my hands on his jaw, I steal sips of virile breaths from strong lips.

The taste of him stirs something wild and instinctual inside of me. "I love to kiss you."

His arms come around me, and he presses in, taking over.

He draws my bottom lip between his and sucks aggressively, bringing blood to the surface of my skin and making it even more sensitive.

I do the same to his top lip. Then we switch. Back and forth, we roll into a sensual glide of mouths and tongues, tangling and gasping into a steamy fog of hunger.

We kiss to the easy-going music. Our hands wander with the heat of the campfire. Hips rocking, reaching, wanting, we melt into flesh and soul and breath.

When the song changes, something completely unexpected thumps from the speaker.

"You have Lady Gaga in your playlist?" I stare into half-lidded eyes.

"The song's called *John Wayne,*" he says, as if that makes all the sense in the world. Then he reclines in the chair, reaches out, and tweaks my nipple hard. "Ride my thigh."

I'm already straddling it, and damn if it doesn't feel like a steel bar wrapped in denim.

The song is racy, the beats high-powered and vibrating with energy. I let it guide my movements and pull my hips into a slow-building grind.

The twisting, rubbing stimulation swells a greedy spasm between my legs, soaking his jeans and working me into panting, needy mindlessness. I slide my hands through my hair and let go, rippling and rolling my body on his leg, my nipples taut and begging.

But he doesn't touch me. Instead, he drinks me in with a look so potent, so gripping, I feel him inside me with phantom fingers, curling and stroking and propelling me toward the edge.

With a moan, I yield to the command in his eyes, falling against his chest as whirls of orgasmic bliss smother me in electric sensation.

Before I can catch my breath, he repositions my legs around his hips while unfastening his jeans. He fumbles with the buckle and zipper and shoves his clothes down his legs.

The hot, hard length of his cock presses against my center, his hips rolling, angling him into the right spot.

He grips the back of my neck, and his other hand wraps around my hip. Then he wrenches me close, our mouths open and touching.

Sinking his velvet tongue past my lips, he flicks it in an arc along the roof of my mouth, once, twice, then he drives his thick cock inside me.

"Fuuuuck." He plunges to the root. Then he thrusts, clutching my neck and hip and using my body to jack off. "Christ, Raina. I love your cunt. You're so tight. So fucking wet."

The space between us detonates. He devours my lips ravenously, licking the hollows of my mouth, his fingers rough and possessive in my hair.

My heart spins, and my breaths try to keep up. He adds pressure to my throat, holding my face an inch from his as he slams his hips, thrusting and forcing himself into me, so hard, so fucking perfect.

"Give it to me, Raina." His eyes glare, his voice an unraveling rope of breath.

"Almost there." I'm falling, trembling against the incoming waves of pleasure.

"I want all of it. All of you. Marriage. Family. Forever."

"You have me."

I surrender to my cowboy, lost in his eyes, wrapped in his love, as he rides me toward a million sunsets.

**ELEVEN YEARS LATER...**

Under a sky of midnight satin, beneath stars so luminous they light up the field, the musical laughter of children overruns the ranch and nestles against my soul.

It's the best sound in the universe.

We've added a lot of seating to the back porch over the past decade. It took a few years for our family of six to grow to seven. A year later, we expanded to ten.

Raina sits beside me on the outdoor couch, with a long sexy leg slung over my knee and huge brown eyes fixed on the never-ending energy of the five- and six-year-olds buzzing through the field behind the estate.

A year after John died, we married right here. Three weddings. One joyful day. Just the six of us and the wedding officiant.

Raina wears my mother's ring. Conor wears Julep's, and Maybe has the one Jarret designed for her all those years ago.

On the other side of the porch, Conor perches on Jake's knee, strumming her guitar while he sings *The Rest of Our Life* by Tim McGraw and Faith Hill. It's the song we played at our wedding.

Today's our ten-year anniversary, and good God, it's been a busy decade.

We dedicated the first few years to growing the cattle operation. We knew we'd eventually have children and would have to enlarge the estate to accommodate our combined families. Four years after we married, we finally had enough time and money to build a third wing.

Jake, Jarret, and I finished the construction just in time for Jake's and Conor's son, Landon, to arrive.

A year later, Maybe gave birth to fraternal twins. Jonah and Jace, now five years old, remind me so much of Jarret and Jake, from their dark eyes and brown hair to their protective rowdiness.

When Maybe isn't chasing them with a paint stick, she's fussing around in the extravagant chicken coop Jarret built for her. While she pampers and coddles her rescued poultry, her white heifer, Chicken, is right there with her.

"Daddy! Daddy!" In a swirl of long black hair, my daughter scampers onto the porch and throws herself against my chest, her arms curling around my neck.

Whenever I hold Julep, I experience a feeling of weightlessness in my lungs that spreads through my limbs. Raina and I made this precious being, and the notion still floats around me like a dream.

She leans back, and I stare into eyes that look so much like my wife's it takes my breath away.

Raina says Julep resembles Tiana. Same sweet temperament, thick inky hair, and bright smile.

But right now, her smile's hiding behind a quivering chin.

# Booted

"What is it?" Raina bends toward her and sweeps tangled black strands from her teary eyes.

"Jace says..." She sniffs and crosses her little arms. "He says he won't marry me."

"Not this again." I rub my forehead and meet Raina's eyes.

She grins.

Jarret ambles out of the field, steps onto the porch, and makes a beeline for Julep.

"Boys are dumb." He crouches beside her. "Give him time. He'll come around."

"But I want to get married today!" She stomps her boot.

"How about instead, we go inside and tear into your mom's biscuits and chocolate gravy?" He stands and holds out a hand.

Her eyes light up, and in an instant, her tears are replaced with a toothy grin. "Yes!"

I shake my head as he leads her inside. He and Jake indulge her the same way they did with Conor.

Across the porch, my sister plucks the song to a close and turns to press a kiss on Jake's lips.

The stars are out, and the night is gleaming with possibilities. Maybe's in the field with the boys. Jarret is occupying Julep, and I have a beautiful woman staring at me with a suggestive smile.

"Hey, Conor. Play that one again." I stand and grip Raina's hand. "Dance with me."

"Under the stars?"

"Always."

I escort her off the porch and bring her in close, lips touching, hips swaying as Conor and Jake serenade us.

Life is good. Better than good.

The cattle ranch is thriving. We're not wealthy. We're comfortable. Happy.

We're doing what we were meant to do.
Working hard.
Loving harder.
In the place we love.

The terrain of childhood shapes the soul, and the soul never forgets.

It doesn't forget the fields of Julep Ranch under a starlit sky.

The laughter of children running though the grass.

The strum of a guitar in the evening summer breeze.

Or Raina Cassidy, the mother of my child, the center of my heart, at home in my arms.

# Other books by
## Pam Godwin

**LOVE TRIANGLE ROMANCE**
TANGLED LIES TRILOGY
One is a Promise
Two is a Lie
Three is a War

**DARK ROMANCE**
DELIVER SERIES
Deliver #1
Vanquish #2
Disclaim #3
Devastate #4
Take #5
Manipulate #6
Unshackle #7
Dominate #8
Complicate #9

**DARK PARANORMAL ROMANCE**
TRILOGY OF EVE
Heart of Eve
Dead of Eve #1
Blood of Eve #2
Dawn of Eve #3

**STUDENT-TEACHER / PRIEST**
Lessons In Sin

**STUDENT-TEACHER ROMANCE**
Dark Notes

**ROCK-STAR DARK ROMANCE**
Beneath the Burn

**ROMANTIC SUSPENSE**
Dirty Ties

**EROTIC ROMANCE**
Incentive

**DARK HISTORICAL PIRATE ROMANCE**
King of Libertines
Sea of Ruin

*Better Man* by Little Big Town
*Hurt* by Johnny Cash
*Cowboy Casanova* by Carrie Underwood
*Just A Kiss* by Lady Antebellum
*Gun Power and Lead* by Miranda Lambert
*Alone With You* by Jake Owen
*Come A Little Closer* by Dierks Bentley
*Eatin' Pussy/Kickin' Ass* by Wheeler Walker Jr.
*Ride* by Chase Rice (Dirty version)
*Like a Wrecking Ball* by Eric Church
*Ain't No Sunshine* by Wovenhand
*John Wayne* by Lady Gaga
*The Rest of Our Life* by Tim McGraw and Faith Hill

# About
## Pam Godwin

New York Times and USA Today Bestselling author, Pam Godwin, lives in the Midwest with her husband, their two children, and a foulmouthed parrot. When she ran away, she traveled fourteen countries across five continents, attended three universities, and married the vocalist of her favorite rock band.

Java, tobacco, and dark romance novels are her favorite indulgences, and might be considered more unhealthy than her aversion to sleeping, eating meat, and dolls with blinking eyes.

EMAIL: pamgodwinauthor@gmail.com

CPSIA information can be obtained
at www.ICGtesting.com
Printed in the USA
LVHW102145180422
716581LV00022B/357